I0565730

DISCOVERING GOLD

What Reviewers Say About
Sam Ledel's Work

Worth a Fortune

"The romance burns tantalizingly slowly as Ledel takes the time to thoroughly explore the ways her well-shaded heroines both complement and clash with each other. This remarkable emotional maturity does not come at the expense of heat, however; when the love scenes come, they steam up the pages. It's subtle, lovely, and stirring. Starred review."—*Publishers Weekly*

"Loved this! It was exciting, down to earth and totally unexpected. Nothing outrageous, just a wonderful connection between two women who find their world has completely changed following the Second World War. I adored the way both of them had to learn new things, take new changes, risks, and try things that weren't known to them, only to find themselves reconnecting in a most lovely way."—*LESBIreviewed*

The Princess and the Odium

"The world-building in the whole trilogy is fantastic, and even if it feels familiar now that we've been navigating it with the characters for a while, it's still surprising and unsettling. All in all, *The Princess and the Odium* is a fitting end to a well-written YA fantasy series."—*Jude in the Stars*

Rocks and Stars

"I think Sam Ledel told a great story. I adored Kyle even though a few times I wanted to shake her and say enough girlfriend. I wish the ending was a bit longer, but that's the romance addict in me. I look forward to Ledel's next book."—*Romantic Reader Blog*

Daughter of No One

"There's a lot of really smart fantasy going on here. …Great start to a (hopefully) long running series."—Colleen Corgel, Librarian, Queens Public Library

"It's full of exciting adventure and the promise of romance. It's sweet, fresh and hopeful. It takes me back to my teenage years, the good parts of those years at least. I read this in a few hours, only stopped long enough to have lunch. I hope I won't have to wait too long for the sequel—I have high hopes for Jastyn, Aurelia, their friend Coran, Eegit the hedgewitch and Rigo the elf."—*Jude in the Stars*

"A fantasy book with MCs in their very early twenties, this book presents a well thought out world of Kingdom of Venostes (shades of The Lord of the Rings here)."—*Best Lesfic Reviews*

"Sam Ledel has definitely set up an epic adventure of star-crossed lovers. This book one of a trilogy doesn't leave you with a cliffhanger but you are definitely going to be left ready for the next book. …As a non-fantasy lover, I adored this book and am ready to read where Ledel takes us next. This book is quality writing, great pacing, and top-notch characters. You cannot go wrong with this one!"—*Romantic Reader Blog*

"If you're a huge fan of fantasy novels, especially if you love stories like this one that contains a host of supernatural beings, quirky characters coupled with action and excitement around every tree, winding path or humble abode, then this is definitely the story for you! This compelling story also deals with poverty, isolation and the huge chasm between the royal family and the low-class villagers. Well, fellow book lovers, it really looks like you've just received a winning ticket to a literary lottery."
—*Lesbian Review*

Broken Reign

"Sam Ledel has created a fascinating and at times terrifying world, filled with elves, sirens, selkies, wood nymphs and many more. ...Going on this journey with both young women and their fellow travellers still has this fresh and exciting quality, all the more so as new characters joined the story, some just as intriguing."—*Jude in the Stars*

Visit us at www.boldstrokesbooks.com

By the Author

Rocks and Stars

Wildflower Words

Worth a Fortune

Heart of Stone

Adrift

Discovering Gold

The Odium Trilogy

Daughter of No One

Broken Reign

The Princess and the Odium

DISCOVERING GOLD

by

Sam Ledel

2025

DISCOVERING GOLD

© 2025 BY SAM LEDEL. ALL RIGHTS RESERVED.

ISBN 13: 978-1-63679-786-1

THIS TRADE PAPERBACK ORIGINAL IS PUBLISHED BY
BOLD STROKES BOOKS, INC.
P.O. BOX 249
VALLEY FALLS, NY 12185

FIRST EDITION: MAY 2025

THIS IS A WORK OF FICTION. NAMES, CHARACTERS, PLACES, AND
INCIDENTS ARE THE PRODUCT OF THE AUTHOR'S IMAGINATION OR
ARE USED FICTITIOUSLY. ANY RESEMBLANCE TO ACTUAL PERSONS,
LIVING OR DEAD, BUSINESS ESTABLISHMENTS, EVENTS, OR LOCALES
IS ENTIRELY COINCIDENTAL.

THIS BOOK, OR PARTS THEREOF, MAY NOT BE REPRODUCED IN ANY
FORM WITHOUT PERMISSION.

CREDITS
EDITOR: BARBARA ANN WRIGHT
PRODUCTION DESIGN: SUSAN RAMUNDO
COVER DESIGN BY TAMMY SEIDICK

Acknowledgments

Special thanks to the city of Idaho Springs. Their well-kept history fueled the characters and stories that came together to form this novel. Thank you to the staff at Argo Gold Mill and Tunnel—the inspiration for Monarch Mill. Thanks to Hidee Gold Mine Tours and the Historical Society of Idaho Springs. And thank you to Beau Jo's for keeping me well-fed during the many research trips I took over the last year and a half.

Thank you to the entire team at Bold Strokes Books. Shout-out to my editor, Barbara Ann Wright. Bringing this story to its full potential was made more fun and educational thanks to your keen eye and hilarious wit.

Dedication

For queer women past, present, and future.
We've always been here.

PROLOGUE

Idaho Springs, Colorado, 1920

Peter's cries woke Eleanor from her dream. She had been staggering through blinding snow, the figures in the distance marred by harsh daggers of white. A frozen lake had groaned beneath her feet. Now, the chill of her visions lingered as she sat up in bed and scanned her dark room, the coals in the fireplace spent. A breeze crept over her shoulders, finding her through her nightshirt. She shivered and glanced at the nearby window only to find it firmly closed.

Bleary-eyed, she went to Peter. His crib was undisturbed in the corner of the room. His little fists fought the air, the blanket tangled at his ankles.

"Shh, my love, don't cry." Eleanor picked him up, placing him against her chest so his cheek rested on her shoulder. She rubbed his back gently, cooing and singing the lullaby Aunt Emily used to sing to her.

That was when the top drawer of the dresser caught her eye.

She didn't recall leaving it open. A *creak* sounded overhead. The lullaby stopped as she studied the ceiling, waiting. The attic often hosted animals seeking shelter from the cold Colorado nights. It was probably another racoon.

The drawer drew her gaze once again. She frowned as Peter's cries softened over her shoulder. The unease she'd felt in her dream returned. "Louis," she said, turning back to the bed. "Louis, wake—"

She froze. Her husband didn't move. There was no gentle rise and fall of his breathing. Her heart raced, and she lifted Peter, securing him against her as she stepped slowly toward the bed. She swallowed, then threw back the quilt to reveal a mass of pillows and a fur blanket.

"Louis?"

Eleanor prodded the quilt, turned it over, then shoved the pillow as if doing so would explain him not being there. She hurried to the front of the house, her quick movements jostling Peter and reigniting his cries. An errant memory flared of Louis insisting on calling the front room of their home the "parlor," even though the space was more a haphazard sitting room that ran into their open kitchen.

"Parlor makes it sound fancy," he had said, smiling after she'd moved in a few short hours following their nuptials two years ago. She had been thrilled to become Mrs. Louis Perry and finally lay claim to a family of her own.

But the parlor was empty, the rocking chair Louis liked to sit in vacant. She felt hot but tried to think through the burning in her mind as she bounced Peter, who was growing angrier by the minute at not being fed. Perhaps Louis was cleaning his rifle, something he did when he couldn't sleep. She'd often found him at the kitchen table idly running a cloth along the barrels. But the moonlight streaming between their curtains fell upon a quiet table. His rifle sat on its perch above the front door.

The pounding of blood in Eleanor's ears rivaled Peter's cries. The house's dark corners revealed nothing, and for a moment, she caught the same shadowy figures of her dreams through the windows. But they were only figments of desperation and fear. She called out again, louder, searching the adjoining washroom, the spare room upstairs, then their bedroom once again.

She found the fireplace, the bed, the window, touching each as if to conjure an explanation for what was happening. "Louis," she said over Peter, "this isn't funny."

No answer came.

Fighting tears, she took a breath and started for the dresser. Hesitating, she pulled the drawer open more.

Peter wailed, and her heart sank at the sight of her husband's clothes missing. She went to the apple crate that held his rucksack. That, too, was gone. She felt dizzy but forced herself to focus on her steps as she returned to the front of the house.

Next to the door, where his hat hung each night when he came home from the mill, sat an empty nail.

Nausea surged in her throat. The horrible haze of her dream rose up from the floorboards, suffocating her in a sheet of white dread. Her vision tunneled as she faced the room and leaned against the door to steady herself. She rearranged Peter, propping him on her left hip.

"This can't be happening." She pulled open the front door, moving onto the planked porch. The dark September night greeted her, ignorant. By the light of the moon, she searched the tall pines, the gravel road running thirty feet ahead, then the towering mountains beyond.

Nothing.

"Louis," she called. Her own voice echoed a sad reply.

She forced down the lump in her throat. Another wail from Peter pierced the night and the panic that ran through her mind. Her chest tight, Eleanor recognized the terrible feeling in her stomach. It was the same feeling she'd had when her father had left her with her aunt and uncle without so much as a hug good-bye.

She had never imagined she would feel that way again, not with Louis.

But this wasn't a dream.

She hugged Peter close as her gaze swept over the wild brush that formed ominous figures across the jagged landscape. She stared into the dark. Deep in her bones, Eleanor knew the truth: her husband was gone.

CHAPTER ONE

Idaho Springs, Colorado 1927

"Come on, nearly there." Julia gritted her teeth, urging the galloping mule on. Thundering hooves sounded over the cobblestone thoroughfare of downtown Idaho Springs on a cool May Thursday night. Under the half-full moon, the streetlamp at the corner of Miner Street beckoned. She grinned, knowing the two dollars would be hers if she reached it first.

When she reached it first.

Over her right shoulder, she found Ralph Davies on his own mule. The poor beast looked haggard beneath Ralph's sturdy, six-foot-three frame. He caught her eye, his twinkling with the moonshine they'd shared before nabbing Mahoney's mules for this impromptu race. It wasn't Ralph but one of the mill men who'd turned from the pool table in the back of Thrasher's and said there was no way in tarnation Julia could outride him. Ralph knew she could ride. He wasn't bad himself, only four paces behind and the closest threat as they and four others hurtled along in the midnight hour.

The other men whooped, hollered, and yipped, the cries bouncing off dormant hardware stores, wagon part depots, and quiet restaurants lining the street. Julia imagined the crowd at Thrasher's nearly a mile away nestled against the adjoining valley on the edge of town. The collection of shanties strung together to create the gin joint hosted patrons eager for a taste of Jay Thrasher's homemade liquor.

Thrasher's was this town's version of a speakeasy that Julia had been thrilled to learn existed. A place to go when her mind wouldn't stop its turning, where she could drown out the dark thoughts that followed her. Now, she grinned, picturing the cheers she'd come back to after she'd won.

Her mule whimpered from her gentle kicks into its side as she urged it onward. Julia wished she had been on one of her father's horses. *These men would be choking on my dust.* She forced herself to focus as she leaned forward, tossing another look over her shoulder. To her delight, the men, including Ralph, had fallen farther behind.

Her smile fell though as she looked ahead. "Whoa," she called, tugging the mule's mane to help it slow.

Sheriff Lee Volz stood alone in the middle of the road just before the cross street and her finish line, hands casually in the pockets of his brown pants. Julia tightened her thighs, calling out again as the mule staggered to a stop just before colliding with him. Volz didn't flinch an inch.

The elation she'd felt moments before vanished with the deafening clamor of the other men halting around her as they recognized the sheriff. Two rode past, then hurried on into the night away from town. Ralph and the rest fell in line behind her, well behind. She glared at each for leaving her to face the sheriff's judgment.

"Miss Holte," he said. His square jaw was stubbled with the start of a beard. She couldn't see his blue gaze beneath his beige cowboy hat, but she didn't need to in order to know it gleamed with the opportunity to reprimand her...again.

"Sheriff Volz." She slowed her breathing as the mule *hee-hawed*, seemingly as eager as her to be anywhere but here. She didn't bother to fix her hair, leaving the strands in a wild mane around her shoulders. She blew some of it out of her face, keeping her gaze fixed on Volz.

He seemed to study her a moment, then tipped his hat to the men. "Good evening, fellas, or..." He pulled a silver pocket watch from his vermillion-colored vest, "Should I say, 'good morning.'"

The men muttered a greeting. Julia rolled her eyes at their pleasantries then cleared her throat, grabbing Volz's attention. "We're in the middle of somethin', Sheriff, if you don't mind." She waved her hand as if to brush him aside. "I've got a bet to win."

His shoulders shook in a silent laugh, and the image made her lip curl. She fought to keep a straight face as he spat just in front of her mule. "I'm afraid the race is over, fellas. Got too many complaints, see. Y'all are disturbing the peace. Townsfolk just trying to get some sleep before work tomorrow."

Julia scoffed, starting to point into the hills behind them where the monstrous Monarch Mill sat. Even now, the machinery echoed around them as the night shift worked. The sounds of crushing rock jarred her to the core, and she imagined the metal and steel working to comb through the stone for crumbs of gold. All the nearby mines sent their ore there to be processed. The din was incessant as the mill worked around the clock. She didn't understand how she was the only one that seemed to be bothered by the never-ending noise.

"Now," Sheriff Volz was saying, "who here's responsible for this race?"

The clatter of hooves started again as the men, except for Ralph, took off down the street from where they'd come.

"Cowards," she shouted after them. Ralph moved his mule closer. She frowned at his look of determination.

Seeming to read her question, he said quietly, "Not gonna leave you high and dry, Holte."

She smiled, then turned to Volz as he spoke. "That's what I thought," he muttered, staring daggers at her. "I'd hoped maybe you'd learned somethin' after our little dance last month."

Her jaw clenched at the memory of the last night she'd spent in jail for what Volz had dubbed "an illegal public display of roughhousing" and property damage. She'd challenged Derek Foresight to a wrestling match after he'd beaten her at poker. He'd lost and thrown a glass at a wall in Thrasher's, but since she was the challenger, Volz had deemed it her need to take the fall.

"Let's just get this over with." Julia dismounted. "Ralph, take these back to the Mahoney ranch. Tell him thanks and that I can pay him once I collect my winnings."

"But—"

"No use both of us going." She softened her tone, giving him what she hoped was a confident smile. "You need to get home anyway."

He looked like he wanted to protest, but Volz added, "She's right. Just think what that poor mother of yours would say if her son spent a night in jail."

Ralph looked ready to reply, his green eyes fiery beneath strands of long brown hair. Julia gave him a reassuring nod until he resigned himself to a glare at Volz before guiding the mules away. Julia's shoulders relaxed as she watched him go. The image she'd crafted of the patrons singing her praises vanished with him into the night. In its place crept the guilt she'd managed to temporarily stifle.

When Volz reached for the handcuffs on his belt, Julia swiped the sweat from her forehead, saying, "No one here to see the show, Volz. That won't be necessary."

He raised a brow, then clenched his jaw, perhaps at her being right that there was no one around to bear witness. Seeming to accept that, he gestured for her to move.

Reluctantly, Julia did, her boots like lead as she headed for the local courthouse and adjoining jail. What was this, her fourth arrest since moving here? She'd lost track. A lick of shame tickled her neck, but she tempered it with anger and clenched her fists at her sides. She nearly asked, "Why is it so difficult to have any fun around here?" before deciding that would probably get her an extra day's time. She didn't want to worry her sister more than she was likely already doing, which was exactly the opposite of why Julia had come to this godforsaken town in the first place.

Her gaze found the hills once again. The harsh music of the mill tolled on, bounding down and diving into every corner of the community, never letting her forget for a second where she was.

When she slowed, Volz prodded her in the back. "Keep moving, Holte. Your cell awaits."

She glared but bit her tongue. God, she thought, I hate this town.

CHAPTER TWO

Pardon me," Eleanor Perry said after bumping into the harried-looking shopkeeper. She helped him readjust the tin trough of iced river trout beneath the shaded awning. He harrumphed before heading inside the fish market. She eyed the row of black eyed, gaping creatures, then pulled the clutch of books tighter to her chest to continue carefully navigating bustling Miner Street on a Friday morning in mid-May. At just after eight-thirty, the quaint mountain town streamed with businessmen traipsing down the sidewalk, shops and markets opening their doors, and women hurrying their children along to the schoolhouse.

Eleanor had just dropped Peter off and was making the walk back through town to the Weldons' home, where her best friend Sue eagerly awaited the return of her books.

"Your boy will love this one," Sue had said last month when Eleanor had gone by to drop off a quilt she'd restitched for the couple. "The Denver library just received a new bin of donations." Eleanor had examined the cover of *The Story of Doctor Dolittle*. "My nephew can't stop talking about it," Sue had gushed. "He's now determined to become a veterinarian and live amongst the apes in Borneo."

Bewildered by such a statement, Eleanor had smiled and told Sue she was sure Peter would enjoy it before accepting the other work, a mystery by Agatha Christie.

Sue had been right. Even Eleanor had enjoyed the tale of the doctor who could converse with animals. What a premise! She had read the tale to Peter before bed when he was too tired to do so himself. She had just finished the Christie tale last night, staying up far later than she should have to figure out who'd done it.

She was thinking about the intricately woven mystery when something jerked her backward. "Oh." Eleanor looked down. She had apparently misjudged things as she'd started across the cobbled street; her skirt had caught the end of a long piece of rebar jutting beyond the end of a wagon bed. The wagon itself was behind a short line of cars all rumbling idly at a cross street, a policeman holding them in wait while cars and mule carts hurried by in the other direction.

Eleanor fumbled a minute with the skirt, managing to untangle herself just as the officer's whistle beckoned the line forward. She stepped into the middle of the road and was about to continue across when she looked down to find only the *Dolittle* book in her arms. "How…" The other must have fallen, and she turned to search for it.

Sure enough, there sat the book atop the dirty street. To her dismay, a horse-drawn cart approached, the book right in its path. Jumping aside as a passing car honked behind her, Eleanor waved and scampered back toward the book, calling out to the cart driver, "Wait, please."

He didn't seem to hear her as his head remained facing forward, his bowler hat so low over his forehead, she couldn't see his eyes. She tried another wave to get his attention. "Please, sir," she shouted, panic rising in her as the horses' mighty hooves stamped closer to the book. *God, Sue is never going to lend me one again.*

Not knowing what to do, Eleanor called out once more when somebody stepped directly into the horses' path.

"Whoa, easy." It was a woman who raised her voice to be heard over the traffic, her arms extended to make her frame seem taller and wider than it was. Her long, ash-brown hair swung down her back in messy tresses. She wore a loose white button-down; smudges of dirt and other stains marred the clean look of it as it fell untucked over the waist of men's trousers. Eleanor gaped at the ensemble that was completed by muddy cowboy boots.

"What the hell you doin'?" the driver cried, finally noticing the woman as his horses neighed, snorted, and came to a halt.

The woman either didn't hear him or chose to ignore him, instead focusing on the pair of brown horses. They shook their dark manes as if flustered by the interruption. She positioned herself to be in their line of sight before patting each above the muzzle, running her hands up and down their coats beneath their eyes. They seemed instantly calmer at her touch. Their tails twitched to-and-fro as she bent and picked up the book.

Eleanor, recovering from the spectacle of the last few moments, hurried forward. The woman extended the book to her. "This yours?"

"Yes, thank you." Eleanor took it, meeting her gaze. Her eyes were bright blue, dazzling, like the cloudless sky overhead. They stood out against the tanned skin in her round face. Eleanor wasn't sure which was brighter, this woman's gaze or the charming smile she wore. "I…" Her throat felt dry. What was she even trying to say? *Thank God you were here to rescue my book? Sue and Agatha would have had my neck?* Every thought seemed foolish. And why did her face feel warm? The woman's eyebrow quirked. Was she amused? "Just…thank you," Eleanor managed to finally say.

"It's my pleasure," the woman replied. She seemed to want to say something else, looking Eleanor over. The act surprised her, as did the growing smile the woman wore.

The horses whinnied as the cart driver snapped the reins. "Pardon me," he bellowed over the sound of passing cars. Eleanor glanced around. She had completely forgotten she was standing in the middle of the road. The horses pulled forward, and the wagon began to move between them. Eleanor looked around, pulling the book close. She was ready to ask after the woman who'd rescued her book, to get her name at least, but when the wagon passed, she wasn't there.

Eleanor glanced right, then left, and spotted her already half a block away, greeting a man in a flat cap who seemed familiar, but his back was to her, and she couldn't make him out. The feeling like she was a stagnant sail hit her, and for a moment, she felt stuck, torn between the urge to follow the woman and carry on with her day. Who was she? Eleanor had never seen her before. Where was she going?

The policeman's whistle sounded, and Eleanor realized he was beckoning for her to move. She apologized and hurried along, glancing back to try to get one more look at the woman whose eyes were as hypnotic as her smile, but she was already gone.

CHAPTER THREE

"Yoo-hoo, Eleanor."

Eleanor smiled at the familiar greeting of Susannah Weldon. "Back here, Sue," she called from around the side of the house where she stood in the expansive field behind her small home. Grabbing a damp linen shirt, she hung it next to the others on one of three clotheslines running between two tall pines. She glanced between swaying sleeves to find Sue traipsing through the tall grass that surrounded the house before she found the path of flat stones Eleanor had laid for Peter.

Sue's low heels *clacked* on the rock as she drew near.

"I see you've put those boots I lent you to good use," Eleanor teased.

Blowing a piece of crimped, strawberry blond hair from her forehead, Sue scoffed. "A manager's wife has certain expectations, even in a mountain town full of mud and snow half the year." She stopped and stood, looking relieved, on the other side of the clothesline. Sue wasn't tall enough to see over it, so she positioned herself just beyond the last shirt. Her pretty oval face shined with perspiration, and she swiped at her hair to ensure the short strands were in place. "Besides," she said, "Isaac loves me in them." She winked. "And I can't deny my husband his little pleasures."

Eleanor laughed and glanced at the fitted blue dress she could see beneath Sue's khaki coat. For a moment, she felt like a rag doll in her old brown dress with patches sewn all over the skirt where she'd torn it on numerous stray nails sticking out from who-knew-where around her house. She let herself admire Sue's coat, too, and tried not to compare it to the five-year-old one sitting in her wardrobe. It was the last Saturday in May, and the sun cast a warm blanket over the valley, but wind kept the residents of Idaho Springs within arm's reach of their jackets even in springtime. "How is Mr. Weldon?"

Sue helped hold a sleeve to the line while Eleanor grabbed another pin from the end of her skirt. "Working himself to the bone, as always. You know he likes to keep a tight ship up there."

Eleanor nodded, recalling Louis's stories of the "red-faced captain" at the helm of the Monarch Mill. Back then, Isaac had only been the manager nine months, but his zealous determination and seemingly boundless energy had shot the mill into record productivity. Monarch Mill had been the jewel of Colorado for some time when it came to gold milling, thanks to its state-of-the-art tunnel system. That, top-notch equipment, and numerous contracts with the area's surrounding mines led to outstanding profits. At first, the workers had been wary of the young New Englander and his penchant for long-winded motivational speeches, but Isaac had quickly become a respected leader who'd polished the mill into an even finer form. He wasn't afraid to get his hands dirty either, something most managers wouldn't dare do in an industry like this. Now, the Weldons were as prominent as the mayor of Idaho Springs and to some, even more revered.

"He's looking for a new file clerk," Sue was saying, pulling Eleanor from her thoughts as she grabbed the final shirt to hang. A trio of robin calls came from a nearby tree. Beyond, the river sang its quiet ballad as it traveled over boulders.

"Another one so soon?"

"Yes." She sighed, standing with her hands on her wide hips and tossing a look to the mountains as if they were to blame. "Young Miss Akins took off with Tommy Brent last week. Off to Reno where Tommy's parents live."

"That's sweet," Eleanor said.

Sue seemed to have other ideas as she huffed again. "That's more work for Isaac is what it is. Down a file clerk and a millman." She *tsked*, her fair cheeks growing flushed in her frustration. Eleanor always appreciated Sue's support of her husband and his work. It was one of the things that had drawn them together as friends in the first place.

"Well, good thing he has you." Eleanor stood, grabbing the empty wicker basket and gesturing for them to head inside.

Sue followed her into the kitchen at the back of the house. "Yes, I'll step in, as I always do. I just wish this didn't keep taking me away from my work with the women's groups in town, not to mention the city council. We're close to getting another street paved."

Eleanor dropped the basket next to the table. Grabbing two clay mugs, she found the kettle—warm from its perch on the stove—and poured them coffee. After taking a sip, her cold hands grateful for the warmth from the steaming mug, she sat at the table and caught Sue's pointed gaze. "What?"

"Well," she said, sitting and running a finger over the rim of her mug, "I was hoping you might be interested in the clerk position."

"Sue."

"Eleanor," she replied quickly, "it could be good for you, what you need."

"I have what I need." She gestured to the tub of clothes soaking in the corner near the back door they'd left open for the sun to stream in.

"And your services as Monarch Mill's laundress are no doubt appreciated by the hardworking men of the mill." She smiled wryly. "The *unmarried* working men."

Eleanor gave her a look, but Sue continued. "You could get to know some of those men better if you were in the office daily." Her eyes lit up. "There's that strapping Mr. Barrow who just joined the team. He's from Texas, and you know what they say about Texas men."

Blushing at the suggestion, Eleanor frowned. "Didn't he move here with his wife?"

Sue waved the comment aside. "Oh, you know what I mean. Men, darling. They're still out there."

"I'm well aware," she replied, pointing at the tub of dirty uniforms. "Intimately."

"Fine. A man in a different line of work, then." Sue glanced around the room, narrowing her gaze. "Oh, what about the sheriff? A man of the law could be interesting." She shimmied her shoulders suggestively.

"No," Eleanor replied immediately. "I don't know what it is about him, but he gives me the willies."

Slumping, Sue said, "I knew it was wrong as soon as I said it. Not like his daddy, that one. Ever since the army didn't take him—flat feet, if you can believe it—he's had a chip on his shoulder. Volz takes his job a little too seriously, like he's a drill sergeant, but you didn't hear that from me. Why last month, I heard he arrested Derek Foresight for public intoxication when he was two steps from his front porch. Was he stumblin' home? Sure, but he was nearly there. Volz Senior would have helped the man inside. No, not like his daddy at all, but you didn't hear it from me."

Eleanor smiled. "I'm doing all right, Sue."

Sue gave a small sigh, her shoulders rising and falling. The crackling of the fire and dissonant birdsong were the only sounds as she reached out toward Eleanor. "Honey, I only want what's best for you."

Eleanor chewed her lip as she studied the modest diamond on Sue's left hand. When was the last time she'd worn her wedding band? One, two years ago? "I know. But what's best for me is keeping a home for my son. Being here for him." Sue opened her mouth, no doubt to pitch the logic behind an office job with higher pay than a laundress could make in a month, but Eleanor shook her head. "I'm not ready to be there anymore than I should be. I'll see you when I drop off and pick up the uniforms on Mondays and Thursdays, like I always do. But, Sue…"

Sue's eyes shined. "I understand." She exhaled, then downed the coffee. "You can't blame a gal for trying."

Eleanor took another drink. "That's why you came by on a Saturday?"

Behind a sheepish smile, Sue said, "And to see my favorite friend, of course." She looked around the modest kitchen and sitting room, her gaze stopping at the tattered rug beneath them, then the mostly bare wooden walls emitting a faint cedar scent. "Where is that boy of yours, anyway?" She snapped her fingers, her eyes alight. "That reminds me, I need to get my sister-in-law to bring another book when she's in town. He liked the *Doctor Dolittle* one, right?"

Eleanor held her mug as the memory from last week returned. She stood in the middle of the road, captivated by the fearless woman who had jumped in front of the horses that day. The woman she hadn't seen since. "Yes," she said, forcing herself to concentrate. "He did."

"We'll try to find another one like it."

"That'd be grand," Eleanor said, then added, "Peter's outside setting some of his traps. He caught us a rabbit just yesterday."

Sue smiled. "Oh, that also reminds me." She found her handbag and set a brown package on the table. "Your boy's medicine."

"Sue," Eleanor said, her face warming. "I told you I could cover the next purchase."

She put her hands up as she stood to go. "I know you did, honey. Consider it a gift for the quilt you stitched up for us."

Eleanor eyed her at the flimsy excuse. She pulled the package closer across the table, shame and gratitude mingling at the back of her neck. "Thank you."

Sue gave her a warm smile. "Happy to help." Her gaze flitted to the back door. "You may want to go check on him. Don't need another incident of him running off."

Eleanor nodded. Since the start of the school year, Peter had wandered across town a handful of times, eluding the schoolmarm after midday recess. Her son's fixation with the mill had intensified since his eighth birthday. Young boys were employed from time to time, but it was a fact Eleanor couldn't reconcile. She knew some of the children from school were skipping days to work a shift, and Peter had noticed, too. She tried to find things to distract him: a steady supply of books, having him help with laundry, and encouraging his trap building went far but not far enough in keeping him occupied.

On top of that, she had his asthma to worry about. She was still learning how to handle his attacks since they'd started two winters ago. The first one had left her terrified as she'd run to his room in the night and found him struggling to breathe. The episodes were few and far between, but they were bad, and medicine was expensive. She'd even tried the local hot springs once. Their waters supposedly cured everything from chronic joint pain to infections to infertility. Eleanor hardly believed in such things—her Aunt Emily had been the most practical of women and had instilled her no-nonsense outlook upon her niece—but Peter was her entire world. Between his health and his reluctance to attend school, she felt stretched thin having to keep an eye on him. Thus far, his expeditions to the mill had resulted in Isaac catching him and sending him home. But it felt like a matter of time until that turned out differently.

After straightening Sue's chair under the table, Eleanor saw her out. The midday sun was high. "Golly," Sue said on the last stair as it wobbled. She jumped down and pointed at the step as if it was a snake. "Honey, you ought to look at that. I about broke my neck."

Eleanor shook her head at the dramatic remark. Granted, the step did look worn, maybe even rotted through. She sighed. It was another to-do to add to her never-ending list.

Sue shielded her eyes as she turned. "Well, anyway, see you Monday morning?"

"See you then," Eleanor said, "Madame File Clerk."

"That's *temporary* Madame File Clerk to you."

Laughing, she waved Sue off before heading back inside.

Chapter Four

"Time to go, Miss Holte." The deputy sheriff's squeaky voice woke her.

Julia blinked at the dim light filtering through the bars of her jail cell. She groaned and sat up. "Thanks, Billy." Stretching, her smile of relief fell at the sight of her brother-in-law, Henry Barrow, on the other side of the open door.

"Lose another bet?" he asked, his voice teasing but kind as she stood, shaking the dirt and bits of straw from the mattress off her long sleeves and pants.

She sniffed, then checked the sole of her boot, frowning at the combination of mud and manure before stomping the clumps free. Henry brushed an errant piece of straw from her shoulder. She ran a hand through her hair, noting the dirt beneath her nails. She scrunched her nose at the stench of herself. "Tried to finish that race last night but may never get the chance to," she replied, "thanks to our favorite town sheriff." She leveled a scathing glare at the vacant desk across the small room, wishing she could burn a hole in the copper nameplate.

"A game of poker would draw a lot less attention."

Julia waved his comment off as they stepped outside. The bright sunlight on a Sunday morning made her squint; the sun seemed to beat down as it rose higher in the blue sky. It was the end of Memorial Day weekend, and summer was right around the corner. She turned and waved to Billy before stretching again. Her navy denim button-down was wrinkled, and she knew everything she wore needed a wash. "Any chump can play poker. Not everyone can ride."

Henry shook his head, and she caught his eye roll.

"C'mon, Henry. Where'd your sense of fun go?" She playfully shoved him as they turned down 5th Street.

He adjusted the lapels of his coat before nodding a good morning to a wagon parts shopkeeper outside his storefront. The look Henry gave her reminded her he could keep up with her antics if he wanted to and had done so plenty of times back in Texas. He had been one of the few of her father's ranch hands to give in to her endless challenges, indulging her need to be just as tough as the men. It was Julia's sister, now Henry's wife, Rose, who had corralled Henry's wild ways and put a lid on his late nights and penchant for whisky-induced brawls.

As they walked, Julia contemplated the changes in Henry as they turned west, farther from the main street. He certainly seemed calmer since marrying Rose, like a sense of peace had locked in place somewhere inside him. Part of her envied that change. She used the toe of her boot to kick at a stray cobblestone.

"Rose will be glad that at least you didn't do nothin' to get yourself booked more than one night."

"She knows I can take care of myself." Julia pulled herself up, but another incredulous look from Henry and the sight of their white, two-story Victorian home made her bravado wilt. The gusto with which she'd attacked last night's bet shrank under the walk up their drive. On the porch steps, she caught movement from the front curtain, no doubt Rose watching and waiting for her return.

Pushing open the front door, Henry called, "Rose, sweetheart, I've found a mutt. She's a bit mangy, but I think we should keep her." Julia shoved him again. He laughed, nearly colliding with the parlor chair.

They moved past the narrow stairs that ran up the wall to their right and into the kitchen at the back of the modest house. They'd gotten lucky, Rose reminded them often, with this home.

Henry had moved to Idaho Springs first after obtaining the assistant manager's position at the Monarch Mill at the start of the year. His experience in helping with bookkeeping as a ranch hand had held great appeal; that, and a sudden vacancy at the mill, prompted his quick hire. The house had belonged to a long-time resident, a widower whose wife had passed a few years before and whose children had all moved on to different parts of the country. The widower, Mr. Franklin, had taken what little belongings he had left and gone to Denver. The mill manager, Mr. Weldon, had notified Henry of the vacancy, knowing he'd have a wife and sister-in-law joining him in the spring. Henry had signed the paperwork, and the house was theirs.

Presently, Rose had her back to them at the sink. Julia could see from her sister's rigid shoulders that this was not going to be a pleasant conversation. "Morning, Rose," she called, crossing the blue linoleum floor patterned with small white flowers, their petals matching the sink and cabinetry running along three of the four walls in the compact space. Henry had had most of the house updated prior to the move, wanting to give Rose as close to her dream home as possible. Only the stove, tucked between counters to Rose's left, was a daunting black amid the bright room.

Julia found a kitchen chair and sat, unlacing her boots. She noted the track of dirt trailing after her. She'd have to clean that up, too. Henry reappeared from the other room having found his black work jacket, swapping it out for the gray one he'd picked her up in. It fell past his hips and made him look trim. A belt with a large brass buckle sat tight around his waist. The blue flat cap was the only touch of color.

"Black is strong," he'd explained to them when they'd joked that he looked like an undertaker. "I need the men in the mill office to take me seriously until I get my feet under me." His dark brown hair and eyes didn't help matters.

Rose remained stubbornly facing the sink and its open window that looked out over their small grassy yard. Julia leaned sideways as she slipped off her boots to discover her sister peeling potatoes. Rose's movements grew more emphatic with each one. Grimacing, Julia glanced at Henry and brought her hands together in a plea not to leave her alone with her sister. Surely, he could spare a little more time before the lunch of mill managers he had scheduled.

To her dismay, he only mouthed, "Sorry," and crossed the kitchen to leave a quick kiss on Rose's cheek before he left.

For a time, the only sound was the swiping of the kitchen blade. Unable to take the quiet, Julia said, "Rose, I—"

"Coffee?" Her sister turned around, not meeting her gaze as she found the tin carafe on the stovetop, then an empty red mug. It was one of several things Julia had brought with her from her family's ranch. She cupped the sides as it rested on the table while Rose poured. "You must be tired. The cell beds are terribly uncomfortable, so you mentioned last week."

Julia looked up, but her sister's blue eyes remained focused anywhere but on her. Tendrils of molasses brown hair had fallen loose from the succinct waves she had spent time delicately arranging. She, like most women, had fallen in line with the decade's trend and cropped her hair short. She had always been one to note what was happening, fashion-wise, when they were in Texas. Though, as Julia constantly reminded her, "By the time those fashions reach us, they're already over." She'd used that often as her excuse for keeping her hair long and not wearing a stitch of makeup.

"Thanks," Julia said, taking a sip. Rose's thin lips were in a hard line as she went back to the sink and continued peeling. "I appreciate Henry picking me up this morning. Glad y'all didn't leave me in there until noon." She gave a laugh, but her sister ignored her.

Searching the room for an idea for an olive branch, Julia said, "Can I help with the food? Looks like we're feeding an army with all those potatoes."

Her sister, who had set the blade aside to dry her hands, spun again, the towel snapping at her side. Julia sat back. Her older sister was typically the sweetest, kindest person she knew. "How's that darling daughter of yours, Rose?" folks back home had asked their parents for as long as Julia could remember. Everyone inquired about her. Men had courted her since she was fourteen. Meanwhile, all people had ever done when Julia walked by was shake their heads, no doubt wondering where things had gone wrong with the Holtes' second child. Unlike Rose, who always looked picture-perfect, Julia usually sported a new bruise from a scuffle with a fellow ranch hand or had a tear in her shirt from scaling fences.

Rose, too, was very much the fierce guardian of the family, the eldest sister to her marrow. While she kept her face clean and a smile at the ready, her gaze perennially held faint concern, the product of familial expectations placed upon her shoulders from a young age. Rose had looked after Julia when her parents had business trips or hosted other well-to-dos in the oil industry at their ranch.

Julia admired the constant calm Rose emitted and how she always seemed to have a plan. Deep down, she craved her sister's approval. The fiery look Rose bore into her now, however, was anything but pride.

"Jules, this has to stop."

"This?"

Rose whipped the towel toward the door. "*This.* This incessant need to prove yourself that inevitably gets you handcuffed and tossed in jail."

"Volz only cuffs me if people are around to watch."

Her sister took a breath before replying sardonically, "How nice of him."

Julia gave half a smile, taking another drink to give herself time to think.

"What was it this time?" Rose asked, crossing her arms.

Julia leaned forward, ready to defend herself. "Remember that hard-boiled sap who thought he could outride me? I was trying to finish that bet."

Rose raised a brow but didn't say anything.

Julia shrugged. "Ralph and some other fellas nabbed a few mules. I would've won if Volz hadn't intervened. Again." She swallowed. "It's not my fault he has it out for me."

Her sister studied her, arms still firmly crossed. Julia tried not to shrink in her seat. Rose's earlier words sank into her skin and made her itch. *This incessant need to prove myself? What do I need to prove to this stupid mountain town?*

"We've been here two months," Rose was saying, pulling Julia's gaze as she took another sip. "Two months and..." She paused, counting on her fingers. "Five arrests. Five." She shoved her open hand forward. "This month, mule races. Last month..." She squinted as if trying to recall.

"Ralph and I tossed Michael Keebo into the river," Julia answered. Sitting up, she explained, finger raised, "We had good reason. He was talking bad about Ralph's sisters, calling them all sorts of names."

Rose only sighed.

Biting her lip, Julia pushed back in her chair. Tension filled the room. As usual, it was Rose who was first to start their reconciliation as she joined Julia at the table. Her voice was softer as she folded the rag in her lap and asked, "Jules, what's going on?"

Uncomfortable sitting in her filth from the night before, Julia became keenly aware of how she must look: a dirty urchin among the pristine appliances in her perfect sister's home. She avoided Rose's gaze and decided to pick at a scab on her left forearm.

"We all agreed that you could come here with us. Remember?"

Sniffling, Julia met her gaze. Their eyes they'd inherited from their mother. Besides that, their similar small noses and petite builds were all they had in common. Rose was willowy everywhere Julia was hard from outdoor labor on their family's ranch, chiseling her arms and legs until she was as fit as any man. Rose had always been more inclined to housework and books. "I remember," she finally said. "I asked to come."

Rose nodded. "Yet you act like we dragged you here kicking and screaming." She licked her lips, leaning forward. "Listen, I know it takes getting used to. My head only now stopped hurting from being up so high in these mountains." She offered a small smile. "Not to mention my lungs. I still need to catch my breath going up and down the stairs."

Julia smiled.

"I thought you wanted this."

"I did." Julia clenched her jaw, rubbing a hand over her forehead. "I do." Rose was right. It had been her idea to join them in Colorado. She'd wanted to go—no, had needed to go—after what had happened last year at the ranch.

She tried to convey this in her gaze as Rose watched her. Finally, her sister's eyes fell as she said, "A file clerk position opened up at the mill office."

Frowning at the change of subject, Julia said, "Okay."

Rose crossed her legs, then ran a hand up and down the material of the blue skirt she wore under a billowy white blouse. "Henry and I put in your name for the position."

"You what?" She stood, nearly knocking the chair back as she gaped.

Rose only lifted her chin, continuing coolly, "You'll start tomorrow if you get the position, which seems promising as you're the only one who's applied."

"I *didn't* apply." Julia felt hot and the room started to spin. "Rose, how could you do this?"

At this, Rose stood, matching Julia's stance. "You did this, Jules. You did this to yourself," she said, pointing. "Yes, that sheriff has you under a microscope. I'll agree with you there." She held up a hand as Julia started to speak. "But you are on a slippery slope, and I won't stand by and watch you fall by the wayside. We're grateful for your help around the house, but it's not enough. You need something else."

Julia clenched her jaw as she stared in disbelief. Eventually, all she could say was, "I hate offices."

Rose's posture softened, her shoulders falling. "I know," she said, almost guilty, "but it's the best I could do."

Julia's chest heaved, and she worked to steady her breathing. Her mind burned. An office job? She could hardly stand to sleep inside, let alone work inside. And Rose knew that. This was punishment, she thought. Punishment for what she'd done.

Before she could say something that she'd regret, Julia snatched up her boots and stormed from the room.

"You'll thank me for this," Rose called after her. But Julia didn't stop; she only focused on the stomping of her feet as she headed for a bath.

Chapter Five

F inished?" Eleanor asked Peter, reaching for his plate. He tossed the last bite of gravy-soaked bread into his mouth, chewing through a grin. "Finished."

She washed the remains of rabbit stew—their traditional Sunday evening meal—from their plates in the sink when Peter asked, "Momma, when can I go to work in the mill?"

She stiffened but took a breath to quiet the uncomfortable fluttering in her chest. She put on a smile and said over her shoulder, "Peter, you know the answer to that."

His face fell, his brown eyes looking dejectedly at his lap. "Not until I'm older."

"Exactly," she said, rinsing the dishes and laying them on a rag to dry. She double-checked that both plates were the same distance apart from the sink. She studied him for a moment while he gently kicked at the air under the table.

He looked up, his gaze bright at a new thought. "But I am older." He lifted his chin. "I'm older every day."

She laughed and went to him, adjusting her cotton skirt to kneel beside his chair. Reaching up, she ran a hand down his pale cheek. His bright red-orange hair was just like hers, though its fineness he'd gotten from Louis. "I can't argue with that, darling, but the answer is still no."

He harrumphed, crossing his gangly arms over his small chest. For a second, she caught a flash of Louis in his determined gaze. "I'm eight now, Momma. Buddy Wilkins and Stephen McCoy both started at the mill."

Eleanor hated to disappoint him, but she shuddered to think of those young boys crawling amidst that dreadful machinery up the mountain. Cupping his cheek, she said, "I'm sorry. The answer is no."

He scrambled out of her reach, moving toward his room upstairs. "That's not fair," he cried.

The sudden outburst startled her. She stood, starting to go to him. "Peter—"

But he stormed away, his tiny stomps echoing up the stairs until his door slammed. Eleanor sighed, turning to replace the lid on the stove pot. Better to let him be for a time, she told herself. He would be fine soon enough. She kept busy in the meantime. She arranged the pot handle to face east, then checked the bins of vegetables were in order. She counted the onions—four—the carrots—six—and the potatoes—two—and made a mental list of what to order from the market on Monday after she dropped the mill uniforms off. She turned to lean against the small gas range and stared at Louis's shotgun above the door.

"You'll never go hungry here," he had stated proudly in their first week together as newlyweds. She'd been there less than a month since leaving Minnesota. "There's so much game on this land, we'll have rabbit and deer coming out of our ears."

She inhaled as the memory shifted, the dark night when her husband had left still as fresh and sharp as a wasp sting. Shaking away the chill that always accompanied such thoughts, she found a teacup and set the water to boil for Peter's tea.

She found him tucked in bed upstairs, washed and in his bedclothes. She smiled. Despite their spat, her son was as responsible as anyone and remained loyal to their routines. Eleanor set the teacup on the bedside table.

She'd wanted to go into town for a photograph with Louis after their marriage, but they'd never done so. A week after that terrible night, she'd found one of his ties mixed up with her things in a drawer. When Peter was old enough for a twin bed in this room upstairs, she'd tied the brown material around the knob on the nightstand drawer in lieu of a photograph. She regaled Peter with tales of Louis when he asked for them, as many as she could supply, anyway. Their time together had been so brief. The older Peter got, the more questions he had. Eleanor's heart sank each time he begged her for another tale, some scrap of what his father was like. The weight of being everything at once to her son was crushing at times, but she would do it forever if it meant keeping him safe and with her.

She reached up to turn off the wall lamp, leaving only the candle on the bedside table for light. The curtains were drawn, and the rushing of the river sounded outside.

She sat and handed him the tea. He took a sip, scrunching his nose. "It's worse than yesterday's."

"Sorry. Doctor's orders. I can't add sugar anymore."

"That's terrible."

She laughed, running a hand through his hair. "I know. But it's to help your breathing."

He downed the tea, giving an exaggerated cough and face of disgust.

"That's a good boy," she said before reaching to rest a hand on his chest. "How do you feel?"

He shrugged. "Fine."

She searched his small frame, knowing it was fruitless to find evidence, a reason, for his weak lungs. Asthma, she believed, was one of the most fearsome maladies in existence. Growing up, her cousins had caught infections, pneumonia, and influenza, all things Eleanor had seen tear through her aunt's home in bouts of fevers and all things doctors could treat. Her cousins had each recovered in due time. But this? She recalled the first asthma episode Peter had had when he was six. She'd been scared to death, carrying him all the way into town to the local physician's house and banging on the poor man's door until he'd let them in. Dr. Wicker had thought it was a reaction to something Peter had encountered at first, but his wife had brewed a cup of Mormon tea that they'd managed to get Peter to drink. Miraculously, his airways had opened, and the incident had passed.

Now, she tried to always have a container of the herb on hand, along with the pills from Denver. His asthma episodes weren't frequent but could be bad enough to leave him bedridden for a day. She worried about him when he went to school, sending him some tea in Louis's old thermos along with lunch when she had enough of the supply. But Peter didn't seem to let it stop him. He was always the last to be called inside in the morning, and she often found him scaling the mountainside or playing by the river on weekends, searching for bugs and squirrels.

"How was your trip to the town hall with Sue this morning?" she asked, sensing he didn't want to talk about his condition.

"Swell," he said. "Uncle Isaac let me stand on the dais and pretend to give a speech. Auntie Sue gave me five cents for carrying her coat all day."

Eleanor raised a brow, following his finger to the coin on the small chair in the corner. "We'll be rich in no time." She smiled, and he beamed proudly. She kissed his forehead. "Sleep well, darling." He rolled over, and she tucked him in before blowing out the candle and returning downstairs.

She rinsed his cup and placed it beside the two others on the shelf above the sink, careful to align things perfectly. Drying her hands on a rag, she studied its cornflower blue pattern. The color reminded her of that woman's eyes, the one from a couple weeks ago who had stopped the wagon from trampling Sue's book. Eleanor couldn't seem to forget her. She wondered if she had been merely passing through. That idea, to her surprise, sent a pang of something odd down the side of her ribs. Sadness? Disappointment? Eleanor wasn't sure, so she dismissed the idea and carried on with her chores.

Later, she dimmed all the lamps on the way to her room. She eyed the bed, then lit the table lamp. The basket of mill uniforms sat on a wooden table next to it. She checked they were still folded neatly when a glint caught her eye. She frowned and pulled the topmost shirt closer to see.

A glistening speck, no bigger than a crumb, sat just outside the collar. Something scrubbed loose, maybe? She pulled the shirt toward the lamp for more light.

Her heart skipped. It was a gold fleck. She threw her gaze at the door as if someone might have been watching. How could this have gotten there? The mill men, of course, worked themselves to the bone sifting through the mountain's rock for this each day. Could some of it have strayed, skipping errantly onto their clothes while they worked?

Quickly, she found a small vial containing the last of her perfume. *I've not worn this in years, anyway.* She dashed the liquid into the kitchen sink. Back in her room, she found a sewing needle and settled near the lamplight. Carefully, she lifted the gold from the linen. With a delicate tap, she dropped it into the vial. It settled against a drop of perfume. She swallowed and looked at the basket of uniforms. Could there be more?

"Don't be greedy, Eleanor," she said to herself. But Peter's cough sounded upstairs. She pursed her lips. Medicine is expensive, a voice in her head reminded her. Surely, it wasn't wrong to save a little for that. The money she brought in for her laundering services at the mill was enough to get by, but with a few of these…

She bit her lip and stoppered the vial. Luck was what this was. And luck didn't come around to people like her often. Tucking the vial into her drawer beneath a pair of stockings, she determined she would take all the luck she could get.

CHAPTER SIX

W hat about a position as a driver?"
"No."
"In the tunnel?"
"No."
"What about—"
"Julia." Henry held up a hand. The silver of his wedding ring glinted in the bright sun where they stood half a mile up the dry, sloping mountainside path that led to Monarch Mill. From here, they could see most of Idaho Springs. The folks below looked like toy soldiers as they started to fill the streets. The surrounding mountains, their tips snowcapped even in late spring, were guards keeping a watchful eye.

Henry's voice broke her thoughts. "You're to look after the files in the office. You'll mind the books and records. No machines. No pickaxes. Just you and the mill ledgers."

She groaned, undoing the top button of her collar to ease the uncomfortable heat on her neck. "Just hand me over to Volz again, why don't you?" She moved to continue their walk, but Henry held her arm. "What?"

Once he had her reluctant gaze, he said, "This is for your sister, not me. It doesn't bother me what you get up to in your free time. The moonshine, the bets..." He hesitated, eyes narrowed as if measuring whether to add to the list before he finally said, "The women."

She raised a brow. "I thought that was you I saw playing Ralph in pool."

He snorted, and a small smile revealed his relief at her casual reply. "I still get out from time to time. And it was impossible to miss that woman pulling you into the back room at Thrasher's."

Her face felt hot, but she cleared her throat at the memory. "I'd had too much to drink. Besides, that was weeks ago, and she was only bein' friendly."

Scoffing, Henry said, "My point is, it doesn't bother me the terms by which you live your life." She opened her mouth to express her gratitude, but he added, "One of those terms, however, was coming here to help Rose see after the house."

Her words fell flat, and she looked down.

"Your sister is worried for you, Jules, and more worry is the last thing she needs after—" She found his gaze. "After everything," he said, his voice low.

"I know."

"This place is a fresh start for all of us." His tone lightened, and he nudged her arm. "Don't go spoilin' things before we've hardly begun."

They started up the path again. The incline leveled out, and the long, fort-style office came into view. Men's voices grew louder from the back of the building. At the same time, a crew of workers came up behind them. Henry added, "Give it a chance. Office work ain't so bad."

She glared, but it was half-hearted. He was right. If this was what she needed to do for Rose to have some faith in her, she had to at least try. The group of men passed, all average height, with scraggly beards and uneven haircuts poking out beneath flat caps. Their plain pants and white shirts surprised her.

At the door, Henry seemed to read her mind. "They have uniforms they change into." He checked his pocket watch. "Mrs. Perry should be by soon to drop them off." He moved inside.

Julia caught the door, peering into the room packed with long cabinets and high shelves. She already felt smothered by the sea of paperwork waiting for her. She turned back for another look around. A memory flashed between the tall pines: endless blue sky, the cold steel of the oil rig as she climbed higher on a mild September day. Higher than she should have…

Julia shook her head, forcing herself back to the present. She replayed what Henry had said: she was here for Rose. To help, not hinder. If this job was what she had to do to regain her sister's trust…she'd bite the bullet. Taking a breath, she stepped inside as the open air disappeared.

❖

"Good morning."

"Mornin'."

Something about the husky voice caught Eleanor's ear, making her pause inside the mill office door. It closed gently at her back. She peered around the stack of uniforms piled up to her forehead and found a pair of bright blue eyes eyeing her. The same eyes she'd found herself thinking about in quiet moments alone the last two weeks. This couldn't be the same woman, could it? Eleanor swallowed as she realized those eyes were settled into the same round, tanned face. The face she hadn't thought she'd see again. "It's you."

Leaning back in the wooden chair, the woman frowned at her statement. She asked, "Can I help you?"

"I…" Eleanor swallowed. *She doesn't remember me.* Her face warmed as the woman's gaze flickered as if trying to understand what probably came across as a strange demeanor. *Maybe she's recalling who I am.* The hopeful thought was dashed though when, to her dismay, the look of recognition never came. Gathering herself, Eleanor said, "I have the uniforms for the men."

The woman nodded, flashing the same charming smile she remembered. "So I see."

The teasing response made Eleanor frown. Was she trying to be smart? Perhaps she did remember Eleanor but didn't want to let on that she did. Maybe she wanted nothing to do with her. Well, if that was the case, Eleanor didn't have time for such antics. She brushed the comment aside and searched the room for Mr. Weldon. She'd hoped to ask him about Sue's recent travels to Wyoming. Not finding him, she scanned for a spot to set the uniforms down and decided to ask an obvious question, "You're new?"

"Just started today. New file clerk."

"You don't—" Eleanor cut herself off, flustered by the woman's continued use of her disarming smile. "You don't look like a file clerk," she said, hitching the basket onto her hip, suddenly aware of its weight. The woman raised a brow and leaned forward. She steepled her fingers under her chin, still grinning. "I mean, you don't look like the last woman who worked here," Eleanor stammered, slamming her lips into a hard line at her own ridiculous remark and the utterly amused smile on the file clerk's face.

She stood, reaching out. "Let me help you with those."

Eleanor turned away. "Thank you, but I've got it. I'm just waiting for Mr. Weldon."

As if on cue, the manager wandered in from the back door across the long room. "Ah, Mrs. Perry, good morning." He set down a clipboard and hurried to her, taking the top stack of uniforms. The woman, she noticed, shrank back into her chair. "Everything in order?"

"Yes, sir. You've got surnames A to H." She lifted the basket, her arms grateful for the lightened load. "I through Z here."

"There's a fella with a surname starts with a Z?" They both turned to the new file clerk's question.

"That would be Thadius Zachary from outside Salt Lake originally," Mr. Weldon answered. His hazel gaze flitted between them. "I take it you've met our new file clerk, then, Mrs. Perry?"

Eleanor handed the basket to a worker whom she recognized. His awkward gait was the result of an injury three years ago in the tunnel. She watched him make his way to the door Mr. Weldon had entered through that led to the men's changing room. Beyond that was the three-quarter mile walk toward the mill. "Actually," she started to say, "we—"

"Julia Holte," the woman said, standing again. Despite being a couple inches shorter than Eleanor, she gave off the confidence of someone closer to six foot. Her dark brown trousers were held up by a leather belt that cinched at her waist, and it seemed she was trying to hide her figure beneath a man's blue button-down and a black vest. All she's missing is a gallon hat, Eleanor thought with a quick glance at her boots, and she'd look like she'd fallen out of a western painting.

Eleanor took her outstretched hand. "How do you do?"

Julia seemed ready to reply when Mr. Weldon said, "Miss Holte came highly recommended from her brother-in-law, Mr. Barrow. We're lucky she wanted the position with the vacancy opening so suddenly."

Retracting her hand, Eleanor wondered at the half-smile Julia gave her. Feeling more offended by the moment at not being remembered, however, she adjusted the knitted green shawl over her shoulders, clasping it tight as she was certain she'd caught Julia's gaze tracing her figure. Everything about Miss Holte was driving her madder by the moment, from her inviting disposition to the way her eyes seemed to take Eleanor in, making her squirm and leaving her uncertain how to feel about such a thing. She tried to track Mr. Weldon's comments, recognizing Mr. Barrow's name as the new assistant manager Sue had mentioned. "Wonderful. I'm glad things worked out."

A millman called from the back. "Well, duty calls," Mr. Weldon said, turning to each of them. "I'll be back soon, Miss Holte. Please start this morning's check-in log for the men, noting anyone who is unaccounted for." He turned, then spotted the clipboard and fetched it for her. Eleanor caught the frown on Julia's face at the sight of the list. "Mrs. Perry, you know where to find the uniforms. We'll see you on Thursday for the next pickup?"

"Yes, sir."

He nodded, then hurried away. Eleanor glanced at Julia, who sighed, then set the clipboard aside. Eleanor pretended to note the time from the wall clock and adjusted her hair as she studied Julia. She tried to reconcile the fact that the same woman from Miner Street was here in front of her. Eleanor had begun to think she was a figment of her imagination. Or maybe a spirit, a guardian angel who'd stepped in one day to rescue a book before vanishing back into the mountain sky. Were there guardian angels for literature? Eleanor shook her head to regain her focus.

The fact was, that same woman was here, and she was the new Monarch Mill file clerk. She even had a name: Julia Holte. How unlike the other file clerks she was, too. Most had been young, not that Julia wasn't. In fact, she seemed in her mid-twenties, a few years younger than Eleanor. But the women before were often newly married, usually the new bride of a mill worker. They found themselves committed to motherhood nine months later, keeping at home to mind their babies. Others, like the previous clerk, Miss Akins, were passing through in search of a husband. Miss Holte didn't seem to fit either profile.

Julia smiled when their gazes found each other. Eleanor felt a small blush at having been caught staring and quickly extended her hand again. "Well, it's a pleasure to make your acquaintance." Eleanor noted the rough skin of blisters on Julia's palm. Like her gaze, her hand was warm. Eleanor found her touch oddly comforting, a bizarre fact as they were practically strangers. A whirl of thoughts circled her. Ultimately, Eleanor landed on the irksome nature of not being remembered. That battled with her insecurity; it was silly to be angry about such a thing when their initial interaction had been so brief. God, she would have to take the long way around to the changing room's exterior door to get out of this situation as quickly as possible.

Unable to handle the whirlwind in her mind, she said, "Good day, then, and good luck," before she turned and hurried out the door.

CHAPTER SEVEN

W ait." Julia's chair scraped over the tile floor, but Eleanor was already gone.

"Julia." She turned to find Henry. He eyed her, then gestured to the door as if asking why she seemed ready to bolt.

"Why aren't you at the mill?" she asked, straightening and glancing at the clipboard, pretending she was reading over it and not fighting the urge to follow Mrs. Perry. She had the nagging feeling they'd seen one another before, but she couldn't put her finger on it.

"I thought I'd give you a tour."

"What happened to 'no machines'?" she asked, smiling.

Rolling his eyes, he waved for her to follow. "Safety precaution in case you must go in for some reason. Don't touch anything," he added at her eager jog to catch up to him.

"Yes, sir," she said and earned a glare for her mocking tone. Laughing, she glanced back at the front door. She couldn't think of when she might have seen Mrs. Perry before. Maybe Rose knew her, and that was why she seemed familiar. She was married, obviously. The thought sent a jolt of dejection through her chest, but she pushed down the feeling as she followed Henry out a side door.

Low-lying brush and scarlet firecrackers dotted the mountain on each side of their walk. The mill loomed closer with each step. She let out a low whistle as they approached.

"She is a beauty," Henry said, admiration clear in his voice. The mill towered over them. Each gargantuan piece of the structure sat like an intricate puzzle as it climbed up the mountainside. Its yellow facade resembled the golden wings of its namesake, which had been emboldened in red letters large enough to read from town. "Construction started in 1891. Took them over a decade to finish." He pointed to a tower of stacked logs, crisscrossed like that of a cabin two stories high. A smaller building sat precariously atop it, connected to a track that disappeared into the mountainside. "The tunnel is state-of-the-art. Over four miles long, it cuts through the hillside to—"

"To drain water to clear paths for the mines," she finished, noting the train that sat on the track below. "Gold is extracted, compiled here at the mill for sifting, then Colorado Railroad takes the product on to Denver for smelting."

Henry gave her an impressed look. "You did your homework."

"I listen when you talk. Sometimes."

They stood in front of the mill's main level. The nearness of grating machinery endlessly turning and crushing the mountain ore set her teeth on edge.

"You get used to the noise," he yelled as he opened the door.

She winced and clamped her hands over her ears. "Jesus, that's terrible."

"What?"

She shook her head, barely able to think. What she wouldn't give for the quiet of the ranch and the sound of cicadas against a tranquil Texas sky. Instead, the piercing squeal of a saw tore through her like a knife. She shivered. Remember why you're here, she told herself as she kept her hands firmly planted over her ears and followed Henry inside.

Eleanor was thinking about her meeting with Julia when she passed the schoolhouse on her way back through town. She was mostly indignant at Julia for not recognizing her. Then again, she reasoned as her anger ebbed, it had been a brief encounter. They'd hardly spoken two sentences to one another. She hadn't even gotten her name. But now, Eleanor knew it: Julia Holte. So she wasn't merely passing through town. She lived here and knew the assistant mill manager. Eleanor wondered what had brought her here. Her mind whirred with possibilities. Eventually, her anger wilted to curiosity. *I'll have to ask Sue if she's met her.*

Admittedly, she didn't ask after folks very often. She'd learned not to since Sue had a knack for arranging a millman, a miner, or a new product manager to be in the office when Eleanor was dropping off the uniforms, her not-so-secret matchmaking attempts. Thankfully, those had waned the last couple of years. Plus, asking after a woman was harmless. Surely, Sue would know something about the new file clerk.

Now, Eleanor shielded her gaze from the sun to scan the group of children clamoring across the field as the schoolmarm came to call them inside. She spotted Peter with another little boy playing with a leather ball. She waved, but he didn't see her before he snatched it up and followed his classmates inside.

A trio of mothers descended the hill from the back of the schoolhouse. Eleanor recognized one of them, Mrs. Henley. Her husband ran the wagon parts store on 4th Street. Mrs. Henley also consistently gave her the cold shoulder when they saw one another at the market and had ever since Louis left. In recent years, sympathy ran in shorter supply than snow-free days in Idaho Springs.

As the women turned toward town, Mrs. Henley's shawl fell from around her shoulders. None of them seemed to notice, so Eleanor hurried forward. "Mrs. Henley." She scooped it up. "You dropped this."

Whatever conversation the women were having paused as they turned. The others pulled back their shoulders, eyeing Eleanor like the most peculiar specimen. Mrs. Henley's pretty, delicate features were downturned as her gaze narrowed at the shawl before she took it back.

"Thank you." She passed it between her hands as if inspecting for damage. The short brunette behind her crossed her arms and smiled tightly.

Tearing through her mind for something to say, Eleanor pointed to the schoolhouse. "Your boy has grown."

The smile returned, and Mrs. Henley's eyes brightened. "Yes. He's taking after his father."

Unsure what else to say, Eleanor smiled and started to go. "Well, have a nice day."

"Mrs. Perry?"

"Yes?" She wasn't sure why, but the prospect of this conversation continuing left her gleeful. It wasn't like this had been a particularly warm exchange. Maybe the awkward meeting with Julia had left her wanting. Was she that hungry for interaction? *God, maybe I do need to get out more.*

"It's a shame we haven't seen you at Sunday service."

As quickly as it came, her joy wilted beneath Mrs. Henley's gaze. Her own fell, and she stammered a reply. "Yes. It's difficult to get away. My work…" Heat filled her cheeks.

"The sermons could be good for someone like you and for that boy of yours."

Eleanor straightened. "Someone like me?"

Mrs. Henley adjusted the shawl around her shoulders, a warrior readying her armor before slinging her next barb. "I just mean a woman out here alone, with a son without a father. The word of God is for even the most forsaken among us, after all."

Anger wriggled in her throat, and she swallowed it to contain her fury. Eleanor's thumb found her forefinger. She inhaled, counting the pine needles scattered between them. A flash of the time she'd gone to church with Sue returned. It had been a few months after Louis had left. Peter had cried through most of the service, drawing furtive glances and judgmental scowls. She didn't recall Mrs. Henley being there, but plenty of folks had made her feel like she was in a fishbowl. Everyone had gawked at the presumed widow whose husband had to have had good reason to leave her. It must have been Eleanor who was the problem; she had to have driven him away. Why else would he have left, abandoning a newborn son?

She counted to twelve before forcing herself back to the present. "Your concern is appreciated but unfounded."

Mrs. Henley's gaze widened, her lips parting in surprise.

"Peter and I are doing just fine, thank you." Eleanor swept her gaze across them, and she gave a curt nod. "Good day."

Rather than head home, Eleanor followed the creek west to the outskirts of Idaho Springs. Her mind spun hotly until she was several blocks from the schoolhouse. The earth felt lush beneath her boots. Open skies overhead were mostly clear, but she could feel rain on the horizon. A spring shower would make its way over the mountain by supper. Mother nature and her beauty quieted the dark thoughts left by Mrs. Henley, and Eleanor relaxed. Drawing nearer to the creek, she pulled a handful of cattails that reminded her she needed to check on the garden when she got home. Maybe she'd get lucky and find a few patches of wild onions along the way. She was mentally counting the strawberry plants behind her house when the hot springs came into view.

Despite having seen them countless times, they remained quite the sight. Three large pools of steaming water at the base of the foothills seemed otherworldly. Their dark waters bubbled, and she understood why they could beckon folks from all over the world. The springs seemed mystical, like a place from a tall tale. Two large pools sat next to each other, slats of slick gray rock separating them. Twenty yards up the grassy slope, a third smaller pool nestled into the mountainside.

Louis had taken her here after she'd arrived in town. "Wait till you see it," he had said excitedly, practically leaping as they walked to the water. "Ain't nothin like it anywhere else." She had kept her mouth closed, knowing there were other hot springs around the country. Her uncle had been a traveling businessman and had regaled her and her cousins with tales of what he'd gotten to see. But Louis's excitement had been so vibrant, she hadn't wanted to dull his enthusiasm.

Once Louis left, Eleanor had fought against being alone. She'd attached herself to Sue at first, who had been lovely in her sympathy. But she still had Peter to raise, and having to do that alone was not what she had planned. It had threatened to break her at times. So when she could, if Sue was willing to watch Peter for an afternoon, she'd sneak out to the hot springs and sit. With each visit, her reality sank in more, and after a year without word from Louis, she'd wept openly for her new life. She'd cried and let the mountains take on her burden, just for a little while as she'd laid her troubles at their feet. Unlike many of the townsfolk, the mountains never judged her. They didn't speak while she relayed her fears. And when she was done, when her tears and cries were spent, they let her go, waiting until she needed them again.

Since taking the laundress job and Peter starting school, she hadn't come by. But now, with him pushing to work at the mill, old fears reared their heads. Mrs. Henley's words echoed, "Someone like you." She found herself in need of quiet support. She clenched her jaw, determined to keep Peter's focus on school and away from that place. Sunlight glinted off the water, reminding her of the minerals trapped within the mountain's rock. The minerals that somehow, though she still couldn't explain exactly how, had broken Louis. The same thing couldn't happen to Peter. She wouldn't let it.

Setting the bundle of cattails at her side, she found a spot on the rocks near the lower pool. She let the water hypnotize her, then spoke, confessing her trepidations.

It surprised her when Julia came to mind. She laughed. "What's the point of her, huh?" she asked the mountains. "Why send such a…" She searched her surroundings for the right word. "A confounding spirit into my life? And why can't I stop thinking about her?"

She waited for a reply, but like always, the mountains only listened.

Chapter Eight

"Cheers to your first day." Ralph clinked their glasses together, and Julia had a long drink. She closed her eyes, savoring the sharp taste.

She turned to him. "I don't know how people do it."

"Office work?" he asked, motioning for another drink after he downed most of the first one. Thrasher's was already busy at five-twenty. The day shift at the mill had just released, and most of the men stopped by before heading home for the night. Lively conversation filled the large establishment. The sound of a game of billiards came from nearby, pool balls clacking off one another. Rowdy shouts were tossed across a game of poker under dimly lit wall lamps. Wood floors creaked under the weight of work boots.

"Yeah. There's no glory in paper pushing, Ralph."

He shrugged, his shoulders like boulders on his large frame. "It ain't so bad if you like what you're doin'."

She mumbled behind her glass, "I think that's my problem." She nudged his arm. "You really like what you do?"

He grinned, his green eyes bright. "Yeah. I'm with my family all day. Can't complain about that." After their first meeting, right here in these exact seats, Ralph had regaled her with the history of the family bakery. His grandparents, Cornish immigrants, had opened a meat pie shop in 1877. His mom had learned the trade, and his father had married into it. Now, Ralph and two younger sisters all helped keep the bakery running like clockwork, making it a staple in Idaho Springs. He'd brought her a pie to try not long after they'd met, and she had to admit, the savory meat wrapped delicately inside flaky dough was delicious. "Plus, it makes me feel good, you know, keepin' the mill men fed. If I'm not gonna be in there with 'em, it's the least I can do."

Julia nodded. This morning, she had noticed a lot of the workers coming in with bandana-wrapped bundles, the scent of meat pies wafting from them as they made their way to change. It was a clever concoction; the pies were easy to transport into the mountain and hearty enough to get the men through the day.

"You're doing the same thing now, helpin' those men," he added, giving her a pleased smile.

"Helping the men?" She snorted. "Organizing papers isn't something to write home about."

He took a big gulp of beer. "Come on, Jules. Lighten up. We're here to celebrate your first day." He clinked their glasses together again. She shook her head, unable to stop her smile at his infectious mood. Ralph always had a way of doing that. She'd been wary when he'd sat next to her that first time here, chatting away like they were old friends. The conversation had come easy though, and since moving to Idaho Springs, he'd proven to be a man she could count on. He wasn't afraid of her wild ideas and could step in if someone was coming on too strong after too many drinks. Not that she needed the help, but it was nice to know he was there.

Her mind drifted back to the office. It hadn't been *all* terrible. Mostly boring. The highlight had been that woman, Mrs. Eleanor Perry. The shade of her hair reminded Julia of the sunsets back in Texas. Warm. Bold. She side-eyed Ralph, who had greeted Willard Hodges taking a seat on his other side when she asked, "You ever met a Mrs. Perry?"

He turned back to her, squinting as he tried to recall the name. "Mrs. Perry? Doesn't ring a bell. But there's always folks passin' through. Plus, I'm not the best with names."

"She lives here, I think." Julia turned her glass, eyeing the white foam of her beer. "Brought the uniforms for the mill men." He shrugged. "I can ask my sisters. Maybe they've seen her at church."

They conversed awhile longer about nothing in particular until Julia finished her drink and bid good night to Ralph. The sun was still setting as she made her way back to the house. Rose was in the kitchen fussing over a boiling pot of what smelled like chicken.

"You're home," her sister exclaimed, her hair frizzing from the heat of the room. "It's nearly six-thirty."

Julia opened a window to let in some air to cool them off. "Stopped by Thrasher's." She caught Rose's pointed look as she sat. "One beer, that's all I had. Well, that and one shot of moonshine." She raised her hands, innocent. "Ralph treated me after my first day."

The mention of Ralph's name seemed to soften Rose's scowl. "Well, that was nice of him. He's a sweet man. His sisters are just as kind. They always save me and Henry seats at church."

"Mm-hm," Julia mused, eyeing the three plates Rose had set. Chicken legs, collard greens, and some kind of fruit puree were for dinner. Her stomach growled in anticipation. "Where's Henry?"

"Washing up," Rose replied, moving the pot to a separate area to cool. She swiped her hands down the white apron tied over a red dress. When Julia reached for her plate of chicken, Rose swatted her hand. "I swear, it's like Mother taught you nothing."

Laughing, Julia sat back, relenting. "You know I was never inside at the first dinner bell for Mother's lectures."

Rose sighed dramatically. "Oh, I remember." Shaking her head, she changed the subject. "Tell me about your first day." She fetched glasses and poured milk for each of them.

Julia leaned forward, resting her elbows on either side of her plate. "It was fine."

Rose gave an incredulous look. "Fine. That's all I get?"

"You did force this job on me," Julia muttered, but her retort crumbled at Rose's withering glare. "It was fine," she said again. "I did file clerk stuff. I…filed."

After another moment of staring, Rose cracked a smile. "I swear, Jules. Sometimes, I don't know what to do with you."

She grinned, relieved the temporary tension had dissipated. "It was work. It was fine, and now I'm home."

Her sister nodded. "I suppose that's all I can ask for."

The sound of the tub draining upstairs caught her ear. Henry would be down soon. Julia found her fork and turned it over, the prongs resting on the table in turn. "I did meet someone who seemed interesting. Mrs. Eleanor Perry." She found Rose's gaze. "Do you know her?

Her sister replaced the milk in the icebox. "That name sounds familiar. Mrs. Perry," she muttered and sat as Henry's footsteps sounded on the stairs. "Red hair?"

"Yes," Julia said as Eleanor's fiery locks moved through her mind like a pleasant picture.

"Oh yes. The mill laundress. I've yet to meet her, though Henry says she's pleasant enough. She lives over on Stanley Road, kind of out of town, if I'm not mistaken."

"Who lives on Stanley Road?" Henry asked, finding his seat after leaving a kiss on Rose's cheek.

"Mrs. Eleanor Perry."

He tucked a linen napkin into his collar. "The laundress? Yes, that's right."

"With her husband?" Julia asked as she sat back. Rose was already enjoying a bite of the greens, but she caught Henry's eye at her question.

He held a chicken leg as he answered. "No. It's a rather tragic story, so I've been told. Susannah Weldon relayed it to me after I was hired on. Bit of a gossip, Mrs. Weldon." He cleared his throat. "Mrs. Perry's husband up and left her only two years after they were married."

"Oh." She had been poking at the questionable puree but now pondered the guarded way Eleanor had spoken to her. Maybe she had thought Julia knew who she was and was fearful of being judged. Another word Henry said struck her then, and it was like a bell clanged. *Story.* "Oh!"

Rose and Henry both looked at her. "Are you all right?" asked Rose.

Julia collapsed back in her chair as the realization hit her. The book. The woman in the middle of the road all those weeks ago. That had been Eleanor. "I'm fine," she said, sitting up again. "Sorry, I just remembered something." She'd been coming from another night in jail that morning. Her mind had been sluggish from too many beers and poor choices. But she remembered now. She'd heard a woman calling out, sounding distressed, when she'd spotted the book in the road. Flashes of that day came back to her: the gentle horses, the book, and Eleanor's relieved face when Julia had handed it back to her.

"Anyway," Rose was saying, waving a skewered piece of collard green around with her fork, "that woman's misfortune is no topic for the dinner table." Henry agreed and bit into his chicken. He squinted, a warning look in his eyes that Rose had, once again, over-salted the meat. "That poor woman," she muttered with a shake of her head.

Julia didn't say anything, but the pieces finally began to fall into place. And her conversation with Eleanor Perry in the mill made much more sense. *She thinks I forgot who she is.* Admittedly, she had. But now Mrs. Perry was at the front of her mind.

CHAPTER NINE

Julia thanked Ralph for the pie before heading up the road toward Monarch Mill on Thursday. She had given him a hard time, insisting he was wasting such a good meal on her. "I'm just sitting all day, you know. Hardly workin' up an appetite in an old chair."

"Don't fuss now, Jules," he'd replied, his large, flour-covered hands pushing the food at her. Admittedly, the scents coming from his family's bakery had been mouthwatering. "Your sister's cookin' can't beat my mom's." At her raised brow, he'd quickly added, "Don't tell Rose I said that," before hurrying back inside the bakery.

She passed Thrasher's on her way. The joint was quiet this early in the day. A woman in a flowing skirt stood outside on the planked porch, leaning casually against a post. She ran a hand through her blond hair as Julia walked by, and the gesture sent a flare of recognition through her. She was the woman Henry had seen her with a couple weeks ago, the one who had pulled her into the back room.

"Hiya, honey," the woman called. In the light of day, she seemed older than Julia remembered. *I wonder how old Eleanor is.* She waved back, and the toe of her boot caught a loose cobblestone, making her stumble. The woman gave a throaty laugh, no doubt mistaking her gaffe for a response to the flirting.

Julia collected herself and continued, surprised at how eager she was to get to the office, knowing Mrs. Perry would be by again. That pleasant thought was interrupted by the voice of Lee Volz.

"What was that?" she asked, slowing her pace outside the residence that doubled as the local barber shop when he sauntered out. He was doing up the final button on his high collar. She could smell the aftershave coming from his smooth jaw.

"I asked where you're headed."

"To work."

"Work?"

"Yep. Headed to the mill." She pointed northward as if knowing the way would slap the stupid look of disbelief from his face.

Volz descended the steps slowly, gripping his vest. She wondered how he managed to look so pompous this early in the morning. He ran a hand over his blond hair, then replaced his hat. "How'd you come by that job?"

"Just lucky, I guess," she replied, not keeping the sarcasm from her tone. "I'm the new file clerk."

He didn't say anything, just eyed her above pursed lips.

"Well, I'll be on my way, Sheriff." She tipped an imaginary hat as he seemed to just register what she was wearing, his eyes wide in surprise at the long skirt she'd paired with a button-down. It was an outfit of compromise after squabbling since sunup with Rose about what she should be wearing at an office job. At least the skirt was loose at the hem, and she could still move about well enough.

"You ain't foolin' no one, Miss Holte," Volz called after her. She half turned but forced herself to continue. *Not worth it.* Besides, she wasn't trying to fool anyone. Was she? All she wanted was to make her sister happy. She glanced down; the material of her skirt had already collected some dirt. She chewed her lip, mulling over his words as she climbed the sloping street and headed for the office.

❖

The flutter in her stomach surprised Eleanor as she reached the mill after dropping a reluctant Peter off at school. She chastised herself for such a frivolous feeling. *Don't be ridiculous.* How difficult was it, really, to make conversation? Granted, she was a bit out of practice. Sue and Isaac were her main associates these days, and both liked the sound of their own voices. *Nonsense.* She shook out her shoulders. Julia was merely another person. There was no reason to be nervous. Taking a breath, she adjusted the basket she carried and opened the door.

Noise bounced off every wall of the office, nearly knocking her back. Despite knowing she was scheduled to pick up the next round of uniforms, Eleanor felt like she was intruding. Instinctively, she shrank back and pressed herself against the door.

Julia's smile eased her worry as their gazes met. "Morning," she called over the din of conversation.

Taking a breath, Eleanor stepped into the room. "It's busy today."

Julia glanced over her shoulder. A couple of men in suits flitted back and forth between desks like the one she sat at. They reminded Eleanor of fireflies Peter had trapped last summer, pinging off one another and the sides of their mason jar. She faced Eleanor. "I was hoping to see you again."

Her face warmed. She bit her lip, taken by the lighter fragments of blue in Julia's wide gaze. Like ice on water, she thought. Wait, wasn't she supposed to be angry? Eleanor blinked, trying to sort out her feelings as Julia stood quickly to hand a folder to one of the harried-looking men behind her. She wore another man's shirt today—this one white—but had paired it with a dark khaki skirt.

"Let me help you with that." Julia took the basket, finding the same gentleman from Monday whom Eleanor had handed them off to.

"Thank you," she said, still distracted and considering the difference in Julia's attire when she noticed Sue near the back left corner of the office. A small stove that held a pot of coffee was simmering behind her. Sue waved eagerly, a concerned look on her face. Confused, Eleanor waved back.

Julia, in her chair again, turned to follow the gesture. "Friend of yours?"

"Yes, I—"

"Julia." Mr. Barrow rushed in from the back room, a frighteningly thick bundle of papers in his arms. Upon reaching them, he greeted Eleanor, then plunked the papers in front of Julia. "I need these alphabetized by last name, then sorted by date." He reached to open the folder, fanning out the papers to better see. "It seems our last file clerk neglected certain aspects of organization." He threw Eleanor a worried look. "We have an auditor coming by in a few months from Chicago."

"I see," she said, now understanding the frenzied situation. Julia, however, seemed unmoved by such news. The look she gave Eleanor seemed like a plea for help.

From behind Mr. Barrow, Eleanor caught another wave from Sue, followed by a *psst* loud enough to be heard across the room.

"If you'll excuse me," she said, not missing the look of disappointment on Julia's face as she scurried past the front desk. The distant pull Eleanor felt as she walked away startled her. She had been upset at Julia for not remembering her, but a deep yearning to talk to her despite that was overwhelming. At the very least, she had hoped for a little more than an exchange of pleasantries. "Hi, Sue," she said upon reaching her friend and trying to push her confusing emotions aside. "Are you here to help with the upcoming audit?"

"Naturally," Sue replied, waving a half-filled coffee mug around. Eleanor leaned back to avoid the flying droplets. "These men couldn't find a mountain in a molehill." One of them going by gave her a look, to which she smiled demurely. Then, she glanced around and pulled Eleanor closer, turning her so she had her back to most of the room.

"Sue," she said, "what's this about? Is everything all right?" Sue's face was near high alarm. Eleanor wondered if something had happened in one of the nearby mines. Her heart raced at the idea of an accident.

"Now, I know I said that I didn't care to be the interim file clerk. It's a terribly dull position," she whispered, still tossing furtive glances behind Eleanor, "but I have no earthly idea what my husband was thinking hiring *that* woman."

Frowning, Eleanor turned. Julia seemed to be listening to further instructions on the alphabetizing process from Mr. Barrow. Turning back, she said, "I thought she came highly recommended?"

"More like desperately recommended."

"What do you mean?"

Sue dropped her voice even lower, raising a hand to shield the sound. "She's a felon, E."

Eleanor blinked, looking again to the front of the office. Sue grabbed her quickly as if afraid of being caught. Eleanor swatted her hand away. "Sue, come now. That's ridiculous. She's…" *Charming. Sweet. Has a terrible memory.* "A woman."

Sue gave her a dubious look. "We aren't all saints, dear. And that Miss Holte has caused nothing but a commotion since moving here."

She considered Sue's comment. While she hadn't heard any local gossip, it wasn't like she was keen on the goings-on around town. If anything, Eleanor kept herself out of town so she wouldn't hear what people thought about her. Unsure what to say, she slowly turned to watch Julia. Presently, she was laughing at something Mr. Barrow said, her smile bright as she gave him a playful shove. Eleanor swallowed at the seemingly insignificant gesture, her gaze lingering on Julia's hands.

"Now, you didn't hear this from me," Sue was saying, pulling her focus, "but I'd wager something's going on between the two of them." She pointed behind Eleanor.

"Mr. Barrow and Miss Holte?"

She nodded. "Why else recommend a woman like that?" She clucked and straightened the collar of her dress. "Honestly, hiring a woman with a criminal record."

Eleanor, still trying to reconcile such information, said, "Sue, doesn't the mill hire on all sorts of folks? A lot of people, men, passing through have...colorful backgrounds."

Sue scoffed. "That's different."

"Is it?"

"She's right there," Sue said, gesturing emphatically. "Right in front. The face of the office."

"Sue, come now."

"Something's funny about this whole thing," Sue said, her gaze fiery and unfocused. Eleanor could see her lost on another thread of fanciful thoughts. She recognized the look. Sue wore it often after finishing a radio program or a scandalous book. "That woman is trouble, E, and trouble isn't something that you need," she added, her voice softening.

Eleanor opened her mouth, then closed it as her reply fell flat. Of course. Sue had a penchant for spewing town secrets, but she also had consistently looked out for Eleanor since Louis had left. Eleanor couldn't forget how the long-standing members of Idaho Springs saw her: the lonely widow with the sickly son, the woman whose husband left her in the middle of the night, no good-bye and no note. Associating with a known felon probably wasn't the best thing for her already tarnished reputation. "I suppose you're right."

Sue patted her arm. "Precisely. I just want what's best for you, E."

Nodding, Eleanor stood back as Sue scampered after Mr. Barrow, who headed for the side door. She studied Julia. Her shoulders rose and fell dramatically as she moved the papers around her desk. Perhaps sensing someone watching her, she turned. Eleanor smiled. Julia waved.

"That's not something you need," replayed in her mind. She hated to admit it, but Sue was right. Eleanor was thinking of herself and her curiosity about Julia when she needed to be thinking about what was best for her family. Peter was old enough now for the talk to fall on him, too. She couldn't stand that.

Eleanor hurried away and ducked toward the changing room door to collect the uniforms. She tried to ignore the confused look on Julia's face and forced herself not to look back.

Chapter Ten

"Have a good day," Eleanor called as Peter started up the hill to the schoolhouse. She'd gotten him to agree to go with a reminder that this was the final week before summer vacation now that it was June. She watched him greet another boy around his age. The two began a quick game of chase. She smiled as a trio of mothers passed, each dropping off their respective children. Eleanor tried to recall their names. All three, in fashionable dresses Eleanor wondered if they'd gotten out of town, eyed her curiously. Mrs. Henley stood behind them, promptly cutting her gaze when Eleanor spotted her.

Giving up on the names of the other women, she was turning to go when the schoolmarm, Mrs. Shearn, called, "Mrs. Perry!" Eleanor spun around to find Mrs. Shearn waving frantically. Her chest sank at the sight of Peter on his knees, his hand on his chest. "Oh God." She sprinted, ignoring the wide-eyed mothers pulling their children aside.

Mrs. Shearn—a middle-aged woman with small eyes— pushed back her frizzy blond hair as she said, "I don't know what happened. He was running with young Stuart, then dropped to the ground just like that."

A high whistle came with each labored breath Peter took. His wide, frenzied gaze found hers. "It's his asthma." The look of confusion wasn't encouraging, so she said, "Please, he needs room."

"Of course." Mrs. Shearn, looking relieved to have received an instruction, beckoned. "Children, please, follow me." She pushed those still outside back, then turned and kept the ones crowding the schoolhouse door inside.

Eleanor sank to her knees in front of Peter. "I'm right here, darling." She put her hand over his. Guiding him, she made circles over his chest. "Keep breathing."

Tears filled his eyes. "It's…hard."

"I know." She kept the motion on his chest, then took a breath. "Breathe with me." She brought his other hand to her sternum. "Match me, darling."

It took one of the longest minutes of Eleanor's life for Peter's breathing to fall in line with hers. Mercifully, the whistling subsided, along with the dread in his gaze. "All right?" she asked. He nodded, and she couldn't help smiling as she pulled him into an embrace. "You're all right, my brave boy."

The tittering of young children, like inquisitive mice, surrounded them. From the doorway, Mrs. Shearn said, "Mrs. Perry, I think it's best Peter return home for the day."

Eleanor wiped her face and stood. "He's fine now," she explained. "These episodes happen now and then. The last teacher, Mrs. Harper, understood."

Unfortunately, Mrs. Shearn only seemed offended at the mention of last year's teacher, who'd left for some place called Seaside, California. Eleanor straightened at the stern look on her face. She also caught the fragment of fear in Mrs. Shearn's eyes. She recognized that look, the look of not understanding what had just transpired, and sadly, the unwillingness to try. Take him away, Eleanor could imagine her saying. Take him away so he's not our problem.

Eleanor helped Peter to stand, noting the flush in his cheeks as he caught classmates watching through the window. Her instinct to berate them all was barely overcome by the need to shield Peter from such judging eyes.

"Very well," she managed to say before leading him away.

At home, Eleanor helped Peter to bed for a precautionary rest. After preparing his tea, she took a moment outside his room at the top of the stairs. She inhaled, anxiety pooling in her chest. It made its way to her hand at her side. Eventually, she couldn't resist the need to count the lines in the planked ceiling. The tea in her left hand, her right forefinger and thumb found one another. *One, two, three.* After reaching twenty, she managed to take another breath and forced herself to move on.

From his bed, Peter glared at the cup. "I hate this."

"I know it's not as good without the sugar, but the doctor says—"

"No. I hate this," he said, his small fist banging on his chest. The gesture startled her, and she set the tea on the side table, quickly grabbing his fist before he could hit himself again.

"Darling, stop."

His eyes were so full of anger, Eleanor wanted to cry out. His bottom lip quivered as he asked, "Why am I like this?"

Eleanor bit her cheek to keep from crying. She swallowed, running a hand down his arm when she was sure he wasn't going to hit himself again. She took a breath and sat next to him. "I don't know."

He seemed to be fighting tears before he turned his back and faced the wall.

"Peter?"

"I don't want to go back."

"Back...to school? It's the final week."

"They hate me."

"No, they don't hate you."

"They always stare at me. Last year, I couldn't breathe after a game of hopscotch. Stuart and everyone said I was a guppy out of water."

Eleanor's blood raged at their cruelty. "Peter—"

"I hate them."

She inhaled to quell her ire. "Darling," she said, trying to keep her tone even, "I know you're angry. It can be hard for people when they don't understand."

With a sniffle, he turned back to face her. Tears streamed freely down his face. The sight threatened to undo her. "Please, Mom, I don't want to go back."

The shortened term of endearment struck her, and she feared he had aged five years at that moment. The knowledge of his own reality wrapped around them both, inescapable. She reached out, running a comforting hand down his arm, his back. What could she do but relent? "All right. You don't have to go tomorrow."

He held her gaze for a moment before turning back over. Eleanor felt lost, watching her son's tiny body rise and fall in his agony. After a time, she said gently, "Don't forget your tea." Then, she kissed his temple and left him alone.

CHAPTER ELEVEN

"Morning, Miss Holte," Ralph's mother, Mrs. Davies, called from behind the bakery counter. Her stout, short frame could hardly be seen above the high glass cases hosting an assortment of pastries and pies. Her blond curly hair bobbed atop her round kind face. The warm smell of yeast and spices wrapped around Julia like a hug, a welcome relief from the cool Colorado morning.

"Hi, Mrs. Davies, how are you?"

"You're here to see my Ralph?"

Julia had been eyeing a tray of fruit tarts when she looked up. "Oh, actually—"

But Mrs. Davies was already scurrying into the back kitchen. Ralph appeared moments later. A green, flour-covered apron was tied over his black pants and light blue shirt, the sleeves rolled up to his elbows.

"Mornin' Jules. I've got your pies ready."

"Thanks." Last week, Henry had smelled her lunch and inquired about the pie's origins. Upon learning it was from the Davies's bakery, he'd asked her to bring him one on Wednesday. This, of course, was unbeknownst to Rose, who faithfully packed Henry with a bundle of rye bread and strips of meat.

"I love your sister," Henry had said on their walk home last Friday, "but sometimes, I can hardly chew through her steak dinner."

"Secret's safe with me," Julia had said. "That fruit puree gave me a run for my money, if you know what I mean." Henry had laughed. "My sister has always had an iron stomach."

Presently, she took the two meat pies wrapped carefully in butcher paper. "I keep this up, I won't fit into Rose's skirts." Ralph laughed. "That ain't so bad." He raised an insinuating brow. "Besides, I like a gal with meat on her bones."

She shoved him for his comment, which only prompted more laughter. Mrs. Davies, apparently lurking behind the counter, caught Julia's gaze. Julia cleared her throat and stepped away from Ralph.

Mrs. Davies practically hopped when she said, "Oh, Ralphie, you ought to invite Miss Holte to the church social."

"Mom." Julia laughed at Ralph's bemoaning tone. Then, she was surprised by the flicker of what looked like hope in his eye.

Her face fell as she asked, "You're not serious, are you?"

He shrugged. "Might not be so bad," he said, suddenly interested in the toe of his boot.

She glanced from him to Mrs. Davies, who looked like she was on the precipice of an earth-shattering breakthrough. All Julia could do was laugh to break the sudden awkwardness. "Ralph—"

"Just think about it." He gave a small smile, then disappeared back into the kitchen.

❖

"Church social?" Julia asked the sky her incredulous question on the final leg of the walk to the mill office. She remembered Rose mentioning the event in passing. When was it, July? Her sister had always been fond of church events and Sunday service. She'd taken quickly to the busy religious community of Idaho Springs and enjoyed the communal aspect. Back in Texas, they'd had to take a car twenty minutes to Amarillo to hear a sermon. Julia had stopped attending years ago; Sunday, much to her mother's chagrin, was for riding and other ranch chores.

Ralph, meanwhile, had never expressed an interest in attending. Granted, they didn't talk much about that sort of thing. Cards, horses, his family's bakery…those were the common topics discussed over a beer at Thrasher's.

Inside the mill office, Julia found Henry pouring a cup of coffee at the stove in the back corner. She wove through the desks and tables, greeting a couple of the junior clerks already filing away. A candlestick phone blared behind her, and a beady-eyed man in a suit answered it.

Julia handed Henry one of the pies. "Is this what I think it is?" He raised it and inhaled, closing his eyes. "Golly, that's good."

"Tastes even better than it smells," she teased.

"Thanks, and my thanks to Ralph." He pulled a handkerchief bundle from inside his jacket pocket, unveiling a brown, rock-shaped thing.

She frowned. "What's that?"

"My breakfast from Rose."

She barked a laugh, then tapped the top of what she realized was solid bread. "She tryin' to take your teeth out?"

"I think she's still getting used to the stove."

Julia raised a brow. "Six months in?"

"Something about the elevation." He shrugged, pocketing the bread and pulling the pie close. "Thank you again." Taking his full coffee mug, he started past her. "I better head up to the mill. There's a new set of records for you to organize."

"Whoopee," she said sarcastically, twirling her pointer finger. She poured herself some coffee, then reluctantly found her desk. Sipping, she eyed the documents when someone imitating the sound of driving a car caught her ear.

She was surprised to find a young boy, maybe eight or nine, plopped at a vacant desk on the opposite side of the room. He pushed a wooden car over every available surface. The color of his hair struck her as familiar, and she thought of Eleanor. His face was elaborately freckled, particularly over his nose and under his eyes.

Curious, she started toward him. "I bet that one wins a lot of races."

He looked up, and Eleanor's eyes looked back at her. She hesitated a moment, surprised. He answered, "I beat Stuart Weekly in a race last month."

Recovered, Julia crouched so she was eye level with the boy, who sat on his knees in a metal chair. "I believe it." She smiled and stuck her hand out. "I'm Julia."

He glanced at her, then vroomed over the top of the desk, driving the car closer. "I'm Peter." He let go of the car and shook her hand before sitting back.

Taking his lead, she examined the toy, giving an exaggerated look of approval. "Sleek build. Newer model. I bet the engine runs smoothly."

He grinned and nodded.

"You know, there's a great course where you could get some practice runs in." She glanced around the office. The last thing she wanted to do was start on those records. They could wait awhile. "It's just outside. I can show you, if you like."

His eyes lit up. "Is it near the mill?"

She wondered at his eagerness. "Well, you can see it, I suppose."

He scrambled out of his chair. "What are we waiting for?"

"All right then," she said, chuckling as he hurried by. She held the door for him. Across the dirt road was an old mineral chute next to an abandoned ore cart. "Over here," she said, leading him. The thirty-yard chute sat idly amongst the brambles and overgrown bushes. At the top of it, she motioned for Peter to stand beside her and smiled at his wide-eyed look. "Think the wheels can handle it?" she asked, gesturing to the chute.

He nodded, running his finger along each of the toy car's wheels as if to test them. "It's ready."

She motioned for him to set the car at the top of the chute. The semi-rusted metal gleamed under the partly cloudy sky. "I'll head to the bottom to catch it." She hurried down the slope then called up. "Ready? On your marks, get set…"

"Go!" called Peter, then let the car fly.

Julia could hear the wooden wheels making their way over the metal track. Within seconds, the toy came into view, traveling at a high speed. It shot out the base of the chute, and she knelt to catch it, raising it high. "Finish!"

Peter whooped and hollered from the top of the slope. He looked ready to run after her when the office door flew open.

"Peter!" Eleanor's face was wild, and Julia's smile fell. For a moment, her sister's voice cried out to her, filled with the same anxiety. Slamming her eyes shut, Julia forced the sounds from her mind. Mercifully, the memory passed, and she started up the hill, her throat dry. "Peter, what are you doing?"

He pointed to the chute. "We were racing."

"We?" Eleanor, who had stooped to grip his shoulders as if to check him for injuries, straightened.

Julia waved, though her bravado withered at the look in Eleanor's eyes. "Hi. We, uh, we were doing a test run." She smiled wide as Eleanor's look of bewilderment and fear shifted. Julia thought she saw pleasant surprise cross her face, but it was gone in a flash, chased out by a formidable glare.

One hand on her hip, she asked, "Do you always wander off like this?"

Julia frowned, mildly offended. "We were only playing." She handed the car back to Peter. "He's practically a professional driver," she added, tossing him a wink.

The muscle in Eleanor's jaw flexed. Despite herself, Julia traced the line of that muscle to her mouth. She forced her gaze to meet Eleanor's, forced herself to pay attention, but…fiery eyes met hers and thick red hair flowed around her soft face. God, she thought, Eleanor was utterly breathtaking.

Blinking and reminding herself to focus, Julia held up her hands. "I didn't mean anything. Just thought we'd have a little fun." She caught Peter's eye. He smiled.

Eleanor pulled him closer. "I think we've had enough fun for the day."

He looked up. "Mom, Julia was helping me win races."

"I'm behind schedule, Peter," Eleanor said, ignoring his comment. "We need to get home. Those uniforms won't clean themselves." She nudged him toward the door.

Julia reached out. "Eleanor, wait."

"Good day, Miss Holte," she said over her shoulder, her voice curt.

Julia stepped back, Eleanor's tone hitting her. It wasn't often women spoke to her like that. Collecting herself, she made sure her voice had an extra layer of jolliness and called, "Have a nice day, then." Her words had their intended surprise effect as she caught Eleanor hesitate and glance back. Julia flashed another smile and waved before Eleanor and Peter disappeared inside.

Sighing, Julia kicked at a loose rock. The jarring sounds of the mill reentered her frame of mind. The few minutes with Peter had been the first moments since moving here that she hadn't felt inundated by the incessant millwork in the background. But now, the machinery pulled her back into the misery of another day here, another day at that desk.

Well, she reasoned, at least she had another piece of the Eleanor puzzle. She had a son whom she was fiercely protective of. So protective that her fair cheeks had flushed, and her eyes had danced with a daring that made Julia's heart race. That image would tide her over until they saw one another again.

CHAPTER TWELVE

"Set those in the wash basin, please, Peter." Eleanor held the front door for him once they arrived home. He did as he was told, untying the canvas bag and dumping the uniforms in. She followed with her own bundle. When he started for the backyard, she called, "And where are you off to, sir?"

He swung back around on the doorjamb, an innocent smile on his face. "Heading to check my traps."

"You can do that later. If you're not going to school today, you're going to help me with the laundry."

"Mom." He dragged out the vowel, leaving Eleanor wondering at how long such a short word could become.

"Peter," she replied. "That seems perfectly fair." A desperate attempt to keep his mind on school found her adding, "And you're going to recite your math facts as we work."

His face fell into disbelief.

"You heard me," she said, trying to keep her tone light. "Now, go fetch the pails so we can boil water and fill these bins to soak."

He harrumphed and set his toy car on the kitchen table before heading outside for the water pail. Eleanor watched him until her gaze found the toy. Her mind drifted to Julia. She grimaced as she replayed their interaction. "Maybe I was a bit hasty in my judgment," she muttered. It wasn't like Julia had taken Peter off the premises. He had disappeared into corners of the office before, and he certainly loved to do so at home on their land. She sighed, realizing Julia probably thought she was one of those awful mothers who never let their children have any sort of fun.

Peter returned, a full bucket sloshing at his side. "Well done," she said, rolling up her sleeves. "Now, let's get to it."

Julia didn't stop at Thrasher's after work, though she was tempted after the day she'd had. Ralph's comment that morning about the church social had left her leery about where he thought they stood. She thought he had known she wouldn't go for a man like him...or any man. She wasn't necessarily subtle in her flirting with women. She dressed like the men, talked like the men. She'd always been free to do so at her family's ranch. Her mother, having dubbed her a lovable heathen since early childhood, had given up trying to change her ways. Julia had rarely gone to town with her parents in Texas since doing so had led to unflattering conversations with other families about how she should present herself. The ranch was her haven to be who she pleased. She hadn't realized how lucky she had been all her life in that respect.

She supposed that was something this mining town had going for it. Big cities were easier to hide in, and she had initially feared sticking out like a sore thumb in Idaho Springs. But maybe, because everyone kept their nose to the ground, its people hardworking and giving everything they had to the mountains, no one had much energy left to bother with what folks should have been wearing. Sheriff Volz being the exception, of course. And despite dressing in the least ladylike way she knew, there always managed to be men who, somehow, never saw the writing on the wall. Ralph being one of those men surprised her.

She was helping chop onions in the kitchen while they waited for Henry to get home and listening as Rose described the neighbor's garden. "It's quite the sight, Jules. Tomatoes, cabbage, carrots, beets, turnips…it's practically a market! Mrs. Jarda and her husband started it fifteen years ago when they first bought land here. These were pulled right out of the ground not fifty yards from this kitchen." She hummed as she chopped. "She helps cook for the church social each summer. I volunteered my efforts. That should keep me busy. Afraid I'm not much use at sewing like some of the ladies who put together a quilt for the donation bin."

Julia looked up. "Church social?"

Rose raised a brow. "Oh, so you were listening?"

"Half listening," she replied. "The church social…when is it?"

Swiping the onion into a bowl, Rose added it to a simmering pot on the stove. "Last Saturday of July. One month away. You're not interested in going, are you?"

"I might be," she said, moving to wash her hands. She could feel Rose's gaze on her, and added, "What? Is that so surprising?"

Placing a hand on her hip, Rose said, "You know it is."

Julia shrugged. "Ralph invited me."

The look of astonishment was followed by a curious frown. "Ralph Davies is a sweet man."

"He is." But Julia wasn't thinking about Ralph. She was thinking about Eleanor and a way to make things up to her after giving her what was apparently quite the scare. An invitation to the social could be just the thing. If she did decide to go with Ralph, she could ensure Eleanor would be there. What better time for them to get to know each other better? Eleanor would see she was harmless. Church seemed like a safe place to do that.

"Well," Rose said, stirring and looking pleased, "how about that? Julia Holte is interested in a community event. Someone better mark the calendar to commemorate such a memorable day."

"All right," Julia said, tossing a piece of carrot at her. She laughed and added it to the pot. "That's enough, now. It's no big deal," she added. "It's just what folks do around here."

She could practically hear Rose's thoughts over the boiling water. *Since when do you care about what most folks do?* Just the idea of being surrounded by bluenose biddies all day made her skin itch, but a plan was forming. Now, she just needed to make sure Eleanor was going to attend.

CHAPTER THIRTEEN

*L*ouis?" *Eleanor leaned against the wall just inside their front door and took several slow, deep breaths. The trek from the market had taken more out of her than she'd expected. As her breathing evened out, she found the underside of her belly, running her hand up and down. Peter kicked twice. She smiled, saying softly, "We made it home, my love." Glancing around, she added, "Now, where's your father?"*

After setting the kettle to boil, she followed a steady hammering sound out the back door to find Louis working on something. "Louis," she called, "I'm home."

He turned, a pleased smile lifting his pale cheeks at the sight of her. The gesture also revealed his work: a wooden crib.

"Oh, Louis." She walked over to join him, crossing a smattering of tall grass and columbine swaying in the breeze.

"Careful," he said, pointing with the hammer. "Few stray nails down there. Mind your steps."

Smiling, she did so, then carefully ran her hands along the wooden frame. "It's beautiful."

He beamed, his brown eyes shining. "I'm glad you like it."

"I love it." She wrapped her arm around him. "Thank you." She kissed his cheek, then ran a hand over his stubble. "My husband, always in need of a shave."

He laughed and stood. After brushing off the crib with a rag, he nodded and said, "I shus a glenip."

Frowning, Eleanor asked, "What was that?"

Louis blinked, shaking his head. He licked his chapped lips, looking uncertain. "I should glenup." His brows furrowed, apparently as confused as she was by his words. He glanced at her, and worry sat in his gaze.

"Did you mean that you should get cleaned up?"

The anxious look lasted only a moment more before he smiled and reached for her hand. Kissing it, he said, "You always know exactly what I'm tryin' to say." He grabbed the crib. "I'll bring this in. Our son will be here before we know it."

Eleanor watched him go, rubbing her belly, pondering his strange phrasing. Louis was just tired, she told herself. Words were hard enough, let alone after a day of labor. She forced the apprehension away and followed him inside.

Eleanor woke with a start. She blinked, orienting herself. The fireplace in her bedroom came into view, then the fading sunlight through the window. The basket of mill uniforms sat at her feet, and the vial with three flecks of gold was tucked beneath her leg. She didn't even remember falling asleep in her chair. The smell of stew wafted through the air. *Peter.*

She made her way through the kitchen. "Peter, time for supper," she called from the open back door before ladling stew into two bowls, placing spoons carefully next to them on the table. When Peter still hadn't come in, she called him again.

No answer, only the wind as the men's uniforms snapped in a strong gust where they hung on the lines. She scanned the wide field, the distant line of trees growing darker as the sun set.

She pressed her thumb to each finger on her right hand. *One, two, three, four.* The rate of her heart slowed, and she stepped outside. "Peter?"

She pushed through the first line of clothes, each brush of cloth like a hand trying to pull her aside. Her stomach sank with each step and still no sign of Peter. She called for him again.

This time, he answered, "Mom!"

"Peter?" She shoved through the last line of laundry and tore toward the river forty yards away.

At the top of the sloping knoll, she stopped, one hand landing on the bark of a pine. Below, near a rocky stretch of boulders lining the water, Peter waved and smiled. "Look!"

She exhaled and wiped the sweat from her brow as he revealed a hare snared in a makeshift trap. Her left hand went to her thundering heart as she called, "Peter Louis Perry, you get up here right now."

His smile fell. She counted each finger touch two times more before Peter grabbed the unfortunate hare and scampered up. She pulled him into a hug.

"Mom," he said, dragging out the vowel again. "You're squishing me."

"You gave me a scare, darling."

"I wanted to show you what I caught."

She held him within arm's reach, kneeling to be eye level with him. "You didn't have to ignore my dinner call. What if something had happened to you?"

The excitement in his face dimmed. He moved out of her grasp and started past her. "Dad would've been proud of me."

A scalding burn shot across her chest. Tears sprang to her eyes, but she kept them at bay. *He's only upset. He knows the rules. He knows to tell me if he wanders to the river.*

She took a breath, slowly starting after him. Her mind cleared. He'd been down to the river hundreds of times. It wasn't a surprise to find him there. Perhaps she had been too quick to chastise him. Perhaps, she thought, rubbing her right hand up and down her left arm, the dream of Louis had left her feeling on edge.

Catching up to Peter, she grabbed his shoulder to slow him. "That is quite the catch," she said.

A smile cracked his sullen face. "Not as big as last summer."

"Well, I think this one will make the tastiest stew yet." She took the hare once they were inside. "You go wash up. I'll get this ready to clean." He headed for the washroom, but she called him. He turned. "I know your father is proud of you. And so am I."

He grinned, but a distant forlornness sat in the back of his gaze. The look felt like Eleanor had stepped in mud, her feet eager to move but her body trapped. She started to go to him when he turned and closed the door.

CHAPTER FOURTEEN

"Here's to another day on the job," Ralph said, clinking his mug against Julia's. "You sure proved me wrong. Thought you'd have cleared out of there by now."

She downed several gulps of beer at the low table where she sat with him on a Friday night. She had to admit, it was a surprise she hadn't quit or been fired after a month and a half. She had been late four times, twice this week, each time on the days Eleanor had come by with the uniforms. Just my luck, Julia had thought, falling into the uncomfortable office chair after Henry had informed her Eleanor had already been by.

"Let's not talk about work," she said, swiping flecks of the drink off her chin. The *clack* of billiard balls echoed nearby among the rowdy voices of men eager for the weekend.

Ralph scanned the crowded room. "All right, then," he said. Someone played a tune on the rickety old piano next to the bar at the front, opposite where they sat. Mill men mingled, and a handful of traveling merchants conversed at tables and at the bar. A couple of women sat amongst everyone here and there, mostly young wives. "You give any thought to the church social?"

Coughing on her drink, Julia asked, "You were serious about that?" Part of her had hoped he would forget about the whole thing. Not because she wasn't planning to go—and make sure Eleanor attended—but she didn't want Ralph to get any ideas.

He shrugged. "Sure, why not?"

"Lots of reasons," she replied, eyeing the crowd over her mug as she took another sip to stall. The same woman from a month ago—the one who had pulled her into the back of the bar—had sidled up to a gentleman near the taps. Her long red skirt matched a ribbon she wore in a braid. She gave a loud laugh to something the man said before catching Julia's eye. Her smile evened out, and her gaze grew sly. Clearing her throat, Julia refocused on Ralph. "Besides, you do everything your mother tells you to do?"

"Hey, ain't nothin' wrong with respecting one's parents." He ignored her scoff. "She likes you, Jules. Yes, it'd make her happy, but it could be fun."

Julia set her mug between them. "You've said that before." She glanced back at the woman at the bar. Her mind shifted to Eleanor. She'd hoped to ask if Eleanor was going to the church social this week but had never gotten the chance.

"It doesn't have to be anything formal," he was saying, looking nervous as he ran his fingers around the base of his glass. His gaze drifted to somewhere near the pool table. "It's just a fun day out." Her mind was stuck, still wondering what Eleanor was up to. She didn't feel like answering Ralph yet and was grateful when he said, "I'm gonna get us another round."

Rose wouldn't be thrilled about her staying for another drink, but it was Friday. She deserved to let loose a little. Besides, she needed the alcohol to dull her thoughts about what the words "church social" meant. She knew what folks would say when she and Ralph showed up together.

She finished her drink, stretching as Ralph waited at the bar. It wasn't long before the woman in the red skirt was in his seat.

"Hiya, honey," she said, her legs crossed toward Julia after scooting Ralph's chair closer.

"Evenin'," she replied, eyeing the line in the woman's stockings that disappeared beneath her skirt. She was trying to recall her name when the woman seemed to read her mind.

"Sylvia," she said, one hand on the very low neck of her blouse. The gesture drew Julia's gaze to the freckles along the top of her chest.

"How're you, Sylvia?"

"Better now," she replied with a Cheshire grin. Julia was accustomed to women like Sylvia finding her in establishments like Thrasher's. Back in Texas, when Julia did go to town, there had been a couple of ladies who, when tired of the men, had sought her out. Julia had been happy to oblige their needs and have hers met in return during late night, clandestine rendezvous. It had been a small point of pride for Julia to please those women the way she had heard most men never bothered to.

Sylvia had a pretty face, with gentle lines around her eyes and smile. Her eyes were a blue green that shone under the hanging lights. Julia wasn't surprised she'd let herself fall into this woman. Her lips were painted a bold shade of red. "Care for another turn tonight?" she asked, her voice low as she leaned next to Julia's ear.

She swallowed, the smell of liquor and heady perfume enveloping her. The scent took her back in time. Fragrant coral bells lined the flower boxes at the ranch. The sun glared. Rose shouted, fearful.

No. She squeezed her eyes closed, forcing herself to the present. "I'm with my friend," she said, placing a hand on Sylvia's bare shoulder to nudge her back.

"That didn't stop you last time." She smiled again. Under the table, Julia felt her heel start up the inside of her calf.

Julia's mouth went dry. "Sylvia—"

"Miss Holte."

Sitting up, Julia turned to find Sheriff Volz standing behind her. He wore black trousers and a white dress shirt. His revolver sat in a holster on his right hip. He looked like a specter with his light eyes shadowed beneath his cowboy hat.

"How you doin', Officer?" Sylvia said, turning her fawning smile at him.

He didn't seem fazed by her charms, though, as he said, "I'm sure Miss Holte was just about to excuse herself."

Frowning, Julia said, "Excuse myself? This is my table, Volz."

"Miss Holte." He used one finger to tilt the end of his hat up ever so slightly. "You know this sort of fraternizing ain't allowed."

"Neither is this 'den of sin,' as I've heard you call it, yet, here we are," she replied. "Here for a drink? Or another secret meeting with Jay?"

His mouth tightened beneath a glare. She glanced from him to Sylvia, who gave her a sympathetic look before standing. "I'll be on my way," she said and wandered away. Julia felt the eyes of patrons on her. She also noticed Sylvia's colleagues draped over several mill men.

"You gonna go after them, too?" she asked, pointing to each in turn.

Volz didn't bother to look. "You know that ain't the same."

"Isn't it?" she fired back, standing to face him. She hated being shorter than him by several inches, but she pulled back her shoulders. The murmur of the room seemed to go a little quieter as she said, "You got a problem with me, Volz, come out and say it."

He only gave a small smile. His right hand went to his holster as he squinted, as if contemplating if it was worth arresting her again. She knew she hadn't done anything wrong, though. Come on, you scoundrel, she thought, matching his gaze. Try me.

"Julia," Ralph said behind her. It was as if his presence broke the spell of their showdown. Sounds rose to their original octave, and conversations resumed.

She sighed, wondering if it wouldn't have been such a terrible thing to punch Volz in his stupid face. "Hi, Ralph," she said. Volz stepped back a bit like most folks did when Ralph was nearby.

"Everything all right?" he asked, setting two full mugs on the table.

An idea struck her then. "Just dandy," she said, then grabbed Ralph's sleeve and tugged him next to her. She wrapped an arm around his back. "I was just telling the sheriff here that I hope to see him at the church social next month. We're going together."

She didn't miss the surprised look on Ralph's face, and she felt a little guilty at the flicker of joy that followed. But if Volz insisted on hounding her for being herself, this could help keep him off her back. And it solidified her reason to be at the social, hoping Eleanor would be there. Two birds, one stone.

Volz looked between them, glaring at Ralph's wide smile. He didn't say anything before mercifully moving on to the back of the room.

Exhaling, Julia fell into her chair. "That man is worse than scum."

"He sure ain't like his dad before him."

Julia shook her head. "I still find it hard to believe his father is the one you named the park after."

"Night and day, those two," Ralph said, pushing a beer toward her. "So," he added, scooting his chair in and raising his mug. "Church social?"

She had been watching Volz, who shook hands with an elderly gentleman watching the billiards game. She clenched her jaw, trying to shake off the nasty feeling he always left her with. She found Ralph's eager gaze. She'd deal with what all this meant later. "Yep," she said, clinking her mug to his. "Looks like it." She downed half her drink, pushing thoughts of Ralph and Volz aside. For the first time, she was eager for the weekend to pass. All she wanted was to get to the office on Monday and see Eleanor again.

CHAPTER FIFTEEN

*B*rought you some broth, honey."
  Eleanor quietly let Sue in, blinking at the bright sunlight she hadn't seen yet today. "Broth?"

"For Louis. Isaac had to send him home this morning." Sue set the pot she carried on the stove.

Confusion trickled up Eleanor's spine. "Louis said that he wasn't needed. Too many men on the clock."

Sue kept her hand on the lid as she turned to Eleanor as if weighing her response against the metal. "Oh, honey." She took off her coat and sat at the table. Eleanor, unsure what else to do, joined her. "Louis came in today and..." She licked her lips, her gaze searching Eleanor's as if the gentlest way to deliver her next news was in there somewhere. "Well, dear, he wasn't himself."

"I don't understand."

"He was mixing things up. Got nearly everyone's name wrong on his shift."

Eleanor straightened, glancing at the grains of wood on the table and starting to count them. Numbers always eased the overwhelming feelings in her mind. "That's hardly cause for dismissal."

"No, but...that isn't all." Sue squinted. "Have you noticed any queer behavior lately?"

Sixteen, seventeen. She met Sue's gaze but kept counting over the instances of Louis being unable to find his words or remember where he kept his clothes.

"He could hardly hold the tools at his station, E. His hands." She held hers out to demonstrate. *"Shaking like a leaf in a hailstorm."*

"He may be coming down with somethin'." Twenty. Twenty-one.

"He snapped at everyone. Yelling like he thought he was my husband, ordering people around." Sue was still watching as she leaned forward and rested a hand on hers. *"Honey, is everything all right at home?"*

He's sick, she thought. *He's not himself.* Eleanor counted thirty when the honest answer surfaced: I have no idea what's happening. *"We all have bad days,"* she finally said.

"This wasn't a bad day, E. He wasn't right. He hasn't been for some time." She glanced at the hall. *"He had to be escorted off the premises."*

Eleanor shook her head, hardly able to stomach Sue's words. Louis hadn't seemed well when he'd returned home after only a half hour shift. He'd had a fitful night's sleep, one of many lately. Maybe he was coming down with something. He'd gone straight to bed once he'd gotten home, closing the door to her and her questions. The misplaced items, the forgotten words, slurred speech...how many things had she brushed aside?

Peter's cries sounded from the bedroom. The kettle whistled. Eleanor's mind flared with the noise and the realization that, above everything, Louis had lied to her.

Sue squeezed her hand. The gesture broke through Eleanor's thoughts. *"Fetch your boy,"* Sue said. *"I'll get the kettle. Then, I want you to tell me everything."*

Eleanor shook herself out of her reverie. Midmorning sun fell gently over the lawn as the final round of uniforms soaked in the tub. She sat on a low wooden stool behind the house under the shade of a sycamore tree that kept the warm sun at bay and stared at the soapy water, the edges of clothing sitting like lopsided icebergs among the suds. A cricket chirped nearby. She thought of the vial tucked into her stocking drawer, eager for another chance to catch a fragment of gold from the clothing. She thought of the five she'd collected so far. Only once had she allowed herself to dream of what she might purchase besides Peter's medicine. Eleanor kept such wishes at arm's length, knowing reality had a way of striking down impossible thoughts.

A cardinal sailed overhead. Its bold feathers awakened the memory of Julia and her daring smile. She bit her lip. Attraction to women wasn't new for Eleanor. She'd had what she dubbed a schoolgirl longing for one of her cousin's friends in Minnesota. Eleanor had followed her around like a puppy for two summers. She'd been positively desolate when the friend had stopped coming around after her engagement. After that, she'd grown fond of a woman who'd come by her aunt and uncle's home to visit. The woman had been older, perhaps forty, and had the ability to command a room with her tales of travel and leisure.

Eleanor had found some men attractive, of course, like Louis. While she didn't quite know what it all meant, she knew there were other women like her out there. Her cousins were progressive and gossiped endlessly about people they knew. She also knew such people weren't always welcome in polite society, so she'd never pursued anything with members of her sex. Julia seemed like one of those women, and her brashness took Eleanor by surprise each time.

This budding attraction battled with Sue's words of caution. While Sue had made a good point, Eleanor didn't want to shun Julia just because of town rumors. Could she really have acquired such a criminal record in so short a time?

Eleanor mulled over these thoughts after she moved inside to make bread. She was kneading dough when footsteps sounded on the pebbled road that led to her front porch. She listened, then wiped her hands on her apron as a gentle knock sounded at the door. It was probably Sue, though it seemed a little early after the ten o'clock church service for her weekly drop-in.

Opening the door, she asked, "Did you skip the sermon this morning? Oh." She blinked at Julia Holte standing on her front porch.

Her posture struck Eleanor first, astoundingly casual now that she was outside of the stuffy mill office. Her right hand slipped easily into her trouser pocket, which drew Eleanor's eye to the snug fit of the pants at Julia's hip. Those were cuffed over a pair of dark leather boots laced high above her ankles. Her other hand ran quickly through her hair that she wore down, the tresses eager to catch each breeze that ran through them. The gesture made the buttons down the front of her shirt pull taut for just a moment around her chest. Eleanor cut her gaze back up to Julia's eyes. Once again, they sat over the most inviting smile.

"I've skipped more than one Sunday sermon," Julia said. "Looks like you're not much for morning service, either."

Eleanor smiled. "Apologies. I thought you were someone else."

"Is now a bad time?" Julia peeked over Eleanor's shoulder. "You busy?"

"I..." Eleanor wanted to say yes. There was no way she should spend time with Julia, the one person she had been warned to stay away from. At her side, her thumb and forefinger met as she silently counted. Sue's voice was in her head: *She's a felon, E.* But curiosity won the internal struggle, along with the tickle of guilt remaining from their last interaction. Eleanor opened the door more. "No. Just preparing a few things while the laundry soaks. Please, come in, Miss Holte."

"Call me Julia." Inside, Julia glanced around. For some reason, Eleanor felt self-conscious of her sparse living space and kitchen. It had been some time since anyone besides Sue had come around. She was a naturally tidy person, but she felt the need to rearrange the few pieces of furniture she did possess. Tucking hair behind her ear, she put the kettle on the stove. "Would you like some tea?"

"Sure." Julia eyed the rocking chair but moved past it to a seat at the table.

Eleanor felt her gaze on her as she found two teacups. "Sue, Mrs. Weldon, typically comes by after church on Sundays. That's who I thought you were."

Julia was looking around the room, seeming to assess the wood floors, the faded, floral-patterned wallpaper above the stairwell, its pink flowers pale, and the open back door, when she said, "I won't keep you long, then. Would hate to intrude on the lady's lunch hour."

Eleanor snorted a laugh, catching Julia's pleased smile. "I'm glad to see you, actually." She felt warm at Julia's expectant brow. She started to count again, then realized her hand was visible. Quickly, she grabbed the kettle and filled the mugs to give her hands something to do. "I meant to apologize for the way I spoke to you the other day at the office. I…well, it had been a rough few days, and I tend to be a bit apprehensive when I don't know where Peter is."

"I'm sure most mothers are like that."

Shaking her head, Eleanor joined her and said, "I snapped at you. I'm sorry." Julia's smile softened as they looked at each other. Realizing she could hear the blood rushing in her ears, Eleanor asked, "What?"

Julia looked down. "It's just funny. I came here for the same reason."

"You did?"

She leaned back in her chair, folding her hands in her lap. *How comfortable she seems.* "I have a reconciliation gift." Julia reached into her pocket, meeting Eleanor's gaze again.

"You really don't have to do that. I'm the one who lost my temper."

Julia presented a handkerchief. She set it on the table, unfolding the cloth to reveal a small pastry. The golden crust gleamed. "It's not much, but my friend insists the blackberries are some of the best in the Rockies."

Eleanor, unsure what to say, only sat looking between the fruit tart and Julia, who pushed it closer.

Seeming to sense her uncertainty, Julia added, "Is Peter home? Thought he might like to try this."

"Oh." *It's for Peter.* Unsure why such a sentiment stung, Eleanor added a bit of sugar to her cup. "He's not home. He sometimes visits the hot springs on Sunday mornings with Mr. Weldon, who takes in the water for his joints."

"I see. Haven't had the pleasure of visiting there yet." Julia tapped the table, leaning forward. "Well, more for you, then."

Passing Julia the sugar, Eleanor said, "That's too kind." Would a felon extend such a gesture? Sue didn't know what she was talking about, Eleanor was certain. Not to mention, Julia had willingly thrown herself in front of a horse. For a book! That was hardly deviant behavior. She stirred a teaspoon of milk into her tea, watching the colors swirl together. "I feel I can hardly accept your gift. I should be the one offering something to you. You've been kind to me twice now."

Julia took a sip of the tea, and Eleanor didn't miss the small scrunch of her nose. It was adorable. "Twice?" Her eyes flashed with recognition. "Oh, that day in the street."

Eleanor studied her cup, her lips pursed, pleased Julia did recall their first meeting. "Yes, you saved me from an awkward encounter with my friend, returning a ruined book."

"Happy I could help," Julia replied, adding quickly, "Not sure how I assisted with Peter, though."

Eleanor wondered at her pushing the subject along. "I was brusque with you when all you were doing was entertaining my son. He ran off with you so willingly." She said the last part quietly, almost absentmindedly.

"He's a sweet kid." She grinned, and Eleanor couldn't resist matching it. "You were only being his mother. You didn't know where he was, and I came in and skipped off with him without your permission. Though…I didn't realize he was yours." She met her gaze, then slid it briefly to Eleanor's left hand. "Might've guessed though from that hair of his. And he has your eyes."

Eleanor felt a blush rise in her cheeks at the observation. "He did get those from me. But that's precisely it, you didn't know."

"Still," Julia said, her gaze falling, and a sudden darkness drifting over her face, "I should've known better. I have a knack for that..." She looked up. "A knack for jumping in before I look at where I'll fall."

Her words were innocuous, but Eleanor felt an undercurrent of something slip through the air between them. It tickled her shoulders. She shivered.

"So this is my truce," said Julia, gesturing to the pastry. She cleared her throat, then seemed to hesitate before adding, "They're from the Davies's bakery on 4th Street. Do you know it?"

"I do. Haven't been by in some time, though." Louis used to love their meat pies.

"Well, that same friend told me about the church social." Julia's bright gaze found hers. "Thought I'd see if you wanted to go?"

Eleanor blinked. Was she asking to accompany her? Or just asking if she planned to attend? "I haven't been to a church social since..." She wondered how much Julia knew about her and Louis. Deciding against sharing too much too soon, she said, "Since before Peter was born. I'm not sure I'd know many people."

"You'd know me." Julia said. "And that friend of yours, Mrs. Weldon."

"That's true." She considered it, running a finger over the handle of her teacup. Maybe it was time, she thought. Peter might enjoy it. Plus, there was always a good homemade meal available. "I'll think about it."

Julia's eyebrow quirked, her lips parting in what seemed like surprise, like she wasn't used to people not saying yes. "Don't think too hard." She stood. "Let me know what you and Peter think of the pastry," she said, pointing to the tart. "There's more where that came from if you like it."

Again, the remark seemed innocent enough, but Eleanor snapped her gaze from the open neck of Julia's shirt back to her eyes that gleamed playfully. All she managed was a nod before Julia thanked her for the tea.

"See you tomorrow, Mrs. Perry."

At the door, Eleanor watched Julia trot down the steps, jumping over the last one. Pointing to it, she said, "I could get some fresh wood to replace that, if you like."

The offer surprised her, another on the long list of surprises today. "Oh, that's very kind. I wouldn't want to burden you with that."

"Henry is friends with a lumberman in town. I'll see what I can do."

"Well, thank you very much." Eleanor smiled, feeling like a schoolgirl. Julia held her gaze. "See you around, Miss Holte." Julia had started to go but turned pointedly. "Sorry, Julia."

Julia grinned and wandered away down the drive.

Returning to the table, Eleanor eyed the pastry a moment before taking a bite. The berries' sweetness burst over her tongue, mingling with the delicately buttered crust. Her eyes closed, and she let the flavors consume her. Her mind cleared, save for one sudden, desperate question: did Julia taste as sweet as this?

Eleanor's eyes flew open. She looked around, worried she'd said such a thing out loud. She felt dizzy. It had been so long since she'd felt any way about anyone. She held the tart in front of her, then quickly wrapped it up and set it out of sight.

A few minutes later, there was another knock on the door. She had hardly opened it before Sue blew through like a windstorm.

"Eleanor," she said, the peach-colored hat she wore to match her Sunday dress askew, "please tell me I was imagining things and that was *not* Miss Holte I saw on the road coming from your house."

She gave a nervous laugh. Oh gosh, how was she going to explain this?

Chapter Sixteen

Julia, do you have those records?"

"Right here." She held up a manilla folder, each paper organized precisely how Henry had requested. He hurried over and grabbed it.

"Bless you. This audit is going to be the death of me." Office managers, clerks, and assistants buzzed around the mill office. A few new ones had come into town at the start of the week. "Experts from Denver," she heard someone say. Experts in what, she wasn't sure, but she assumed they had to know what they were doing because Henry seemed less wound up since they had arrived. Julia had met each of them on Monday but had promptly forgotten their names when Eleanor had arrived to pick up the uniforms. She'd been pleased to learn both she and Peter had enjoyed the blackberry tart.

Now, Thursday morning had been a blur, and Julia was surprised when the cuckoo clock struck eleven. She glanced at the front door. "Has Mrs. Perry come by for the uniforms?"

Henry, who had been reading through some of the papers she'd handed him, looked up, frown lines heavy on his forehead. "I don't think so." His concentrated gaze cleared a little as he said, "You two seem to be getting along."

She smiled and shrugged casually. "She's sweet. So is that kid of hers."

"You're also attending the church social with Ralph Davies, I hear."

Julia's blissful thoughts of Eleanor dissipated. She sighed and sat back in her chair. "That's right."

He gave her a look that said, "Be careful, Jules."

She nodded and waved him away. "I need more coffee. That file was a doozy."

"I've got three more for you to finish by the end of the day. Let me go find them."

"Can't wait," she said, standing and stretching. She flattened her long skirt, readjusting the material to fall over her boots. She'd borrowed one of Rose's blouses. The sleeves fell to her elbows and flowed in ways she wasn't used to. She was fiddling with the hem, trying to decide if it should be tucked in, when a man's voice said, "How ya doin', doll?"

Julia frowned and looked around. About ten different men were scattered throughout the office. She finally made eye contact with a fella who was a little taller than her. He was clean-shaven, with a head of oiled brown curls. She squinted, trying to recall his name. David? Daniel?

"Damian," he said, pointing at himself. "I work under Mr. Barrow."

She nodded. "Right."

He licked his lips, seeming to gather some courage, then asked, "Some friends and I are headed to Denver this weekend to catch the latest Chaplin flick. You, uh, you interested in joining?"

She raised a brow. "Sorry, don't care much for that sort of thing."

His dark eyes looked confused. "Don't much care for movies or trips to Denver?"

She started for the coffee at the back of the room. Pointing at him, she replied, "Yes," and smiled at the perplexed look on his face before she turned her back and found the coffee carafe. She exhaled, closing her eyes and shaking her shoulders. "Men," she muttered. Someone walked past, and she quickly recognized the head of gorgeous hair. "Eleanor," she called.

Eleanor was almost at the door that led to the changing room when she paused. Julia grinned and waved. Eleanor waved back before throwing a wary glance around the office. Half the men watched them curiously for a time. Eleanor seemed to contemplate whether to continue or go to her. Julia smiled even wider when Eleanor found her way through the desks and filing cabinets to join her.

"I thought maybe you weren't coming by today," Julia said, turning to lean against the edge of the counter.

Eleanor had a pair of empty canvas bags in her right hand. Her left seemed to tic at her side. She'd noticed the gesture at Eleanor's house the other day, too. While Eleanor seemed pleased to see her, there was a hint of fatigue around her eyes. "It's been a long morning. Peter..." She trailed off, chewing her lip.

Julia straightened. "Is he okay?"

Eleanor searched her gaze. "He is now. He's...well, he was sick this morning. That's why I'm late. I had to see to him. He's sleeping at home."

Nodding, Julia reached for her hand. Eleanor looked at the gesture, then met her gaze. A distant wonderment sat in her eyes. "Is there anything I can do?"

"No." Eleanor pulled back her hand. "But thank you." She gave a small smile. "You've already been too generous to us."

Julia wondered if Eleanor knew just how generous she could be. The thought surprised her a little here, in this office, under bright wall lamps while a phone rang, and men's voices called every which way.

They stood quietly for a time. Julia wasn't sure what to do. Offer her coffee? Eleanor had a job to get to. And she surely was worried about Peter and was probably eager to get back to him. Julia thought of making broth when she got home tonight, then blinked at the thought. She'd never entertained the idea of making something in the kitchen in her life.

A man walked behind Eleanor, putting his hand on the small of her back to push her forward so he could get by. Two things happened then: a flare of jealousy sang in Julia's mind at someone laying a hand on Eleanor, even an insignificant gesture like that. She clenched her jaw at the sight. At the same time, Eleanor was nudged forward, and for the briefest of moments, her chest brushed Julia's in the tight space. Julia caught a scent of soap and something else she couldn't name, but it was gone when Eleanor stepped back.

Still reeling, Julia felt a bit dizzy when Eleanor said, "Well, it was good seeing you."

Managing to collect herself, Julia asked, "Will I see you at the social in two weeks?"

Eleanor smiled. "It's possible."

Julia bit her lip at the playful look in Eleanor's eyes. "Is that a yes?"

Eleanor didn't say anything as she moved back to the changing room door. She only flashed a smile before disappearing, leaving Julia in a state of happy expectation.

Chapter Seventeen

"Slow down, Peter," Eleanor called. Hurrying after him, she lifted the end of her skirt to avoid the muddy patches that littered the grassland leading to the hot springs. It had rained last night, the sky now lined with streaks of gray clouds.

Peter, ten feet ahead, waved toward the first pool. "Mr. Weldon."

Isaac sat in the steaming water, his forehead shining. Cottonwoods encircled the pools and dotted the nearby slopes. "Good morning, Peter." He greeted Eleanor a moment later.

"Morning," she said, hands on her hips as Peter plopped down, quickly shedding his shoes and long socks. "How's the water today?"

"Just dandy."

She often forgot that Isaac had been an athlete in his younger years, but the evidence remained in his strong shoulders and broad build. He wore the same navy blue swimsuit he always did when he took in the water. "I swear, I buy him a new one every other year, but he refuses to wear them," Sue had told her once. "Thinks he's still twenty, that man." The tank top was snug on his chest as he moved to help Peter ease his feet in.

"Not too long, now, Peter," she said.

He kicked gently at the bubbles. "I know, Mom."

Isaac stretched his arms out across the edges of the pool, leaning back with his eyes closed. "Sue is helping some of the women's group prepare for the social. She's also working on getting some new books from the library."

"Can she get *Huckleberry Finn*?" Peter asked.

Eleanor found a dry spot on a large boulder and sat across from them. "You've read that one twice already."

Isaac chuckled. "I'll see what we can do." He faced Eleanor, his eyes opening wide like he remembered something. "Mr. Chisholm was here a few minutes ago. You just missed him."

"The fisherman?" Eleanor recalled a futile matchmaking attempt by Sue with Mr. Chisholm about five years earlier. He'd been kind enough but not terribly fond of children.

"Yes. He joins me some mornings. Told me about his brother who works in the mill, Don."

Eleanor nodded. "I know the name."

Isaac glanced at Peter, then said, "Don's had to miss work recently. Fallen ill."

"Ill?"

He nodded. In the quiet, knowing stretched between them. He didn't have to say it: like Louis.

"How many is that now, Isaac?"

He frowned, deep wrinkles creasing his forehead. "Third this year."

"Don is one of the ones sifting through the ore?"

"Yes."

She took a breath, watching Peter bring his feet closer, wiggling his toes on the grass. "Does Don have children?"

"No, not married."

"That's a blessing," she said, cutting her gaze to Isaac.

He gave a small nod. "Sue thinks it has something to do with the milling process."

"Sue has a good mind for that sort of thing."

He smiled. "That she does." He sighed, his palm cutting slowly through the water in front of him. "Once this damn audit is over, maybe I can look into it."

A faint voice inside her shouted joyfully at the idea. She'd long mourned Louis and knew he wasn't coming back, if he was even still alive. She also knew that what happened to him wasn't normal. Body tremors, garbled speech, erratic behavior... those weren't the symptoms of a typical malady. Since him, more men had succumbed to similar signs, but their families—and the mill—had chalked it up to other culprits. Bad meat. Spoiled milk. Tainted liquor. After all, it wasn't possible that what gave so many of these men their livelihood was simultaneously turning on them, poisoning their minds. That sort of injustice seemed unfathomable.

Finally, Eleanor said, "Well, if I know Sue, she won't let you forget it."

He stood, water dripping off the ends of his swimsuit trunks. "That she won't."

She contemplated the possibility of some sort of justice for Louis and the other poor souls like him. Meanwhile, Isaac fetched his towel from a low-hanging branch. Peter was arranging several small rocks into what she presumed was a fort. Beyond, in the farthest pool, movement caught her eye. She was about to ask who else was there when the figure stood. Her back was to them, but Eleanor recognized Julia. Her hair was wet and slicked behind her shoulders, and she must have borrowed a swimsuit from Henry as it was very similar to the one Isaac wore, only striped. It clung to her hips, and when she turned, twisting her hair to squeeze out the water, the cut of the tank top revealed the side of her breast.

Eleanor averted her gaze as Julia got out of the pool and found her towel. She forced herself to focus on Isaac, asking something about the audit to give herself something else to think about besides Julia, wet and coming their way.

"Oh, Miss Holte. I didn't know you were here." Isaac wrapped the towel around his waist. Eleanor turned, hoping her expression feigned surprise.

Julia had drawn her own towel over her shoulders, holding it closed across her chest. She grinned at Eleanor before answering. "Kept hearing so much about this place, I had to check it out."

"Hi, Julia," Peter said, waving before returning to his construction.

"Hey, Peter," she replied. "Nice fort you got there."

"Thanks."

Eleanor glanced at Julia's bare feet, tracing her gaze up her calves when Isaac said, "The springs can't be beaten. These are local treasures. The health benefits are unmatched. And that's not just my word. Experts from New York have said as much after visiting." He stretched. "My body feels ten years younger."

Julia still looked amused as Eleanor dared a glance at her. "I certainly do feel refreshed. May just have to come back." She seemed to want to say something else, licking her lips. Finally, all she said was, "Well, have a nice Saturday," before heading on to the main dirt road.

"Where are her shoes?" Peter asked, adding a final rock to his creation.

Eleanor was watching her when Isaac said, "Bit of a wild one, Miss Holte. Hard enough to get her to wear proper office attire, so I hear."

She scoffed, knowing it was Sue spreading that rumor. Maybe Julia was a bit of a wild card. Maybe, Eleanor thought, meeting her at the church social next week wasn't a terrible idea. She could get to know her, see if all that talk from Sue was a bluff. Then again, Eleanor thought, glancing at Peter, perhaps it wasn't the best plan. A worried voice in the back of her mind warned against plunging her reputation even further into the mud if the rumors about Julia were true.

But the image of Julia in that swimsuit lingered. Eleanor's mind buzzed, a distant hope pleading with her to do something for herself. It asked the question of her, leaving her to wonder if for once it was worth it to pursue…whatever it was she felt starting between them. How bad could getting to know Julia be, really?

CHAPTER EIGHTEEN

"Come here, Peter. I need to fix your collar." Eleanor pulled him close, adjusting the ironed shirt for the third time outside the church. People streamed into and around the building. Lines of cars and the occasional wagon were parked along the road.

"Mom, can we go in already? I'm hungry."

Tossing a glance around, Eleanor swallowed the nerves in her throat. She tried to soak up Peter's enthusiasm. It was his first community event. She tried to focus on that and not the shrieking fear in her gut at how little socializing she'd done in the last eight years. "Very well," she said, "let's go."

They headed inside where she was told to drop off their contribution: a few bundles of deer and rabbit jerky she'd been saving. The main atrium was small but funneled everyone into the larger sanctuary. Pews had been pushed to the walls, creating a vast open space where tables with everyone's donation items were on display. Women sat behind their handiwork, mostly patchwork quilts and a few stacks of knitted sweaters and fur-trimmed gloves. Eleanor smiled politely to everyone as they passed. Mrs. Shearn stood in one corner, and the schoolmarm seemed to hesitate before giving a polite nod.

"Come on, Mom," Peter said eagerly, tugging her toward the back exit. "Everyone's out here."

After dropping the jerky with a man she recognized as the local butcher, she was hit by the din of cheerful conversation drifting across the church's back lawn. The vast, two-acre lot brimmed with townsfolk, and for a moment, Eleanor fought the urge to run home. Peter's hand in hers reminded her to be brave. She also reminded herself that Julia was here somewhere, and the thought of seeing her again helped to overrun the trepidation in her mind.

More cars had pulled onto the grounds near the road along the edges of the church lawn. Men in pressed pants and shirts leaned casually against them, conversing and opening their car doors and hoods to compare machines. To her right, long picnic tables had been set up to host the day's food. Handkerchiefs lay over them to keep the summer flies at bay amid the hot July air. In between the cars and tables and out over the grass, people sat on dozens of blankets, taking in the warm weather.

Unsure where to go, Eleanor pulled Peter close. She held him to her, and to her relief, he let her. She squeezed his shoulders. *One, two, three.* He leaned back to meet her gaze. She smiled, and the buzzing in her mind quieted.

"Eleanor, you made it." Sue wore a flattering lavender dress that featured a delicate floral pattern. Her matching hat looked new, and she knelt to hug Peter, who smiled up at her.

"Hi, Auntie Sue."

She stepped back, taking them in. "My, you two look a picture."

Eleanor ran a sweaty hand down the skirt of her dress. She'd let it out around her waist after Peter was born, but it was still her finest. The green color, a deep forest shade, was one of her favorites. She'd pinned a white prickly poppy near her left shoulder to hide a grease stain. "Thanks, Sue. You look lovely."

Peter pointed to a line of men about thirty yards away. They all stood a few feet from each other. Eleanor squinted, but it didn't seem like they were doing much else. "What's over there?" he asked.

Sue turned and answered. "That's the gum chewing contest. Been going on twenty minutes now."

Behind that, several games of horseshoes were afoot. Eleanor frowned as there was still no sign of Julia.

"Looking for someone?"

She met Sue's curious gaze and swallowed. She'd shared Julia's peace offering from earlier in the month and had since defended her character. Still, Sue hadn't bought it. "A tiger can't change its stripes, E," Sue had said after catching Julia leaving her house. Admittedly, Eleanor really didn't know Julia that well. They'd only seen each other at work and the hot springs last week, besides the previous two instances. Part of her had hoped to get to know Julia better today.

"Mr. Keen is here," Sue was saying, pulling Eleanor's attention. The name didn't ring a bell, so Sue added, "The expert from Denver. He's been helping to prepare for the audit."

"Oh, right," she said.

Sue turned, seemingly ready to go fetch Mr. Keen when Peter took off, calling, "Julia!" He ran between a collection of picnic blankets toward the back half of the grounds. Sure enough, there was Julia. She lay on her side talking to a woman with short, stylish hair and Mr. Barrow.

Sue sighed and stepped closer to speak under her breath. "You didn't hear it from me, but the sheriff has had his eye on Miss Holte. And not in the way any lady wants a man's eyes on her. She hangs around Thrasher's more than a respectable woman should." Eleanor shot her a look. Sue raised her hands and retreated into the crowd. "You didn't hear it from me," she called again.

Eleanor shooed her off before following Peter. She waved as Julia noticed them. A look of surprise filled Julia's face as she sat up just in time for Peter to barrel into her with a hug.

"Peter," Eleanor called, hurrying to reach them. "So sorry," she said to their group. "Peter, you know how to greet people. Where are your manners?"

He stepped back, moving to Mr. Barrow for a handshake. "How do you do?"

Mr. Barrow grinned. "How do you do, good sir? I'm Henry."

"My, what a gentleman," the woman next to him said, taking Peter's hand in turn. Her eyes were the same as Julia's, though something more solemn and distant sat in them.

"Mrs. Perry," Henry said, setting down his bottle of Coca-Cola and standing to greet her. "It's good to see you."

"Hello," she said, glancing at Julia. Eleanor had found herself daydreaming recently about what Julia might be wearing today. To her delight, she sported trousers and a powder blue button-down. As always, her hair was down and flowing freely.

"My wife, Rose," Henry was saying, motioning to the woman on his right. While Henry wore what Eleanor had often seen him in at work, a drearily dark pair of trousers and jacket, Rose was dressed for the occasion in a light day dress and matching hat.

"How do you do? It's nice to make your acquaintance," Rose said, her tone lilting carefully.

"My sister the debutante," Julia teased. Rose gave her a look, but Eleanor sensed a playful nature between them.

"I take it you know my unruly younger sister, Mrs. Perry?" Rose asked.

Eleanor couldn't stop her blush. "Yes. We've seen one another at the mill office."

"Julia, can we race again?" Peter asked, tired of the adult pleasantries. He fished the small toy car out of his pocket.

"You betcha," Julia replied, starting to stand. "If it's all right with your mom."

Eleanor smiled. "Yes, go ahead."

Julia held her gaze for a moment, and Eleanor wanted her to stay right there. She wanted to sit with Julia, talk to her, explore the depths of blue in her eyes. Realizing the others were staring, she nodded politely and moved aside for Julia to pass.

"Let's go see the big cars," Peter said, pulling Julia away.

Henry called, "Careful with mine."

Julia hollered over her shoulder, "We'll mind the paint job," before letting Peter lead her away.

"Come," said Rose, sitting and patting the checked blanket, "join us."

Eleanor did, glancing once more to see Julia and Peter disappear into the crowd.

"How old is your boy?" Rose asked, pushing a plate of grapes and apple slices toward her.

"He'll be nine in August," she said, taking a red slice.

Rose smiled and shared a look with Henry. "How wonderful. You seem to have done a good job by him."

The comment surprised Eleanor. She wondered how much the Barrows knew of her life. There was always gossip, she knew, most of it coming from Sue. Still, Rose seemed genuine in her sentiment. "I do what I can, though it hasn't been easy." They nodded. She sat back and asked, "Do you have children?"

A dark look flickered over Rose's face. That solemn note in her eyes was pulled forward as she exchanged another look with Henry. Eleanor had a feeling she shouldn't have asked.

"No," Henry answered. "Not yet." His smile, like the faint lines around Rose's eyes, held sadness.

Eager to change the subject, Eleanor asked, "How do you like Colorado? You've all been here six, seven months?"

"The weather is grand," said Henry, munching on a crust of bread. "Not as sweltering as Texas this time of year."

Was that where Julia was from? Eleanor smiled to herself at the image of Julia's boots, when she had looked ever the cowgirl. Perhaps sensing the question, Rose added, "We lived on my family's ranch outside of Amarillo. Do you know it?"

Eleanor shook her head.

"Dry as a bone and dust like you wouldn't believe," Henry said, which earned him a playful swat from Rose. "Well, isn't it?"

"My husband is from Ohio originally," Rose explained. "Never quite took to Texas."

"Well," he said, finding Rose's hand and kissing it, "I took to some things, didn't I?"

Eleanor looked down as they shared a moment. She admired how utterly smitten they seemed and wondered how long they'd been married when Peter came running back with Julia on his heels.

Henry finished off his soda pop and asked, "Back so soon?"

Peter pulled up to a stop, catching his breath. Eleanor watched his chest expand, resisting the urge to go to him until his breathing evened out.

"Lunch break," Julia said, tossing Eleanor a wink.

"Oh, that's right," she said. "Your whole reason for being here...the food."

They all chuckled as Henry stood. "Here, Peter, why don't you and I go find you a lunch?"

Eleanor stepped forward as Peter moved toward him. Julia reached out, placing a gentle hand on her arm. "I can show your mom around while you do that," she said. Eleanor found the reassuring look in Julia's eyes and was surprised as it eased the nervy bundle in her gut at Peter going off with someone else.

"You really should take in the games," Rose said. "Pole sitting should start soon."

Julia sidled up to Eleanor. "What do you say?"

She looked from Julia to Peter.

"Go on," Henry said as Rose joined him. Eleanor wondered if she sensed her unease. She placed a hand on Peter's shoulder. "We'll see after Peter for a time." He smiled and asked, "What do you say to some fried chicken?"

Peter's eyes bulged. "Fried chicken!" He grabbed each of the Barrows by the hand and pulled them toward the food tables. "See you soon, Mom," he called. "I'll get you some, don't worry."

Anticipation and a wave of something else mixed in Eleanor's chest as Julia took her hand. "Come on," she said, "this way."

❖

"You ever driven a car?" Julia asked, leading Eleanor through the crowds. Kids hurried past in a game of chase. "Peter seems fascinated by them."

"No. I took trains from Minnesota when I moved here to meet Louis."

Julia glanced over her shoulder. She presumed Louis had been Eleanor's husband, but Eleanor continued before she could ask:

"Peter and I have ridden along plenty, though, with Sue and Mr. Weldon. They took me to Denver to see a specialist when Peter was six."

"A specialist?" The throngs of picnic goers thinned, and Julia released Eleanor's hand so they could walk side by side.

Eleanor nodded and slowed her pace to observe a pie eating contest. Each of the contestants sank face-first into several inches of meringue to the cheers of onlookers. Julia recognized Isaac Weldon from the bald patch on his head. "He has asthma," Eleanor said, still watching the contest. "It can get bad at times. Medicine and tea help."

Julia started to understand the protective net Eleanor cast over Peter. It had been flung out just moments ago when Peter had gone with Rose and Henry. Julia had been surprised she'd let him go but pleasantly so since Julia was eager to be alone with her.

"Is that why he wasn't in school that day in the office? His asthma?"

Eleanor, who was applauding the contestants' efforts as they neared the end of their pies said, "Yes. It's been difficult lately between his health and his stubbornness to get him to go to school at all. Of course, now we're into summer vacation." She sighed. "He's insecure about his health, about what his peers think. The teacher this year was no help." The sharpness of her tone surprised Julia, and she followed Eleanor's gaze to the east where the mill sat against the mountainside. "He'd rather work than learn."

Julia had seen a few young boys coming and going in the office. It had been startling at first to see such young, stone-faced children as they followed the men into the mill. Some, she knew, went into the mountain itself. While she didn't agree with children doing such work, she did understand not wanting to be in school. "I get where he's coming from. School was never my cup of tea," she said, flashing a grin. "Not much for books." Julia felt a surge of longing at the look in Eleanor's stunning eyes.

"Well, you respect books enough to save them."

Laughing, Julia was about to suggest they continue walking when Ralph's voice cut in.

"Jules, there you are." He moved through the nearby circles of people, a bowl of something in hand.

She forced a smile, realizing she'd forgotten all about Ralph. He'd gone to help his family at the serving tables when they'd first arrived. She'd been so focused on Eleanor, she'd forgotten he'd accompanied her here.

"Hey, Ralph. What's that?" she asked.

He picked up a spoonful. "Date pudding from Mrs. Jarda, your neighbor. Really good stuff." He took a bite and held the bowl out to her. "Wanna try?"

What she wanted to do was disappear with Eleanor. Run her fingers through Eleanor's hair and discover every shade of red it possessed. She clenched her jaw, trying to think of an excuse to give to Ralph. Admittedly, she felt a tad guilty at leaving him hanging, but surely, he would understand.

She caught Eleanor's patient smile. "You know Mrs. Perry?" she decided to ask.

Ralph, seeming to just realize Eleanor was there, replaced the spoon and wiped his hand on his hip. "Ralph Davies, friend of Julia's."

"Eleanor Perry, new friend of Julia's."

Standing between them, Julia's pulse quickened at the look Eleanor gave her.

"Ralph, dear." They turned to find Mrs. Davies waving from behind a food table. She smiled at Julia before beckoning for Ralph.

He sighed. "Duty calls." Seeming to hesitate, he took a step to Julia, then said, "The Blackstreets have homemade ice cream across the lawn. You oughta check it out."

"Good idea," Eleanor said. "It is a rather warm day."

With Ralph gone, Julia asked, "Fan of dessert?"

"I like anything sweet."

Julia swallowed. "Well, let's go satisfy that sweet tooth, then."

CHAPTER NINETEEN

Eleanor reminded herself to breathe as Julia led her to a circle of chairs. It was the second time this afternoon Julia had taken her hand to direct them. Eleanor had to admit she rather liked such an act. Louis, while attentive, had always been timid in his decision-making, often relying on her to know the best thing to eat, what to do on a quiet Sunday, or how to take care of a newborn. His need for a wife—anyone, really—to make a choice for him had made sense quickly after their wedding. Julia, on the other hand, always seemed to have a plan in mind, and Eleanor happily let herself be guided.

The circle of chairs surrounded a large brown bucket where a matronly lady with strong arms stood manning the ice cream maker's hand crank. "Hiya, girls," she said, looking up beneath a head of bouncing brown curls. "Sally, get each of these ladies a cup."

A girl of maybe ten in a polka-dot dress passed two paper cups with wooden spoons in them.

"Thank you," Eleanor said. She searched for a free seat when Julia nudged her elbow.

"Over here."

Eleanor followed, pleased to catch a glimpse of Peter on the lawn behind them. He and the Barrows were back on the blanket. She struggled against the need to go to him, knowing he was fine. He certainly looked pleased as punch as he gnawed on a drumstick. Unfortunately, she also locked eyes with Mrs. Henley, who strolled arm in arm with her husband. Eleanor looked away, shoving aside the disdain she felt trailing after her.

She focused instead on the flutter near her ribs as she and Julia settled on a patch of grass beneath a large sycamore. The broad limbs provided ample shade and a sense of privacy as they sat a good twenty yards from the nearest social goers.

"I can't remember the last time I had ice cream," Eleanor said, careful to tug the hem of her dress over her knees.

"We always had some at the ranch growing up. Can't get through most of the year in Texas without it."

Eleanor closed her eyes at the first bite of sweet vanilla.

"Good?" Julia asked as she opened them. Eleanor didn't miss Julia's gaze lingering on her mouth.

"Divine." A curious look crossed Julia's face that intensified the flutter near Eleanor's ribs. She seemed to collect herself though and took a bite. "So you grew up on a ranch? With horses and all that?"

"Horses, sheep, cattle, you name it." Julia spooned another healthy bite. "I was surrounded by noise but nothing like that." She pointed toward the mill. Eleanor wondered at the edge to Julia's tone before she seemed to shrug off the idea of the mill and continued. "Rose is my only sibling, but my dad hired so many hands, it always felt like I had twenty cousins hanging around. Most of the men knew us well and lived in bunkhouses near our property."

Eleanor nodded, noting the strong look of Julia's shoulders and the way her trousers were tight along her thighs. No doubt from the work she'd grown up doing. Forcing herself away from the vision of what Julia's arms might look like beneath that shirt, Eleanor said, "I see why you weren't prone to schooling." She smiled. "Much to do on a ranch."

"The chores never end," she said, shaking her head to move hair from her face. "I learned how to ride before I could read a line by Shakespeare. Rose always wanted to put on an act from stories like that at parties and whatnot, but I usually ended up turning it into a vaudeville routine." She smiled, and Eleanor envied the look of fondness on her face when it came to her sister.

"You're lucky to have Rose," she said.

Julia's smile faltered before she asked, "No siblings?"

Eleanor shook her head. "Just me. I..." She licked her lips, wondering how to explain her childhood. "My mother...well, I don't know much about her. But after having me, she..." Eleanor lowered her ice cream. For a moment, the dreadful vision of that frozen lake returned, the one from her dreams. "My aunt said she fell ill and never recovered. She died not long after I was born. My father didn't..."

Julia set her own cup down and moved to sit cross-legged, listening.

"He was a busy businessman. No time for children. He left me with my Aunt Emily when I was just a few years old. She raised me with my cousins."

Eleanor's throat felt dry. She'd only shared that once before with Louis. But even he didn't know the whole truth of how her mother had died. Now was hardly the time or place for such a tragic tale, though. She smiled and said, "When I was nineteen, I answered an advertisement for a wife in Idaho Springs, and here I am."

Julia's brow rose as she seemed to take in Eleanor's story and change of demeanor. Feeling uncomfortable at having shared so much, Eleanor said, "I bet you're an excellent horseback rider."

Julia squinted, her lip quirking in a smile at her change of subject. "Can ride circles around every man in town."

Eleanor took another bite. The ice cream was mostly melted now, and she felt it dribble down her chin.

Julia reached out. "I've got it."

Eleanor let Julia trace her thumb from her chin to her lip. Her chest felt hot when Julia held her hand between them. They both looked at the line of vanilla sliding down her thumb. A vision struck Eleanor. She imagined taking Julia's hand and bringing her thumb into her mouth, letting her tongue take back the sweet dessert while discovering the taste of Julia's flesh. The image was so vivid, Eleanor thought for a moment she'd done just that. But the dryness of her mouth proved it was only a fantasy, a hungry fantasy that seemed to reflect at her in Julia's gaze.

Finally, Julia brought her thumb to her own mouth and behind a devilish grin, made quick work of the ice cream. Long dormant want surged in Eleanor's abdomen. Her heart raced, and she leaned forward.

"Mom!"

Eleanor pulled back, turning to find Peter skipping over to them. The world that had gone unfocused in their shady den beneath the sycamore realigned as her heart pounded. She swallowed, glancing at Julia, who looked somewhere between disappointed and bemused as Henry followed Peter.

She reached for him as he plopped down beside her. "Hi, sweetheart, have a good lunch?"

"It was so good. We had fried chicken and corn and date pudding, and Mr. Barrow let me have a Coca-Cola."

She smiled and hugged him, tossing a grateful look to Henry. "How nice."

Peter noticed their cups after flourishing a drumstick she took from him. "You got ice cream?"

"We were waiting for you," Julia said, passing her cup to him.

He thanked her and started in on the rest of the dessert. Meanwhile, Eleanor sat back, taking a breath to slow her heart rate. She tried not to replay how close she'd been to kissing Julia right here in the middle of the church social. *Maybe this is why I never leave the house.*

"Jules," Henry said, "I think we're heading home soon."

Disappointment settled over Eleanor when Julia said, "All right." She and Henry exchanged looks, and Eleanor wondered if the Barrows and Holtes practiced conversing in furtive glances with how often it seemed to happen. "See you on Monday?" Julia asked once she stood.

Eleanor looked up. Julia was a shadowy figure with the sun at her back. The image beckoned the shapes from her dreams, and for the first time, Eleanor considered the possibility that the nature of those dreams could be something other than sinister. Perhaps those figures were only the unknown, the often-terrifying prospect of what she didn't know, of ways she wasn't sure how to be.

Now, she found she wanted to learn more about so much... the Barrows, Texas, and one Miss Julia Holte. "See you then," she said before Julia gave her one more smile and followed Henry into the crowd.

CHAPTER TWENTY

Julia was no stranger to women. She might not have been well-read, but she did consider herself well-versed in matters of female pursuits. In particular, she adored the starting off point, that delicious in-between after she'd connected with a woman, and they were yet to act on their attraction. At times, it felt like she was living for that part...the tantalizing chase. It was as good as any drink or dessert, as wonderful as any high she'd hunted.

Nothing, however, compared to this in-between with Eleanor. A tense, sensual tightrope stretched between them. Eleanor Perry was different. Something about her demure nature, her unexpected guile, kept Julia guessing. Eleanor was beautiful, and the physical attraction Julia had felt didn't surprise her initially. It was the intrigue that followed that captured her attention. She hadn't been sure if Eleanor was even interested in her like that. She'd had a husband, after all. Not that married women hadn't taken an interest in Julia before, but Eleanor had kept her cards close to her chest.

Finally, though, Eleanor had showed her hand. The church social had solidified Julia's notion that Eleanor was, in fact, interested. She had a good laugh about such a realization coming at a church sanctioned event. *Maybe I should go to services more often.*

It had taken a lot of willpower not to kiss Eleanor beneath that sycamore, to not lay her down upon the thick grass and breathe her in. Like most of their time together thus far, the day had been cut short.

"Don't forget your breakfast," Rose called the final Monday in July. "I can't believe you beat me downstairs," she added, still in her robe, her hair in pins as she yawned and rummaged through the icebox. Julia noted the hinges no longer squeaked after she'd oiled them yesterday. Rose wrapped two boiled eggs in a bundle. Julia took them, dodging Rose's attempt to pack a slice of unsavory banana bread.

"Gotta run," she said before hurrying out the door. She was eager to get to the office and could even stomach the idea of sorting papers on such a beautiful day if it meant seeing Eleanor again.

Over the next two weeks, however, it seemed Eleanor had taken hold of that tension between them. Julia was the one grappling with ways to get her alone or finding herself unsure how to even stand when Eleanor came around. Sly quips of, "Good morning, Miss Holte," and, "How's your sister, Miss Holte?" were the extent of their pleasantries inside the mill office. The teasing nature Eleanor had adopted was unexpected, and it left Julia's head spinning in the best of ways. Of course, she understood Eleanor was likely trying to be cautious when they were at work. It was probably best to minimize attention from the men.

Henry, keen-eyed as ever, didn't let their charged moments go unnoticed. "What're you doing, Jules?" he asked on the second Wednesday in August, handing her another file. They were a month away from the audit, and the filing seemed to never end.

"Nothing I haven't done before," she replied with a confident grin.

Henry sighed. "Just be careful. Volz has been hanging around Thrasher's a lot lately."

Julia scoffed. "I hear he's there to dip his sticky fingers into Jay's funds. Hush money to keep the joint running."

Narrowing his eyes, a look like he wasn't sure whether to believe her, crossed his face. "Well, they say he's been cracking down on gambling and other activity." His voice dropped on the last word. "Mind yourself."

"Yeah, yeah."

Julia could handle Volz. It was this new, enticing world of Eleanor Perry that left her in wonderfully uncharted territory. Finally, on Thursday, Eleanor came in and beckoned for Julia to join her at the back for some coffee. "I was afraid you were avoiding me," she said.

Eleanor smiled and picked up an empty mug, pretending to study it. When she still didn't say anything, Julia glanced around then quietly said, "I want to see you again."

"Isn't that what we're doing now, Miss Holte?"

Julia bit her lip to contain a smile. "I want to see you properly, outside of this office."

Eleanor replaced the mug. "Maybe," she said behind a coy smile before heading off to collect the uniforms and leaving Julia in a state of yearning.

August seemed to drag along in her agony. The following Monday, Julia had an invitation to dinner prepared when Eleanor arrived at the office. She'd managed to convince Rose to throw a get-together, so her sister believed it was fully her idea to invite the Perrys over. Surely, Eleanor wouldn't refuse that.

When twelve o'clock rolled around, though, and there was no sign of Eleanor, Julia's excitement dwindled. At ten after, she called to Henry that she was taking lunch.

Outside, the warm midday sun hit her, and she blinked at the brightness when somebody grabbed her arm.

"Hey, watch—" She was pulled around the back of the building. Her gaze adjusted to the dimness, and she registered old machine parts and dilapidated mining tools in heaps along the wall. Those and the hedge of wild overgrowth at the base of the sloping mountainside created a narrow tunnel. All that fell away as she realized who had pulled her into the shadows. "Eleanor?"

Eleanor released her, wearing a look of surprise that no doubt mirrored the one on Julia's face. "Sorry," she said, reaching out as if to apologize. "I didn't mean to startle you."

"What did you mean to do?" Julia asked, tugging the middle of her shirt to straighten it. She didn't miss Eleanor following the movement. Her gaze traced the shirt buttons, lingering on the hollow at the base of Julia's neck before snapping back to look at her.

She smiled sheepishly. "I...I heard you take lunch at Thrasher's most days around this time."

Raising a brow, Julia replied. "A little birdy named Sue tell you that?"

"She may have." Eleanor cut her gaze sideways toward the corner she'd pulled Julia around. Doing the same, Julia noted the swath of sunlight. It was mere feet away yet felt so far, as if Eleanor had pulled her through a looking glass into a shady dreamscape all their own. She chose to ignore the fact that they were surrounded by rusted cogs and errant pickaxes. Eleanor stepped closer, and Julia felt the cool brick at her back.

"So you waited until you knew I'd be gone for lunch to come by?"

Eleanor looked down, seemingly embarrassed at her own plan.

Julia lifted her chin. "I was afraid you didn't want to see me." She swallowed at the shine to Eleanor's lips. "Is Peter okay?"

She nodded. "He's fine. He's in town with Sue."

Julia wasn't sure what to say. The dinner invitation she'd carefully crafted seemed unreachable, like it had slipped from her tongue to the recesses of her mind now thick with desire as Eleanor stood close.

"I wanted to see you and..." She hesitated, seeming to admire Julia's face, her body. Julia let herself be taken in by Eleanor's hungry gaze. "I wanted to continue what we started."

"And what exactly did we start, Mrs. Perry?"

Julia caught the rise and fall of Eleanor's chest beneath her blue dress. "Please," she said, moving to whisper next to Julia's ear, "I've been dying to kiss you."

Julia didn't hesitate, finding Eleanor's lips and doing just as she wished. She kissed Eleanor hard as she pressed closer. Exquisitely soft lips moved against hers. The surprise of what was happening crashed over Julia like a wave until she managed to set that surprise aside. She cupped Eleanor's cheeks. Their kiss deepened. Julia couldn't recall the last time she'd been so taken aback by a kiss, despite the hope that this very moment would happen.

A series of voices sounded around the building, and they pulled apart. Eleanor rested against Julia's temple as they waited for the group of men to leave. Julia found Eleanor's gaze. She smiled, a relieved laugh preceding another quick kiss.

"Come to lunch with me?" Julia asked.

Eleanor seemed to consider it before a small frown turned down her lips. "I should get back. I'm supposed to meet Peter and Sue downtown."

Julia found her right hand as she touched her fingers to her thumb. It was the same rhythmic tic from before. *Was she nervous?* "Dinner then?"

"Tonight?"

"Saturday. Rose's invite. It seems she's quite taken by you."

Eleanor's brow rose at the comment, and Julia hoped she could see how true that sentiment was for more than just her sister. Finally, she smiled. "Okay."

"Okay? Yes?"

Laughing, Eleanor kissed her again. "Yes, Julia. I'll see you Saturday."

Julia fell back against the wall as Eleanor moved out into the sunlight after checking that the coast was clear. She waved and disappeared, leaving Julia in a whirl of hope. To the cool shadows that had engulfed them, she said, "See you then, Eleanor."

Chapter Twenty-one

"Peter, hon, can you get the door?" Eleanor called as she held the repurposed perfume bottle to the light and tapped another fleck of gold into her collection. *Eight, nine pieces?* She wasn't quite sure, but she did like the way the late afternoon light glinted off them. Part of her wished she hadn't dashed the remnants of her perfume out that day. Would Julia have liked that scent on her? The question sent a quiver through her stomach as Eleanor tucked such thoughts alongside the bottle before adjusting her hair in the mirror.

"It's Auntie Sue," Peter called from the main room.

Eleanor stepped back to see more of herself in the vanity. She had decided on an old dress in her wardrobe and had furiously tried to let it out a bit. It was a cornflower blue and made her think of Julia's eyes. After washing Peter's hair this morning, she'd done the same with hers, and it had, mercifully, dried and fallen just the way she'd hoped.

Sue's sing-song voice neared. "I come bearing books." Eleanor turned as Sue appeared in her bedroom doorway. She gasped and clutched the books to her chest. "E, dear, you look positively radiant."

"You think?" she asked, giving a small turn. "This dress is so old, is it presentable enough?"

"Absolutely." Sue looked utterly delighted. "Don't tell me you have a gentleman caller?"

"No." Sue's face fell. Eleanor laughed. "The Barrows invited us to dinner."

Sue, who had wandered in to adjust her earring in the mirror, froze. Her wide gaze slid to Eleanor. "Oh?"

Eleanor smiled but could sense Sue's questions. She decided to avert them with facts. "That nonsense you mentioned about something between Miss Holte and Mr. Barrow can leave your mind right now, by the way." Sue looked only mildly offended as her brow rose in curiosity. "He's utterly taken with his wife. She's the kindest woman, Rose Holte. They seem entirely in love."

She moved into the kitchen where Peter sat at the table. He was in his finest brown patterned shorts that fell to his knees where they met his matching socks. He wore a jacket that had come with the shorts when she'd bought the suit two years ago. Now it fit snugly over his chest, only one button able to close over the white shirt with a large collar. She helped him with the buckle on his shoe. "Peter, what happened to your hair?"

"What?" He ran a hand over it. "Do I need to comb it again?"

"Yes, please," she said, sending him off to the washroom once more. "And hurry or we'll be late."

Sue met her near the kitchen table. Eleanor gestured to the books, pleasantly surprised at her lack of engagement in the matter of the Barrows. "The latest from Denver?"

Setting them on the table, Sue said, "Yes. The top one is for you, it's another Christie." She glanced toward where Peter had gone, then stepped closer and lowered her voice. "E, I know thus far my warnings have gone unheeded regarding one Miss Julia Holte. But do you really think going to dinner there is wise?"

Eleanor sighed. There it was. "Sue, I know you're looking out for me, but…" Eleanor tried to figure out how to explain the thrill and joy that came with being around Julia. It was a feeling she hadn't experienced in so long. Surely, she deserved that again.

"You didn't hear this from me," Sue started to say, "but Sheriff Volz has told some of the city council to keep watch of Miss Holte and her behavior."

"Behavior? You mean that whole getting arrested business that I've seen none of since she started at the mill office?"

Sue shot her a look. "I mean…a different kind of behavior." She looked around again, then said, "*Irregular* behavior. But you didn't hear it from me."

Eleanor's chest tightened as she had a feeling she understood. "You mean…"

"Come on, E. You've seen the way she dresses, the way she hangs around Thrasher's." She waved a hand at her own dress that gave her a boyish figure to go along with her short haircut. "I know this look has been all the rage, but Miss Holte takes it to an extreme." She raised a hand and whispered, "They say she fraternizes with the same sex."

It wasn't surprise that hit Eleanor, though that was the emotion she tried to convey on her face at Sue's comment. Rather, a snaking of jealousy coiled in her chest at the idea of Julia and other women.

"You see," Sue was saying, pointing at the blush filling Eleanor's cheeks. "Scandalous behavior. More scandalous than last month's radio program. Did you hear it?"

Eleanor focused on a different question. "Do you think the Barrows know?" she asked, more to give herself time to recover, but she had been wondering as much since meeting them at the church social.

Sue barked a laugh. "That whole family is teeming with secrets. I can feel it."

"Oh, Sue." Eleanor took a breath, deciding it was best to keep Sue and her fanciful gossip moving forward and away from Julia. "You know there's more to life than drama and sordid affairs. Sometimes I wonder if you lose the difference between fiction and reality."

Sue put a hand to her chest, looking mock offended. "Eleanor Perry, it's as if you don't know me at all."

They both laughed as Peter scurried out. Eleanor hoped the levity chased away any hint that she was eager to avoid any more of that conversation. She herself had engaged in so-called irregular behavior just the other day. Sue had always been a progressive woman, fighting for women's rights and more opportunities when it came to work. Cutting her gaze to Sue now, she suddenly wondered just how open-minded Sue was.

"Are you coming with us, Auntie Sue?" Peter asked.

"No, my boy," she said, patting the shoulders of his jacket approvingly. "You'll have to tell me all about your evening with the Barrows when you join me at the town hall next week."

He nodded and hurried to the door.

"That goes for you, too, E," Sue said as she walked with them outside. When the third porch step held firm beneath them, Sue looked up, surprised. "You fixed it."

"Julia did. Last week on her lunch break."

That reproving brow rose once again, but Sue remained quiet.

"Come on," Eleanor said, wrapping an arm around her. "I'm sure it'll be a perfectly boring dinner. The Barrows and Miss Holte are lovely people. You'll see."

Chapter Twenty-two

"Julia, they're here!"

Smoothing her hair, Julia called back to Rose. "Here, here, or coming up the road?" She let a smile slip into her voice, picturing Rose peering out the window, eagerly anticipating her guests.

"Just rounding the corner!"

Julia chuckled and finished tugging on her boots. She'd spent most of the day shining them. They'd been a gift from her parents before she'd left for Colorado. "Think of us," her father had said gruffly when she'd pulled the pair of cowhide boots out of their box. She'd asked Rose to iron her whitest collared shirt for the evening. Her sister had happily done so as she'd busied herself all day, swatting away the summer flies and Julia's sporadic teasing.

"Just like your mother," Henry had said when he and Julia had paused outside the kitchen to watch Rose fuss over the stove where several pots stood boiling. Bits of chopped carrots, onions, and something else Julia didn't recognize had lain in heaps atop a cutting board.

"Any more stewing about and she'll be as steamed as those vegetables," Julia had said.

Henry had worn a proud smile. "She always puts her best foot forward, doesn't she?" Julia had glanced at him. The way he looked at Rose was so full of love. Could anyone look at her that way? Could Eleanor?

Despite her joking, Julia had also found herself wanting to be sure everything was in order for the Perrys' visit. When Rose had blown through the hallway upstairs at midmorning, feather duster in hand, she'd skidded to a halt outside Julia's room. "You cleaned?"

Julia, lining her boots up below the window, had tossed her gaze to the made bed and swept floor and shrugged. "Looks like it."

After the look of shock settled, Rose had smiled and moved on.

Now, Julia waited until she heard Eleanor's voice before starting downstairs. She hesitated halfway down, taken by the shine in Eleanor's hair that fell like a luscious mane. Her dress seemed to fit her like a glove, and Julia stared at the way it clung to her hips and breasts.

Henry's booming greeting tore her from her thoughts. "Is that young Mr. Perry? Come in." He shook Peter's hand and bowed. "How are you, my good sir?"

Peter straightened. "Just dandy, Mr. Barrow."

"Oh, please, call me Henry." He bent and presented a spiral, rainbow-colored lollipop. Julia chuckled at Peter's wide eyes.

"For me?"

"For you."

Rose cleared her throat. Henry hesitated, glancing from her to Eleanor. "As long as it's all right with Mom."

Eleanor smiled, a gentle hand on Peter's shoulder. "Of course. For dessert," she added. Peter took the lollipop, stashing it in his jacket pocket.

Rose spotted her on the stairs. "Jules, what are you doing lurking? Come say hello."

Julia rolled her eyes but enjoyed the look Eleanor gave her as she descended: a mixture of intrigue and appreciation went from her boots to the open collar of her shirt.

"Good evening," said Eleanor.

"Howdy, Mrs. Perry." Julia tipped an imaginary hat. Henry snorted, but she ignored him. "Hi, Peter."

"Hi, Julia." He ran over and hugged her. "What's 'howdy'?"

"It's how Texans say hi."

He nodded seriously, then looked around the parlor. Rose, who had disappeared into the kitchen, reappeared in the atrium. "Well, Henry, pour our guests some tea. Peter, we also have lemonade if that's to your liking?"

"Yes, ma'am."

Rose beamed. "Dinner will be on soon."

Henry led them into the parlor. He stood near the small fireplace while Eleanor and Peter sat on the ornate love seat. Julia took the leather wingback they'd had shipped in from Dallas. The smell of it reminded her of the ranch, and it was one of several rustic touches adorning her sister's home. "So, Peter," Henry said, handing him and Eleanor their drinks, "what do the young men of Idaho Springs get up to now? I take it you're getting ready for another school year?"

Peter gulped down half his lemonade before answering. "School's all right. I'd rather work in the mill like you."

Henry cast his surprised look at Eleanor. Julia caught a slight shake of her head. "Well, the mill is exciting at times, but you know what I had to do to get that job?"

"What?"

"Finish my schooling."

Peter slumped. "You sound like my mom."

They all laughed.

Peter looked around. "Stuart Weekly works in the mine."

Henry took a drink, his brow low in thought. "He does. I'm sure he has a good reason for not being in school."

"I could help," Peter said, glancing around eagerly. "I could earn my keep."

Eleanor reached out, pulling him into a hug. "Children should enjoy their time, not concern themselves with work."

"I could buy you something nice," he said to Eleanor, who smiled, but Julia could see the embarrassed flush in her cheeks.

"We're all right, Peter, don't you worry about such things."

"You're lucky to have such a strong mother," Julia said. "Hardworking, dedicated..." She stopped herself before adding "beautiful." Peter frowned and crossed his arms, looking ready to move on from the conversation that wasn't turning out to his liking. Julia cleared her throat to gather her thoughts. She found Eleanor watching her when Henry coughed. She'd forgotten he was there.

"Dinner is served," Rose called, reappearing in a flurry.

Julia spent most of the meal listening to Rose and Eleanor exchange histories. She noted how Eleanor remained tight-lipped about her time in Idaho Springs, sharing most about her childhood in Minnesota. Peter focused on his food, finishing it quickly and using his dinner roll to soak up the gravy and remnants of mashed potatoes on his plate.

Julia pushed the aspic around with her fork. She'd never much cared for the dish when her mother had made it. Rose didn't seem to have the recipe down; the veggies were undercooked and the broth oversalted. Eleanor, to her credit, had eaten half of it, but Julia could see her struggling to finish. Henry shot her a look as Rose cleaned her plate and said, "We'll have to get up to Minnesota some time if it's as beautiful as you say."

Eleanor finished her glass of tea before replying. "Summer and fall are idyllic. There are more lakes than one knows what to do with."

Rose shook her head. "Can you imagine?" She looked at Henry and Julia. "We hardly had a drop of water in summer growing up."

"Just what was comin' out of the sink," Julia said, pushing her plate forward.

Henry added, "The land here is nice. Green, plenty of natural water. Those hot springs are a sight. Have you taken them in, Mrs. Perry?"

"From time to time." She kept her gaze on her plate, and Julia wondered if she recalled their run-in there all those weeks ago. "They say the waters are good for so many things." She reached out to Peter sitting next to her on the long side of the table and ran a hand over his hair. He smiled and moved to sit on his knees, looking anxious to move on from dinner.

Julia wanted to ask after Peter's health but wasn't sure how to do so. She smiled and looked at Rose over her glass. Her sister caught her eye. "Well, Texas had its pleasures. No unreasonable mountains to climb." Henry laughed, and she gave him a playful slap. "My husband the explorer. He was a ranch hand back in Texas. Strong as an ox, though he doesn't look it."

Henry coughed into his tea. "Rose, come now."

She laughed. "Oh, darling you know I tease. Come, tell us, how many trails have you walked since we moved here?"

Henry—whose aspic was mashed into pieces to hide it in his potatoes—hummed thoughtfully. "Twenty? Thirty?"

"The adventurer, this one," Rose said.

He leaned over and kissed her cheek. "I do miss the sunsets, though," he said.

Julia leaned forward, resting her elbows on the table. "Hear, hear."

Eleanor smiled, looking between them. "Better than here?"

"Absolutely," Julia said. "The sky there is so big, it feels like it goes on forever. Like you could fall into it. Blues, yellows, and pinks rest over popcorn clouds, streaks of orange running through them. All of that as far as you can see. And when it gets darker, the shades of carmine, scarlet…" She found Eleanor with a distant look in her eyes as she listened. "The most incredible golden copper," she added as Eleanor ran a hand through her hair. "Absolutely stunning."

They fell quiet for a time. Henry wore a reminiscent look. Rose smiled softly at Julia. Eventually, Eleanor said, "Maybe I'll get to see it sometime."

Julia swallowed as their gazes locked.

Eleanor's chest rose and fell. She blinked and seemed to force herself to look away. "You all have plans to get back there?"

"Oh no," Rose said. "Besides, we just got here. "Maybe one day," she added with a look at Henry. Julia noted how her posture shifted as she started to clear their plates. "Peter," she said, blinking back what looked like tears, "there's a plum tree I've yet to pick out back. If I get you a basket, would you go and fetch some? I can make a pie and send it to you next week. How does that sound?"

He grinned and hopped down. "Yes, ma'am," he said and followed Rose into the kitchen.

"Take Julia with you," Rose added. "She can show you where the blackberries are. You can take some home with you tonight."

Julia frowned at her sister pushing her outside but decided she did want to spend some time with Peter. Eleanor hadn't shared much about her life in Idaho Springs at dinner, and she was hoping Peter might be a good source to learn more.

Eleanor stood. "I'll help clean up."

"Nonsense." Henry took her plate. "What you can do is keep Rose and me company. I'd love to hear more about the lakes. Is it true they're full of walleye?"

Julia shared a look with Eleanor before meeting Peter outside. "I heard you enjoyed that tart I brought you," she said as they walked over the lawn.

"Sure did."

"I'll tell my friend Ralph you approve." They strode twenty yards to the back of the property. Bushes and fruit trees sat in patches near the northeast corner. To their left was a timber-framed garden twenty feet long. Julia recalled setting the wood into the earth with Henry shortly after moving in.

"Rose will like this," Henry had said as they'd toiled away each evening before sunset earlier that year. Now, it sat mostly vacant since they'd missed most of the planting season. Rose aspired to have it as overgrown as their neighbors. The trees were here when they'd moved in and bore lovely fruit.

"Do you get to work in the mill every day?" Peter asked, hopping over a patch of wild mushrooms.

"Yes." She sighed. "Though I'd rather be anywhere else."

Peter looked at her. The sun was just starting to set behind them. "What do you mean?"

"My job is boring."

"What would you rather do?"

She frowned, thinking. She couldn't stand the machinery sounds. Maybe a place in one of the mines? Stuck underground sounded even worse. "Why do you want to work there so bad, huh?" She gave him a playful shove.

"My dad worked there."

Julia turned as they approached the fruit tree. "He did?"

"Mom says he worked with the gold. Pulling it out of the rock."

"Did he work there…I mean…how long was he there?"

Peter set the basket down and studied the plums. "I don't know. He left when I was little."

Julia smiled, wanting to explain he was still little, but something about the look on his face made her think better of it. The breeze grew stronger, and they picked together in silence.

"You know, your mom just wants you to be able to do things like this," Julia said after a time. "Things kids should do." He didn't say anything. "Imagine working all day. You'd be dog tired and couldn't do fun things like come to dinner at our house. Or pick this fruit. Or…" She poked his jacket. "Enjoy that sweet from Henry."

His face brightened. "I forgot!" He was reaching into his pocket as the wind kicked up again. It was cooler now that the sun dipped lower, and Julia shivered. Peter's gaze was on the tree when his face changed.

"Peter?"

He licked his lips, and his chest expanded slowly, the expression on his face drawing inward. He dropped the plum in his right hand and found his chest.

"Peter, what's going on?"

His jaw set, and he seemed to try to take in air between his teeth. Tears welled in his eyes as his gaze found hers. Julia's stomach dropped. Peter's breath turned labored, a high wheezing accompanying each desperate intake for air.

"Oh no," she said. It seemed the sky darkened. She wanted to reach out, to comfort him, but her body was heavy. She was frozen, petrified at not knowing how to help. She tried to recall if Eleanor had ever shared about what she did for him when an attack came on. They hadn't had time to share such things...no time. "No," she said, shaking her head. The darkness around her shifted to the open landscape of the ranch. Its low fences surrounded her vision, barricading her as an oil rig towered above. She stood, stuck, at its base, the cold metal looming overhead.

"Julia, get down from there."

The image shifted. She was atop the rig, her hands unwilling to let go of the metal. Rose's voice echoed again.

"Julia, don't make me come up there."

The darkness whipped around her, lashing against her. She was twenty feet up. When she did look down, Rose was beneath her. Her sister clung to the metal, her face frightened.

"No, Rose. Don't."

Her sister reached for her.

"Julia?" Rose's voice broke the vision. Julia blinked. Peter's face was red, and his breathing staggered. Rose must have registered the dread on her face as she ran to them. "Julia, what's happening?"

She stepped back as Rose knelt in front of Peter. "I think..." She blinked, shaking the vision from her mind. "I think it's his asthma."

"Asthma?" Rose looked from her to Peter. "Ssh, it's okay," Rose said, swiping a hand over Peter's forehead. "It's okay."

"Rose, is everything all right? I heard—" Henry spotted them halfway across the lawn. His face fell, and he turned back to the house, calling for Eleanor.

Rose rubbed her hands down Peter's shoulders. "It's okay, sweetheart, it'll be okay."

Julia moved farther back, fear and guilt driving her steps when Eleanor came flying toward them, a pill bottle in hand. Rose moved to stand behind Peter as Eleanor asked, "How long has he been like this?"

Julia shrank under her worried gaze. "I…" She shook her head. "I don't…"

Eleanor's look shifted from worry to disbelief. She glanced at Rose. "A couple of minutes, maybe," Rose said softly. "I can't say."

Eleanor unscrewed the lid of the bottle, dropping a small white pill into her palm. "Peter, love, please. Take this."

Henry ran to join them, water sloshing out from a glass until he reached them.

"Thank you," Eleanor said. "Peter, it's all right. Take this."

He did, managing to swallow enough water to get the pill down. The sound of his breathing echoed the whir of the mill machinery, and Julia felt sick. She lifted her hands to her ears, her heart pounding. Flashes of that day at the ranch tried to force themselves to the front of her mind. She closed her eyes to keep them at bay.

Eleanor spoke gently to Peter. Julia forced herself to be present as Eleanor pressed her palm to his chest, rubbing circles until his breathing eased and matched hers.

As Peter recovered, he broke into quiet sobs and fell into Eleanor's arms. "It's all right, sweetheart," Eleanor said. "It's okay."

Rose wiped silent tears from her cheeks, and Henry moved to wrap an arm around her. "You're all right, Peter," Rose said, bending to place a quick kiss on top of his head.

Julia felt small as thoughts that haunted her months ago returned. *It's my fault. I shouldn't be here.*

"Julia," Henry said, still holding a bereft-looking Rose, "can you help them inside?"

She started to reply when Eleanor said, "We should go." She seemed to avoid their gazes. "Peter will need to rest."

Finally, it was like the earth released Julia, and she stepped forward. Reaching out a hand, she said, "Eleanor, wait—"

"Don't," she snapped, sniffling and tossing an apologetic look at Rose and Henry. Softer, she said, "Don't, Julia."

Julia's heart sank at the sharp glint in Eleanor's gaze. But it was deserved. Nodding, Julia stepped aside and let Eleanor lead Peter inside.

CHAPTER TWENTY-THREE

After getting Peter to bed, Eleanor retreated to her room with a cup of tea. She felt fraught, like she'd been clinging to the edge of a cliff. Her limbs ached. A cool wind blew through the open curtain near her bed, and she let the air soothe her. Her mind had been hot—irritated, terrified, confused—too many things at once since leaving the Barrows.

Everything had been so pleasant. Lovely, even, before the world had turned on its head. *Well, besides the food.* But the conversation with the Barrows, Peter's joy at being around people, and Julia...

"Julia." Eleanor leaned back in the rocking chair, her gaze unfocused. Why did it always seem like each step forward between them resulted in two steps back? Once again, Eleanor had found herself storming off with Peter. What had happened out near the garden? Julia had seemed shaken, petrified almost, by Peter's attack.

"She's probably never seen one before," Eleanor reasoned, taking a sip of chamomile. She reminded herself how shocked she had been when his first attack had happened. Still...Julia had done nothing? Thank goodness for the Barrows. They were wonderful people, and so was Julia, but...each time together seemed to lead to more questions.

Exhaling, Eleanor closed her eyes. The image of Julia on the stairs, shoulders pulled back confidently, that effervescent grin, and those boots. Eleanor's attraction seemed to have grown tenfold. The looks they'd shared over the dinner table had sent anticipation over her skin. Julia was a good listener, too, sitting back and taking in everything Eleanor had to share about growing up with her aunt and uncle. Her questions were few but insightful.

She returned to her picture of Julia on the stairs. A thought hit her…what if all that bravado was a cover? And if it was, what was she hiding?

Sue's gossip of jail time and other hearsay regarding Julia since she'd arrived in town returned to her mind. "Perhaps it's time to get some answers once and for all," she said. If she was going to figure out Julia Holte, she would have to go directly to the source.

Over the next week, however, that proved difficult to accomplish.

"Miss Holte," she called, finding Julia pouring coffee at the back of the mill office on Monday. The bags under her eyes surprised Eleanor, and a guilty look sat in Julia's tired gaze.

"Mrs. Perry," she said before skirting around her and returning to her desk. "I've much to do today. The audit and all."

Eleanor stood with her mouth open in surprise as Julia slumped over a pile of papers. She caught Henry's gaze. He gave her a sympathetic look before returning to his conversation.

Thursday was much the same, so Eleanor decided to take matters into her own hands. The second weekend in September, she dropped Peter off with Sue, determined to find and speak to Julia.

"I hate to say I told you so," Sue said as she opened her front door to let Peter inside. Eleanor handed her the bottle of pills to have on hand just in case. Eleanor had come by after sunup and a trip to the market for eggs to see if Sue could see after Peter while she went to the Barrows.

"Sue…"

"I'm not one to judge," Sue said, and Eleanor gave her a look. "I'm not," she insisted. "But I don't see why you're putting such effort into that woman."

Eleanor cut her gaze sideways, hoping Sue didn't catch the reason in her eyes. "She's new in town," she decided to say. "I remember what that's like. You took me in, helped me get settled." Sue seemed to relax, nodding as a reminiscent look filled her gaze. "It's not easy out here on your own."

Sue crossed her arms. She studied Eleanor for a time, her gaze narrowed. Eleanor retreated, calling a good-bye to Peter. "I'll be back after lunch," she said. "Thank you."

Eleanor wasn't sure what she was going to say when she stood on the Barrows' porch and knocked. Rose answered, her short hair framing wide eyes and a kind but surprised smile. "Eleanor?"

"Hi, Rose."

She slipped a dishrag onto her shoulder, moving a hand over her heart. "How's Peter?"

"Better now, thank you." She felt suddenly self-conscious and looked down. "I'm sorry about last week."

"Sorry?" Rose reached out and placed a hand on her forearm. "Eleanor, don't be sorry. Your son…well, those are things that can't be helped. I'm just glad he's doing better."

Eleanor smiled, grateful for the never-ending kindness of the Barrows. Taking a breath, she summoned the courage to ask if Julia was home.

"Julia?" Rose found the dishrag on her shoulder, running her hand over it. Her tone changed slightly, dipping from surprise to a knowing warmth. "She's still sleeping." She pursed her lips, glancing over her shoulder, then back at Eleanor. Then, she stepped outside and lowered her voice. "Between you and me, she hasn't been that well the last week. Staying out late. Spending time at Thrasher's."

"Oh?"

Rose nodded solemnly. "She does this from time to time. Last time was…" Rose seemed to cut herself off. "Well, it's a habit that's hard to shake, it seems. And that sheriff doesn't give her an inch."

Eleanor frowned. "Sheriff Volz?"

"Watches her like a hawk, that man. Just because she's…" Rose cut her gaze to Eleanor. *So she does know.* "Well," Rose said, smiling. "I imagine you understand."

Eleanor blinked. Wait…Rose knew she was like that, too? Her mind spinning, she could only manage a smile as Rose seemed to contemplate something, then said, "Let me wake Jules. I think it'll be good for her."

"Oh no, you don't have to do that."

Rose reached out, a gentle but firm hand keeping Eleanor in place. "Trust me." Then, she disappeared inside.

Eleanor walked slowly along the edge of the planked front porch. She felt dizzy after that exchange. Did that mean Rose knew what was happening between her and Julia? And was she… all right with it?

She contemplated such a situation when the front door opened again. Julia seemed to be shoved outside as she stumbled through the doorway, tucking what looked like the same white shirt from dinner—albeit wrinkled—into a pair of overalls that fell over her boots. She ran a hand through her hair. How did it always seem to fall perfectly around her face? The strands caught the late morning sun as her gaze found Eleanor.

"Hi."

Julia kept her distance. "Hi. What are you doing here?"

What *was* she doing here? Eleanor ran through the last week in her mind. Right…trying to get to the bottom of the mystery that was Julia Holte.

"I wanted to see you." Julia's brow rose, a hopeful look in her eyes. "Last week at dinner, outside with Peter, you seemed… um…"

Julia shook her head. "I was awful."

Surprised by the comment, Eleanor moved closer. "No. You seemed...frightened, maybe?" She found Julia's hand, pulling her gaze. "I understand. I was the same way when Peter had his first attack." She laughed dryly. "Ran him through town in the middle of the night, all the way to Dr. Wicker's house. I must have looked like a madwoman in my nightgown."

A small smile was all Julia gave as she stood quietly, averting her gaze.

"Walk with me?" Eleanor said, tugging on Julia's sleeve before starting down the steps. "Please."

Julia glanced back at the house as if searching for approval from the shutters. "All right."

They walked in companiable silence for a couple blocks. Each house seemed to trill with life; children played in the front lawns, elderly folk sat on the porch, waving as they passed.

"I've forgotten what it's like," she said as they took a right toward town. At Julia's inquiring look she added, "I'd forgotten what it's like to be around all this. The sense of community...it's nice."

Julia looked around at the homes, the people. "Guess I haven't given that much of a chance since moving here."

"Why *did* you move here?" Eleanor asked, stepping closer. Their shoulders bumped, and Eleanor felt the leap of anticipation run over her body at their touch.

Julia was quiet a long time.

When she still didn't answer, Eleanor decided to fill the quiet. "I told you before that I answered an ad." They started past the row of shops on Main Street. The sidewalks were moderately crowded on a Saturday. The sun cast a strong heat over the town from its perch among a smattering of clouds. "One of those advertisements for a man seeking a wife." She laughed off how ridiculous such a thing seemed. "I was young." She looked down, watching her steps. "I was lonely."

"I thought you lived with your aunt and uncle and...fifteen cousins."

Eleanor laughed. "Five cousins. It was a terribly busy household, but…as much as I loved them and they loved me, it wasn't home. Not really. I needed something of my own. A family to call mine. Moving here to marry Louis felt like that chance for me."

They crossed Miner Street. It was the same spot where Julia had stopped that wagon from trampling Sue's book. Eleanor smiled at the memory and caught Julia's distant gaze. Did she recall it too?

"What happened to him?"

"Louis?" Julia nodded. "He left." They turned toward the residential streets, looping back toward the Barrows'. "I wish I knew why. There was no note. I tried to find him, but his kin were all gone, so there was no one to ask. He never telegrammed. He just…left." Her voice broke, and she slowed to clear her throat. A large tree shaded that part of the street, and she paused to stand beneath it.

"Peter said he worked at the mill."

"He did." She squinted as memories resurfaced. "I don't know what happened, but he changed. Right before Peter was born, he fell sick of the mind or something. Struggled to collect his thoughts, to speak. At times, his hands shook terribly. As far as I know, he never saw anyone about it. I only discovered it myself toward…toward the end."

Julia was watching her. "That must've been difficult for him to have you see him like that."

Eleanor met her gaze. A sudden beam cut through the memories of Louis like someone slashing through a canvas, revealing a thought she hadn't let herself have before. *Is that why he left? His pride?* Surely, whatever had a hold of him would have only gotten worse. But if he'd stayed, they could have gotten help. Surely…

She shook her head. There was no point in what-ifs, she reminded herself. Not for Louis. Not for her parents. What-ifs only led to pain.

Julia's hand on hers brought her back to the present. She hadn't shared that much in a long time. Not since Louis had left and Eleanor had to lean on Sue as she willed herself to go on as a single mother to Peter. A few cars passed on the street, and she squeezed Julia's hand. "Please," she said, "I want to know. Why did you move here?"

A collection of emotions crossed Julia's face. What looked like yearning and possibility were followed by doubt. Fear trailed quickly before she motioned for them to continue. They walked side by side, the Barrows' house coming into view.

Finally, Julia said, "I moved here for my sister."

"For Rose?" She hadn't been sure what answer she'd expected, but that wasn't it. "Is she ill?" Rose didn't seem sick, but Eleanor knew well that certain ailments could hide themselves in plain sight.

Julia's face scrunched, lines forming around her eyes as a wave of pain seemed to overcome her. "No."

"You don't seem like the type to want to keep house," Eleanor said, trying a light-hearted approach as they walked down the house's drive.

Julia chuckled. "That's definitely Rose's territory." Up on the porch, she turned. Fear returned and climbed higher in her gaze. Eleanor wanted to reach out, to assure Julia that whatever it was that scared her, she could offer it up. She could lay it before her and let it be seen. There was nothing more, Eleanor realized, nothing more she craved than for someone she cared about to trust her with such secrets. Louis had never been able to do that, but maybe this time…

"Julia," she said, stepping onto the porch and closing the space between them. "Please."

Julia looked so young at that moment, so terrified. "I'm sorry for last week," she finally said. "I'm not…I'm no good."

"That's not true."

She cast another sad look to the house. "I should get inside. I'm glad to hear Peter is well." She pulled away.

"Julia, wait—"

But the door closed, and she was gone, leaving Eleanor hovering once again on the precipice of something good. Something that could have been hers. But that chance fell away as she stood alone on the Barrows' front porch, leaving her to wonder for how much longer she was willing to hang on.

CHAPTER TWENTY-FOUR

I'll take another," Julia said, siding up to the counter at Thrasher's. The bartender looked up from the glass he was cleaning, scanning the chairs behind her packed tight with patrons on a Friday night.

Looking at her, he grunted, "I think you've had enough."

"That so?" she asked, leaning forward to be heard over the racket of conversation. The striped pattern of his shirt seemed to waver, and she blinked to refocus her gaze. The wall lamps flickered, teasing her vision more. "What makes you the expert on my tolerance?"

He only gave her a look and wandered down to help a man at the end of the bar. Julia thought she recognized him as one of the visitors from Denver in town to help with the audit. She blinked, and his face changed. He was one of her father's ranch hands. She took a deep breath, fighting the memory. She felt hot as the Texas sun burned her neck.

"Let one of the men handle it, Julia," Rose said.

She ignored her, starting up the rig.

I'm not there, Julia reminded herself. Taking a shaky breath, she turned around to lean against the bar and take in the room. Visions of the ranch fell away. She grinned when she spotted Ralph at a card table.

"Hey," she said, running into the back of his chair and waving to the group.

Ralph turned, surprised. "Jules?" He looked her up and down, and she unsuccessfully tried to suppress a hiccup. His face fell, and he stood. "How long have you been here?"

She pushed against his chest. "Longer than you." Hitching a thumb over her shoulder, she said, "Fella won't take my money." She fished in her trouser pocket, producing a few coins. "Get me a beer, Ralphie? Here." She produced two more. "Treat yourself while you're at it."

His face, which had been an expression of concern and surprise, shifted to what looked like anger. Julia's head began to spin, and she couldn't put together what exactly he'd be upset about. She was going to buy him a drink; what wasn't there to like?

He turned to say something to the table. "What are you looking at?" Julia quipped over his shoulder to a large man she didn't recognize. His thick goatee and bushy eyebrows reminded her of a woodsman. Guiding her away from the table, Ralph led her back toward the bar.

"Keep your money," he said, placing the coins she'd handed him on the counter.

Julia's back itched at his terseness. She'd never seen him be short with anyone. "Hey," she said, pocketing the money. "Who put a bee in your bonnet?"

He looked at her like he couldn't believe the question. Behind him, a woman walked by. Her hair was cut short, and the color reminded her of Eleanor. Julia wondered what she was doing now. What would she say if Julia showed up at her house? Maybe not the best idea, she reasoned, swaying a little as Ralph shook his head.

"What?" she asked, blinking and realizing she'd completely missed his response.

"You, Jules. You put a bee in my bonnet."

She burped. "Me?"

He glanced around, then lowered his voice as the bartender passed. "We've hardly seen each other since the church social. I thought…" He licked his lips, reaching out to her, then stopping himself. "I thought that was gonna be a nice time for us."

Us? "Ralph—"

"But you spent most of the day with the Barrows. I get it, they're nice people. But you've only stopped by the bakery once since then. I didn't even know you'd be here tonight."

His hurt tone prompted a wriggle of guilt in her gut. She swallowed, trying to focus on him as the room tilted. She hadn't meant to ignore him; she'd only wanted to get to know Eleanor in the last few weeks. They'd been…what had they been doing? Stealing clandestine kisses behind the mill office? Always dancing around each other? At present, Julia wasn't sure how she felt. She liked Eleanor a lot, but twice now, she'd driven Eleanor off. Yes, she'd come back to talk things out. Was it worth it, though? What if she saw Julia for who she really was? What if she learned that how she'd been with Peter that night was how she always was when things got tough? She'd acted cowardly, just like when Rose…

"Maybe I got my numbers crossed," Ralph said dejectedly, pulling her from her thoughts.

She found his kind eyes. Finally, his words settled over her. "You…you thought that we…" She pointed between herself and him, eyes widening.

He shrugged. "I like you, Jules."

She had to close her mouth when she realized she was gawking at him. A nervous laugh escaped her, though she regretted it at his crestfallen face. "Ralph." She looked around. "I thought…" She turned and spoke low. "You've seen me, right? You've seen how I dress, how I speak." She punched his shoulder. "How I drink."

"That's why I like you. You don't give a fig what people think. My sisters say women will be wearing trousers on the regular by next decade."

Julia could hardly believe what she was hearing. Conversation grew louder around her, and she scraped a hand down her face, then pinched the bridge of her nose. "Ralph, I'm…I'm not…like you."

His brow furrowed, and she sighed, realizing she'd have to spell it out for him. "I like you Ralph but only as a friend." Someone left a glass on the bar on their way out. She grabbed it and downed the watery backwash for courage, receiving a glare from the bartender. Swiping her mouth clean, she said, "Ralph, I fancy women."

He stared. For a long moment, Julia wasn't sure he heard her. She searched his face for a sign of recognition and was about to repeat herself when his gaze finally shifted. A strange smile lifted his lips.

"Ralph?"

The smile grew, and he laughed, low at first, almost incredulous. It escalated into a bellow, drawing the gazes of nearby patrons.

"Hey, Ralph."

But his laughter continued as he turned and ordered another drink. She felt small as he took his beer and downed half. He turned to face her.

"Ralph, are you okay?"

His gaze turned hard, and his lips fell into a straight line. "I'm fine, Jules."

She exhaled. "Good."

"I think…" He hesitated; his eyes narrowed as he studied the floor. "I think I better get back to my game."

She nodded, recognizing through her drunken haze that he wasn't ready to talk about it. Now probably wasn't the best time anyway. He moved on, and Julia slumped over the bar, a strange combination of relief and uncertainty washing over her. That mixing with the alcohol in her stomach made her insides churn.

Glancing sideways, she spotted Sylvia at the end of the bar. She was chatting up a gentleman but caught Julia's eye over his shoulder. For the briefest moment, Julia imagined going over to her. She imagined telling that man that he could never satisfy

Sylvia, and that she was twice the man he'd ever be. She closed her eyes and held her head in her hands. *Why would I do that?* Why did she feel the need to say those things? Was she that insecure, that bothered, that she had to belittle men to feel better about herself? Not all of them deserved that. Not men like Ralph.

Besides, being with Sylvia wasn't what she wanted. She wanted Eleanor. But not like this. She needed to sober up. She needed to go home. Rose would be waiting.

"Hiya, hon," Sylvia said.

Julia was surprised to find her at her side. "Hi."

"Why so glum? Fight with your fella?" She gestured to Ralph, who had been watching her but returned his focus to his cards.

Julia gave a sardonic laugh. "Something like that."

"Anything I can do to help?" she asked, her breathy voice caressing her neck.

Julia felt sick now. She clenched her jaw as a wave of nausea hit her. "Listen, Sylvia." She put a hand on her waist to create space between them. Right as she did, though, a hard hand came down on her shoulder.

"Miss Holte."

She turned, stumbling into Sylvia at the sight of Sheriff Volz. "What are you…when did you get here?" she asked, cursing the slur that accompanied her words. God, how was this night going from bad to worse?

"Been here awhile," he said, his voice slinking out between his chapped lips, his eyes hooded under the wide brim of his hat. She hated that hat and the gall he exuded to never remove it.

Julia scoffed and gave what she hoped was an apologetic look to Sylvia, who returned to the other end of the bar. "Well, I was just leaving."

"Now that's something you and I can agree on." Volz reached behind his back, producing his handcuffs.

Julia stepped back but ran into another patron standing at the bar. To Volz she asked, "What did I do?"

"Public intoxication," he stated, reaching for her.

"Public? I ain't been outside in hours."

He ignored her, grabbing her arm and turning her. Placing the cuffs on her wrists, he stepped close. She winced at the feel of his breath near her ear. "Deviant behavior is a worse offense, Miss Holte. Everyone saw you put your hands on Sylvia."

"Are you kidding me?" she asked. "She came on to me." Julia wobbled, her vision wavering as old voices screamed.

"What did you do, Julia?" Her mother and Henry stared, fear and blame burning in their eyes.

She shook away the memories, trying desperately to cling to the present.

All protests were fruitless though as Volz nodded to the bartender and pushed her forward. "You can't do this," Julia cried over her shoulder. How was this night unraveling so quickly? "It ain't fair." Passing the card table, she tried to catch Ralph's eye, but he kept his steady gaze on the table. Her heart sank. "Sheriff, wait—"

"You can go home tomorrow, Miss Holte. Your jail cell awaits."

She forced him to push or drag her out of Thrasher's and toward the jailhouse. She needed to get home. Trying again to wriggle free, she ended up tripping onto her backside.

"Listen here, Holte." Volz's voice yanked her from her miserable thoughts as he made her stand. Her boots scuffed over the cobblestone until he tugged her to face him. His predatory teeth shone beneath the streetlamp. She tried to pull back as he spoke, spittle hitting her face. "You wanna know why this town has boomed like it has?"

"The mill, obviously," she replied, finding his question funny as she laughed.

"It's boomed because I keep vermin from crawling in and chewing away at the foundation. The foundation my father laid, may he rest in peace." His lip curled as his gaze traced her figure.

"I spotted a rodent the moment I laid eyes on you. Nothin' but trouble and sin, you are."

"Nice to know how you really feel," she spat back. "Jesus, you're so stuck in the past. Why not just challenge me to a duel and get it over with?" She grinned, drunk with desperation. "Afraid you'd lose?"

He ignored her, saying instead, "Don't know how you came from the same branch as that sister of yours."

"Every family has their black sheep. I hear that's something you and I have in common." His eyes widened, and she felt tall at his surprised look. A reckless fervor overtook her, and she stepped closer. "*Baah*," she mocked, getting in his face, relishing the fury filling his gaze.

She grinned. "You can't do what you really want to me." She rocked back a little, fighting to keep her balance. "Can't throw me in the river or toss me onto a train. Not when my brother-in-law works at the mill. Not when my sister is a God-fearing Christian. And 'cause when it comes down to it, you're a man of the law. Despite how crooked you are. So," she said, turning her back to him. "Take me in, Sheriff. And when that sun comes up, let me go."

She glanced over her shoulder to find his face twisted with rage. Red filled his cheeks, and she knew she'd gotten under his skin in a way she never had before. Maybe she'd regret all this in the morning. Add it to the list, she thought as he shoved her hard, and they headed for the jailhouse.

Chapter Twenty-five

Julia's body ached. Harsh morning light streamed in through the brick-sized window near the top of her cell. She groaned and rolled over.

"Been a while, Miss Holte," Billy said, the sound of keys jangling with his voice.

She inhaled sharply and sat up. Her head pounded. She ran a hand through her hair as he opened the cell door, and the gesture sent an ache through her shoulder.

"Bar fight?" he asked as nonchalantly as if asking how she took her tea.

She blinked, trying to bring his face into focus. Why was her vision blurry? And wait, why could she barely see out of her right eye? Quickly, she reached up. "Goddammit," she screamed, immediately regretting touching her eyelid. It felt swollen. How the hell did she get a black eye? She stood, and her right knee shrieked in protest. She could feel bruises already forming on the parts of her body that felt like she'd been hit by a car. She found her lip next. Yep, swollen, too.

"I didn't...I wasn't in a fight." She would have remembered something like that, wouldn't she?

He laughed, holding the door open. "Coulda fooled me. Good thing Sheriff Volz pulled you outta Thrasher's when he did."

Standing just inside the cell, Julia froze. *Volz.* Flashes from the end of the night flooded her mind. She'd been ornery the entire walk to the jailhouse. He had thrown her inside. She'd yelled something at him. *Did he kick me?* She thought the image of her fist flying toward him had been a dream. Touching her busted lip, she remembered: he'd taken the rage from their walk out on her in the privacy of the jail cell. She'd been too drunk to put up a fight.

"Where is our lord and savior this morning?" she asked, blinking at the light and adjusting her sullied shirt.

"On his way to Sunday service, o' course."

"Of course." She looked around. "My brother-in-law here?"

Billy gestured to the door. "Waitin' for ya outside."

Julia took a shaky breath. She wasn't sure what was worse, the way she felt or the look she knew would be on Henry's face when he saw her.

It didn't take long to get her answer. "Jesus, Jules." Henry reached up, but she moved his hand away from her temple. She could feel the bruise deepening around her eye. "What the hell happened?"

"I happened," she muttered, tugging the cuff of her pants out of her boot. A few passersby stared, and she leaned against the brick wall, a futile attempt to avoid their gazes. Across the street, she caught Sue Weldon scurrying ahead of a trio of other biddies on their way to church. Great, she thought, I wonder how long it'll take her to report to Eleanor.

Henry looked like he wanted to say something. Instead, he only scratched his head, his oily locks coming up in the back. The sound of hooves over the road caught Julia's ear. The horses and wagon reminded her of another one; the heavy fog in her mind cleared as she recalled the first run-in with Eleanor. It was right there on that street. She'd had no idea they'd continue running into each other, could never have anticipated what would happen between them. A familiar voice caught her ear. "Julia?"

"Oh boy," Henry said. Julia lifted her head and looked around. Eleanor waved from the corner at the end of the block.

Her bright smile sent a burst of warmth through Julia, and for a moment, she forgot how much pain she was in. Oh God...how she must look. She shot a worried glance to Henry as Eleanor started for them.

"Julia, hi. How are—" Eleanor stopped in her tracks, the canvas bag she carried swaying dully at her side. Julia gave her a tight-lipped smile, though that sent a jolt of pain through her jaw. "Julia," she said, her voice full of concern as she stepped closer. "What happened?"

Henry started back. "Good morning, Eleanor." He found Julia's gaze. "I'll, um, just be...I have to..." He scampered across the street.

Julia sighed, then flinched when Eleanor reached out. "Don't." She said, her hand finding Eleanor's before it could cup her cheek.

"What happened?" More passersby wandered past. Julia felt hot, so she led Eleanor toward the narrow alley between the jail and courthouse. "You're starting to worry me."

Julia searched Eleanor's gaze. She did see worry and concern pouring out. But also, something else. Something Julia didn't dare hope could be real. "Sheriff Volz," she said, gesturing to her face.

Eleanor's lips parted in surprise. "He...he did this to you?"

She swallowed. It would be easy to blame Volz for everything. Yes, he'd hit her. But she'd provoked him. The sheriff was dirty and took the law into his own hands too often. Still, Julia had to face the fact that she could've gone quietly. She could have kept her mouth shut for once. Instead, like always, she'd taken the option that had landed her in the worst position.

But how to express that? Who could understand the fear she held close to her heart, the fear of being seen for who she really was? "You should go," Julia said quietly, avoiding Eleanor's gaze.

"What?"

"I appreciate you trying, Eleanor." She sniffed. "I do, but..."

"Julia." Eleanor was closer now. Julia could smell the fresh soap on her skin. "You're hurt."

Tears filled Julia's eyes, and she looked skyward to try to keep them at bay. "I don't..." She tried to speak, desperately wanting to explain herself. *I'm not good. I don't deserve you. You don't deserve this.* "I was in jail," she finally said. "Henry was picking me up."

Eleanor's face went still. She blinked, seeming to take in Julia's words. The distant spark of what they were building, of that beautiful potential they shared, was marred by confusion.

Better to snuff it out now. Julia took a deep breath, then said, "I've been arrested six times since moving here." She laughed wryly. "I was leaving the jailhouse this morning." She forced herself to meet Eleanor's gaze. "Remember when we first met? Right out there?' She pointed toward the street. "I had left the jailhouse that morning, too." She swiped her nose, then winced as she tried to stop the tears. "So you can tell your little birdy Sue I'm exactly who she thinks I am. I'm a felon. I cause trouble. I'm not worthy of anyone's time." Her voice trembled. "I'm nobody."

Eleanor was very still as she listened. Her fingers ticked at her side. A knot twisted itself in Julia's chest. She reminded herself this was for the best. Pushing Eleanor away was the best thing for her. If Julia got too close, she could hurt her. She could hurt Peter.

To her surprise, Eleanor's cool palm found her neck. Her hand rested there before moving to her sternum. Eleanor's gaze remained there a long time before meeting hers. Julia's heart raced. "Julia, I—"

But Julia wouldn't hear her. She shook her head, forcing Eleanor's hand away. "No. I'm sorry Eleanor." She hurried out of the alley, forcing herself not to look back.

Chapter Twenty-six

Eleanor hung the last batch of shirts on the line. The late September day was unusually warm. She used the skirt of her apron to wipe sweat from her brow. Exhaling, she scanned the grounds. Peter was between the trees toward the creek, setting another trap. She'd discovered his makeshift gold dish near the wildflowers toward the top of the hill where he often played. Evidently, he'd gotten hold of a misshaped pan she hadn't used in a year, puncturing it with rocks to create a sieve. Asking him about it, he'd explained, "To look for gold. They have to hire me if I find some way out here."

She'd smiled at his answer. Little did he know she had her own stash hiding in a bureau drawer. Still, the lingering dread of his fixation on the mill worried her. At the market the other day, she'd heard the cashier talking with another customer about an incident with a young boy. He'd gone up the mountain with a group of powder monkeys, young children nimble enough to place dynamite sticks into the hard-to-reach parts of the mountain to make way for a new mineshaft to open. The others had made it out unscathed, but he'd fallen behind and was badly wounded, unable to get out of the blast radius in time. Now the poor child was in a hospital in Denver.

She shuddered at the thought as she pinned a sleeve to the line. The mill liked to keep such instances quiet. Henry was terribly upset at the news when she'd seen him that morning. Eleanor had hoped to run into Julia, but she wasn't back to work.

"Resting," Henry had told her when she'd asked on Monday. Eleanor could imagine she needed it; she'd looked awful that morning outside the jailhouse. Eleanor had never put much thought toward Sheriff Lee Volz before. Stories had circulated, of course. Sue had shared some things that had given Eleanor pause: throwing the book at people for seemingly small offenses, an intolerance for certain folks who passed through town, often people who didn't look like him. Her skin felt hot at the idea of him laying hands on Julia. Maybe, she thought, it was time they all took another look at their local law enforcement.

Feeling overwhelmed at the idea, Eleanor found her stool near the back door. A wave of tiredness hit her as she sat. Closing her eyes, she let her mind wander while the next round of clothes soaked. She'd been fighting the urge to visit the Barrows for over a week now. She wanted to honor Julia's wishes, to give her space, but she also wanted to see her. She still had so many questions. Most importantly, what was Julia so afraid of, and why did she keep pushing her away?

It would be easy to give her up. The harder thing would be to fight for whatever it was they were building. To fight for their feelings. The last few nights had found Eleanor pondering this, leading her to the realization that this was something Louis couldn't, or wouldn't, have done. Eleanor had her fears. She knew she was protective of Peter, maybe too much. She knew she had secluded herself from town, creating tension between her and most of Idaho Springs. She was also terribly afraid of being abandoned again. Maybe Julia knew something she didn't. Did she have plans to leave town? Her behavior certainly was erratic, but when they were together…Julia seemed calm. She seemed at ease and like she wanted more time together. Eleanor wanted the same.

"God, I don't know what I'm doing," she muttered, leaning her head back against the wall of the house.

"Not many of us do, honey."

Sitting up, Eleanor found Sue ducking under a clothesline. "I didn't hear you come by."

"I can see that. Spent five minutes knockin' on an empty house." She adjusted her cloche hat and smoothed her dress, looking ever the busy councilwoman.

"Come from a women's group meeting?"

"I did," she said. "We're trying to get a library established right here in Idaho Springs. Some of the men on city council are opposed, but I think we can convince them." She smiled slyly.

Eleanor laughed. "That'd be grand." An idea struck her then. "Sue, you're on the city council."

"Since 1925."

"You all organize the election for the local sheriff, correct?"

Sue, who had been searching inside her open handbag, looked up curiously. "Yes, that's right, though we haven't had any formal election in some time." She puckered her lips as she recalled. "Last time there was an election was closer to the turn of the century, when Volz Senior got the position, may he rest in peace."

Eleanor sat up. "Lee Volz wasn't elected?"

"Don't you remember?" Sue asked. Eleanor shook her head. She'd just moved to town when Lee Volz had taken over. "Oh, that's right. Well, there was no formal election for him. No one else wanted the job. Folks saw the name Volz and thought, why bother? Besides, his daddy was a jewel of a man." She sighed and placed a hand on her hip. "Not many could've predicted how unlike his father he'd turn out to be."

Nodding, Eleanor mused, "I wonder if someone would run opposite him."

"Oppose the standing sheriff?" Sue looked intrigued, her eyes bright. "My, that would be something. Who would do that?" She raised her brows. "You know someone?"

"No," she said, slumping back. "Just thinking out loud. I hear…" She glanced up, wondering how much to explain. "I hear he's let some of that power go to his head."

Sue only hummed softly and looked around the lawn. The lines of laundry waved gently in the breeze. Another chill wrapped around Eleanor's shoulders. She adjusted her stool to be more in the sun. When Sue still hadn't met her gaze, only standing awkwardly a few feet away, wringing her hands, Eleanor asked, "What brings you around today, then?"

When Sue finally looked at her, her face drew into a concerned frown. "E, you look flushed." She hurried forward, pressing the back of her hand to Eleanor's cheek. "Are you well?"

Eleanor felt her forehead. She did seem warm, and that chill lingered. "I may be coming down with something." She tossed Sue a grin. "Are you avoiding my question?"

Sue laughed, but it was nervous, and she looked around. "Isaac is bringing in some more tea from Denver. We can drop it off on Friday if you like."

"Mr. Jarda just gave me another batch." Eleanor felt a strange unease settle in her stomach. "Sue?"

Sue threw her gaze toward Peter across the lawn when he skipped by and waved. "Hi, Auntie Sue," he called before vanishing beneath the tall grass again, chasing something.

Sue waved back, then said, "E, darling, there's…well, I suppose there's no good way to say this."

Eleanor sat up straighter. "What is it?"

Sue studied her for a moment, hands on her hips. Finally, she said, "The Judsons, over on 6th Street, saw you and Miss Holte last month."

Eleanor frowned, trying to recall. It had felt like ages since she'd seen Julia. Then, she remembered. "I'd gone to see her. We'd…we'd left things on the wrong foot after dinner."

"Yes," Sue said, "that seems to happen often." Eleanor shot her a look, even if Sue had a point. "She also hasn't been at work in nearly two weeks."

"I'm aware," Eleanor said, glancing at the line of clothes. "She's recovering."

"From a bar fight, so the story goes."

Eleanor snapped her gaze to Sue. "Bar fight? No, it was—" She cut herself off at Sue's expectant gaze. It wasn't her story to tell. Then again…why not share the truth? If Julia was afraid to, somebody should. She kept her voice low when she said, "Sheriff Volz beat her, Sue."

Her eyes widened. "That why you brought up that city council business?" Feeling her face warm, Eleanor nodded. To her dismay though, the look of shock on Sue's face shifted, her eyes narrowing. She was quiet a time before she asked, "Did you see it?"

"Him? No." She stammered. "But Julia told me."

"Oh, did she now."

"Sue." Eleanor stood, and Sue stepped back, a startled look on her face. "Sue Weldon, what are you implying?"

Her mouth had fallen open as she looked up to meet Eleanor's gaze. She recovered quickly, adjusting her stance. "Why are you so quick to defend that woman?"

Eleanor scoffed. A quick reply found her tongue: *Because I like her. Because there is something magnificent and daring in her eyes, something sacred and wholesome in her smile, and it's like nothing I've known before.* "Because," she finally managed to say, "she's a friend."

Sue pulled her shoulders back, a challenging look mixed with disbelief on her face. "You and I are friends, E. She's…"

"What?" Eleanor made herself as tall as possible, daring Sue to finish her thought. Her body hot, she continued. "You and I have been friends a long time. You have a kind heart beneath the pretense you carry around. I've seen you stand up for the women in this town, like those who find themselves in the family way. You stood by my side when the rest of this place labeled me a pariah. What is it about Julia Holte that has you so twisted up you can't give her an ounce of sympathy?"

Sue's face was a mask of shock. "I…" She swallowed, one hand on her chest to gather herself. The challenge in her eyes faded. "Eleanor, I only want what's best for you. That's all I've ever wanted. You know that."

Eleanor took a breath. "Then what is it you can't stand about Julia?"

"She's not…she's not right."

Eleanor could hardly believe what she was hearing. "Why, Sue?"

Her startled face shifted to skepticism. "You know why."

"Because she fancies women?"

Mouth agape, Sue rocked back, looking alarmed at such a statement being spoken aloud. "Eleanor."

She could only stare before a dark laugh crawled out of her throat. "For someone who claims to love the details of others' lives, someone who lives for drama, when faced with something real right in your backyard you…" Eleanor squinted. "You turn the other way, pretend it's a sordid story on your precious radio. Well, people's lives aren't for your amusement, Sue." She could hardly believe the words coming out of her mouth. Perhaps she'd been on the edge this entire time, eager to let this out, and had just needed an injustice to take the leap.

Sue paled. Steeling herself, Eleanor decided she had nothing else to lose. "Guess what, Sue? Reality is a lot more complicated than people think. People are messy, but they deserve love. And I…" She took a breath. "I'm a lot more like Julia than even you know."

Sue, clutching the collar of her dress, stared. "What are you saying?"

Peter called them and started their way. Eleanor kept her gaze on Sue. "I think you know." Her friend searched her face, licking her lips as if she wanted to say something. Eleanor shivered again, feeling drained as more chills ran down her back. She wiped another layer of perspiration from her forehead.

"Mom, Auntie Sue, look what I found!" Peter bounded toward them, a frog in hand.

Sue stepped toward Eleanor, shrinking away. "My, Peter, how lovely."

Eleanor didn't miss how Sue skirted around her, stepping back toward the way she came. "Auntie Sue was just leaving," Eleanor said as Peter studied the frog.

"Oh, okay."

Sue caught her gaze. Eleanor couldn't read the look in it before she said, "Peter, you should make your mom some tea. I fear she's catching a cold," before ducking behind the clothes and hurrying away.

CHAPTER TWENTY-SEVEN

Daylight spilled across Julia's room. "Hey," she protested, rolling over.

Rose gave her a pointed look from the window. "It's time to get up."

"I'm tired."

"I don't care."

Through her bleary vision, she found her sister's face as serious as she'd ever seen it, reminiscent of the day she'd put Julia's name in to be the mill's new file clerk.

Julia scooted back to lean against the headboard. Tangled blankets and discarded clothing lay in heaps on the floor. She rolled her shoulders, relieved at the lack of pain. Her facial swelling had gone down, too, and she could almost see completely out of her eye.

"Rose," she finally said, "I told you, I'll go back to work on Monday. It's only Friday."

Her sister gathered items scattered around the room. "Good. You can help me get this place in order until then." She tossed clothes into the hall before returning to open the window. "This room needs fresh air." Then, seeming to gather herself, she moved to the bed. Hesitating, she pointed to Julia's eye. "The compresses have helped."

Carefully feeling around her brow bone, Julia nodded. It was significantly less tender. When she found Rose's gaze again, anger poured out. "Rose?"

"I still can't believe he did that to you."

Embarrassment warmed her cheeks, though she hated that was how Volz left her feeling. Picking at the sheet, she said, "I provoked him." It had become a sad mantra the last couple of weeks.

Rose shook her head. "I don't care what you said or did. No man should lay hands on a woman that way."

"Not even a woman like me?"

A small vee formed between Rose's brows. "What a thing to ask, Jules. You know that's made no difference to me."

Julia swallowed the emotions that threatened in her throat. "I know, but…"

"No," Rose said, sitting on the edge of the bed to face her. "Henry's had his reservations about that man. So have several folks at church. He claims to be a Christian, but there's a difference between respecting the Bible's teachings and playing God." She took a breath. "Your friend, Ralph, has voiced his reservations, too, right?"

She sniffled. "Yeah."

"Even if the way you are does bother Volz, he has no right. He should just keep it to himself," she said primly, as if saying so should solve the issue. Reality drew over her face, though, and she rested a hand on Julia's leg. "I don't know what can be done about him."

"Maybe someone should run against him for sheriff."

Rose smiled. "And who would do that, you?"

Julia snorted. "A good man. Maybe Ralph."

"That's an idea."

Feeling uncomfortable at the swell of emotions circling them, Julia shifted. She brought her knee up to her chest.

"Why don't you get cleaned up? I'll make you some eggs."

"It's midday."

"There's no timetable on breakfast, Jules, remember? Momma always said so."

Smiling, Julia agreed.

Later, she'd stripped her bed and had set the sheets to soak out back. Henry was still at work. She found Rose in the kitchen chopping tomatoes. Thoughts of Eleanor returned. Julia wondered how she was doing. She imagined Peter playing in the backyard. She pictured soft sunlight dabbled over their land, lighting Eleanor's hair in stunning shades of crimson.

"What's that smile for?"

Julia took a seat at the table, catching Rose's curious look. Folding the clean pile of napkins, she replied, "No reason."

Rose's look said she didn't believe her. "Peter Perry came by yesterday."

Julia looked up. "He did?"

"Said he had hoped to get a test drive in, but you weren't at the office." She smiled. "That boy sure is the sweetest."

"He's a good kid."

Rose dropped the tomatoes into a pot and set it to boil. Julia vaguely recalled her mentioning wanting to make katsup. She hoped this batch wasn't as sour as the last. After joining Julia at the table, she said, "I imagine Eleanor will be glad to see you back at the office next week."

She kept her gaze on the napkins. "I don't know about that."

Rose stole a drink from the glass of iced tea between them. She tossed Julia an incredulous look. "You'd have to be blind to miss the way that woman looks at you."

There it was again: hope. It tiptoed around the edges of her heart. Julia tried to focus on her breath and not the quickening of her pulse.

Perhaps sensing her overwhelm, Rose said softly, "I know you've grown close with her. Have you two...you know..." She let her voice trail off.

Julia shook her head. "No."

Rose's look said she understood, but Julia caught the surprise in her face. She always pushed things along quickly with paramours. Perhaps there was a reason she was taking things slowly with Eleanor.

Tapping a finger on the table, she added, "We did kiss."

Rose grinned and slapped her knee emphatically. "I knew it. Henry owes me a foot rub."

Despite herself, Julia laughed. "You two were betting on me?"

Rose waved a napkin at her in lieu of a response. Julia's mood lifted momentarily but darkened when she recalled her last interaction with Eleanor. "She doesn't want to see me."

"Why wouldn't she with that delightful personality of yours?"

Julia, surprised by Rose's jab, tossed a napkin at her. They laughed, and for a moment, it was like they were kids again, giggling and hiding in the front room of their parents' ranch house. "Why bother? I'll only add to her stress." She met Rose's gaze. "You saw me with Peter that day. I completely froze."

"It was a frightening situation, Jules."

"You and Henry knew what to do."

Rose studied her, tapping the glass thoughtfully. "Jules, no one knows what they're doing the first time something like that happens. There's a learning curve."

"I don't feel like I ever learn."

"Have you tried?"

The sounds of the house settled around them. Julia's mind felt stuck again. She saw Peter as he struggled to breathe, Eleanor's alarmed eyes. That image shifted to a different time and place. Julia was atop the rig. Rose was below when her hand slipped…

"Jules."

She wiped a tear away. "I'm afraid."

"Of what?"

"I'm afraid that I'm always going to be the problem."

"What are you talking about?"

Reluctantly, Julia met her gaze. Rose's brows relaxed as understanding settled across her face. "Jules."

"I came here to support you after what happened at the ranch." More tears fell. "It was all my fault. Everything that happened to you. It was my fault."

"I climbed up after you that day. I climbed up of my own free will."

"If I hadn't been up there in the first place like you told me." She swiped at her nose. "If my damn pants wouldn't have gotten snagged. If I wouldn't have gotten stuck, then you wouldn't—"

"I wouldn't have fallen."

Julia looked up. Rose's jaw was set tight. She ran a hand over her hair, the memory seeming to crash over her. Quietly, Julia said, "I didn't know."

Rose wiped at her own tears now. "We hadn't told anyone." She found her abdomen, a gesture Julia had seen her do in quiet moments. "It had only been a couple of months."

"Still, I—"

"No." Rose brought her hand firmly down on the table. "Jules, we've done this. You apologized when it happened, then at the hospital when they examined me, and then again after Henry…when he told you that I was pregnant. You apologized a hundred times."

"I know."

"Then," she said, taking a deep breath, "what's all this for? Why are you really here?" Julia wiped her face on her sleeve. "Did you think if you came with me, you could"—Rose narrowed her gaze—"protect me? Watch me to make sure nothing like that would happen again?" Julia only swallowed. "I hate to break it to you, Sis, but people are going to get hurt. I'm going to get hurt, whether you like it or not." She reached out. "Seems to me, you came here to run away from your problems. Drown out your guilt with those antics of yours. A change of scene to try to forget?"

Julia felt hot at her recognition of the truth.

Rose nodded. "I don't blame you. That's why I asked Henry if we could leave. It was too hard." Her voice trembled. "Too hard being there after…" She blinked to collect herself. "But, Jules, you're not doing yourself any favors pushing people away and hanging around this house or places like Thrasher's like a shadow."

Julia wanted to cry out, wanted to lie down and let herself feel everything she'd been pushing away for the last year. All the guilt, all the awful nagging from her conscience for what had happened…she knew Rose had forgiven her, but it wasn't until now that Julia let that forgiveness start to sink in. Only now did she let it begin to chip away at the awful walls she'd built around her heart. As usual, her sister was right. About everything.

Clearing her throat, Julia started to speak. "I'm—"

"Julia Hesther Holte, if you say you're sorry one more time…"

Smiling, Julia found Rose's raised hand, cupping it in her own. "I was going to say, I'm glad that you're my sister."

Rose's small smile quivered, tears in her eyes. "You are one stubborn spirit, you know that?"

Looking down through her laughter, Julia sat for a moment before she said, "I really like Eleanor, Rose. She makes me feel…" She reached for her chest, trying to find the words. Julia recalled the way her sister and Henry always were together. "She makes me feel calm. Like things are going to be okay."

"I know." Rose smiled, and that sliver of hope expanded in Julia's chest. "What are you waiting for? Go get her."

Julia smiled through the final rush of tears, grateful. Rose scooted her chair around and pulled her into an embrace. After a while, Julia said, "You're not going to believe this."

"What?"

Leaning into Rose, the image of Eleanor back in her mind, she said, "I can't wait to go to work on Monday."

CHAPTER TWENTY-EIGHT

Eleanor had to force herself out of bed for work the following week. The chill had settled into her bones, making her ache with each step. She didn't have the energy to argue with Peter about school, so she was grateful when he went without protest. At the mill, Henry spotted her first. He frowned, looking over the top of his papers. "Eleanor, I'm afraid you don't look well."

She tried to give him an optimistic smile before continuing to collect the uniforms. On her way back to the front office, Julia came in, but her smile quickly fell as she laid eyes on Eleanor.

"Are you all right?" Julia asked, hurrying over. She reached out but seemed to force her hands back to her sides.

The weight of the uniforms felt enormous as Eleanor struggled to carry them. "I have a little cold, I think. I'll be all right."

Julia looked like she wanted to say a thousand things at once, concern and affection flashing through her eyes. Eleanor hadn't realized how much she'd missed those eyes. If only they didn't look so worried. She would be fine; this was merely a little malady.

"I'll see you on Thursday." She headed outside. Julia called after her. Turning, Eleanor was pleasantly startled when Julia ran up to leave a quick kiss on her cheek. Eleanor glanced around, but the coast was clear.

"You're burning up."

Eleanor brushed the comment aside. "I'll be fine, really." She tried to give Julia a playful nudge, but she was so weak, the gesture ended up being more of a timid bump. "See you in a few days."

A few days later, though, things had gotten worse.

"Mom," Peter said, standing at her bedside. He jostled her. "Mom, wake up."

She forced her eyes open. *Why was it so cold?* "Peter, close the window, please, darling."

"It is closed."

"Would you put the kettle on? I'll make some tea. I just need some tea."

He remained in the same spot. She found his concerned face. "I think we need Auntie Sue," he said.

Eleanor wanted to tell him she did not need Auntie Sue. She was still angry with her. But she had no energy to oppose the idea. She managed to reach up and cup his cheek. "The kettle, please, sweetheart. You don't have to go to school today if you don't want to."

His face was still solemn as he ran into the kitchen, and Eleanor fell back into a fitful sleep.

On Saturday, Julia knocked on the Perrys' door. It wasn't Eleanor, or even Peter, who opened it, but Sue Weldon. "Oh, hello."

Mrs. Weldon was an inch shorter than Julia, but she stood with the prowess of a titan. Julia stepped back as Sue closed the gap in the door, blocking her view. "Can I help you?"

"I know Eleanor is sick. She didn't come by the office on Thursday. I wanted...I made her this." Julia extended the small pot of soup. "Well, Rose, my sister, did most of the cooking, but

I helped. So it's not bad," she explained, giving a proud grin. It shrank at Mrs. Weldon's cold stare.

"Auntie Sue," Peter called, and Mrs. Weldon turned, opening the door wider. When Peter spotted Julia, his face lit up. She couldn't help but smile at the sight of him.

"Hi, Peter."

"Julia!" He hurried over, but Mrs. Weldon kept him inside.

"It's good to see you, Peter."

"And you," he said before Mrs. Weldon squeezed his shoulder.

"What was it you needed, dear?" she asked him.

He replied, "The bathroom sink is leaking."

She exhaled, and Julia realized how frazzled she looked. She was without a hat, and her cheeks were flushed. Errant strands of hair stuck out around her face. "We'll have to find someone in town to look at it, dear."

Pulling the pot of soup closer, Julia said, "I could take a look at it." Mrs. Weldon eyed her as if she had just said the wildest thing. "The ranch hands back in Texas showed me how to do it. Ours acted up all the time. You got a wrench?"

Mrs. Weldon found her collar, then her earrings, seeming at a loss. "Well—"

"We have one," Peter said. "My dad had tools. I'll show you where they are." He scampered away.

Julia started inside, but Mrs. Weldon stepped in front of her, glancing over her shoulder before saying, "Listen here, Miss Holte." Julia stepped back, baffled and intrigued by the spitfire that was Mrs. Weldon. "I'll let you in but only to take care of this little sink business." Seeming to remember the soup, she grabbed it quickly. "And we'll take this. Thank you." Julia smiled. "After that, you'll be on your way. Understood?"

"You know, Sue," she said with the sounds of Peter rummaging through something in the distance, "can I call you Sue? I feel like I can since I've heard so much about you. And I imagine you've heard plenty about me." Sue blinked, bewilderment in her gaze.

"Eleanor speaks very highly of you." At this, her face softened. "I can see why she values your friendship. You're protective of her and fiercely loyal."

Sue lifted her chin. "That's right."

"I respect that," Julia said. "So I'll come in and fix the sink and leave the soup. I'll thank you for looking after Eleanor. She's..." Sue studied her, waiting. "She's a special woman."

A small smile lifted Sue's lips. "That is something we agree upon." She seemed to size Julia up again before saying, "Very well, then. This way."

CHAPTER TWENTY-NINE

Eleanor shuddered against the pale cold. She twisted in her sheets, part of her knowing she was safe at home while the other, louder, part of her mind screamed, why was it always this place? Why was she always lost amid a blazing sea of white, alone?

She was always alone.

"Mom, wake up."

Eleanor followed Peter's voice, forcing her eyes open. She smiled at the sight of his face. When had he gotten so big? "Peter?" Her throat felt like broken glass, her voice scraping against the shards. She trembled as cold pulled at her limbs.

"She's burning up."

That voice. Eleanor knew that voice. *I love that voice.*

"Here, put this on her forehead."

Her blurry vision kept Julia's figure at a distance. It was Julia's voice she heard, wasn't it? How she longed for that to be true. She reached out, but her arm fell, heavy, as her eyes followed suit, and she drifted back into the cold and dark.

"How long has it been now?" Rose asked over the dinner table, biting into her roast beef.

"Feverish for nearly a week."

They exchanged worried glances when Henry asked, "Has the physician been by?"

Julia said, "Yes. He'd been in Denver on business, but Sue called him back, thank goodness. He was there this morning when I went by with more soup." She picked at her food but couldn't bring herself to eat. She'd stood in the open doorway that morning while Sue had brought in some broth to try to get something into Eleanor's stomach. The image of Eleanor, pale, her chest rising and falling in shallow breaths, had shaken Julia to her core. Helplessness threatened to drag her down when the physician shared his diagnosis.

"Pneumonia?" Rose said, her voice a fearful whisper.

Julia nodded.

They sat quietly, knowing the grim reality of what that meant. But Julia could hardly fathom such an outcome. She had just found Eleanor. Surely, this world wouldn't take her away now and leave Peter without any parents. She clenched her jaw and didn't realize she was stabbing the prongs of her fork into the table.

"We'll get her better," Rose said, resting a hand on hers. "Have faith."

Over the next week, Julia tried to do just that. She went to the office each day, stopping by Eleanor's in the morning to walk Peter to school. He seemed terribly glum, and she tried to keep his spirits up.

"Your mom will be okay, you know," she said as the schoolhouse came into view on Tuesday. It was early October, and she tightened her jacket around her in the wind. "She's strong."

He didn't say anything but grabbed her hand as they finished the walk. Warmth spread through her at the gesture, and something small kindled in her chest. "I'll see you after school. Sue will pick you up, and I'll come by the house after work." She handed him his thermos of tea. He hugged her and hurried off after his classmates.

A vision struck her as the future projected itself across her mind. She stood arm in arm with Eleanor as they waved Peter off to school. She inhaled, trying to reconcile the deep yearning against ominous prospects of reality.

Turning to go, Julia collided with someone. "Pardon me," she said, stepping back to find one of the mothers she'd seen regularly since taking Peter to school. It was Mrs. Henley, if she recalled correctly.

Mrs. Henley looked startled, urging her child on to the schoolhouse before pulling her shawl tighter. They stared at one another for a moment, Julia unsure what to say. Finally, Mrs. Henley spoke. "I hear young Peter's mother has fallen ill." Her tone was even, the lack of sympathy in her voice and gaze unnerving. Julia had seen the way many townsfolk—mainly women—kept their distance from Eleanor, like she carried some disease they were afraid to catch.

"Yes," Julia said, hands in her pockets. "I'm helping to see after Peter while she rests."

Mrs. Henley's brow rose. Her lips pursed as she scanned Julia's pants and men's shirt. "Well, I am sorry to hear that." Julia frowned at the reply as Mrs. Henley started to go. She turned back though, adding, "Prayer is the Lord's best medicine, you know. I do hope you're placing Mrs. Perry's health in His hands."

Smiling, Julia said, "Dr. Wicker is working diligently to help. But I'll be sure to put a good word in with the man upstairs."

Mrs. Henley's eyes widened momentarily before she shook her head and left.

"Have a nice day," Julia called after her.

The final week before the audit had arrived. A strange quiet settled over the mill office. Henry was terribly busy while Mr. Weldon read and reread all the files. Now that everything was in order for the auditor's visit, Julia was left with little to do besides the daily employee logs. She tried to keep herself busy with a mental to-do list. With each visit to Eleanor's, she noticed more and more things that needed tending around the house. Peter and Sue had taken on most of the laundry work, and Julia had helped with basic house tasks and keeping things clean.

On Wednesday, the office door opened as she sat penciling a sketch of what to plant in Rose's garden next spring. She looked up, the far-flung hope at seeing Eleanor walk in, healthy and glowing, vibrant in her mind. It wasn't her, of course, but rather Ralph who stepped inside.

She sat back in her chair. They hadn't spoken since that night in the bar when she'd told him the truth about who she was. He hesitated before stepping to the other side of her desk, hands in his pockets. He stooped a little at the low ceiling.

"Hi, Jules."

"Hi."

A couple of the office men glanced in their direction, so she scooted closer to ask, "What are you doing here?"

He licked his lips and ran a hand through his hair. "I, uh, I heard Mrs. Perry was sick." He spoke to the desk, avoiding her gaze. "My mom made these for her and her son." He reached into his jacket and presented two small bundles. She could smell the meat pies through the handkerchiefs.

"That's really swell."

"I added a new spice to them. Turned out well, I'd say."

She smiled at the pride in his eyes. Taking the bundles, she said, "Listen, Ralph—"

"Hold on," he said, raising a hand. "Let me say something first." She swallowed and sat back. "I'll admit, what you told me that night at Thrasher's surprised me." He glanced at one of the men who stood nearby and lowered his voice. "You know, about…"

"I remember," she said.

"But I started thinking how hard it must've been for you to tell me that. And that got me thinking how nice it was you trusted me with it." He smiled and met her gaze. In it, she saw understanding and acceptance.

"I didn't mean to hurt you, Ralph. I was rotten that night." She took a breath, reminding herself to be brave. "I shouldn't have agreed to go to the social with you." His brow furrowed as she continued. "I wasn't doing it for the right reasons. I led you on, and I'm sorry."

His gaze fell, and he nodded solemnly. "I kinda figured that out. Guess I didn't want to admit it to myself." Then, he stuck out his hand over the desk. "Still friends?"

She smiled, relief washing over her. "Still friends."

They shook hands. He turned hers over, seemingly noting the bruises on her knuckles. He looked at her face and surely noticed the faded shade of purple around her eye. "Are those from…"

"That night. Yeah."

He stooped and spoke lower. "I heard about Volz. Rose mentioned it to my sisters at church. Could hardly believe it when they told me."

She glanced over her shoulder, afraid the sheriff was lurking in the corner, waiting to pounce. "It's done now, Ralph."

"Is it? Jules, what's to stop him from doing that again?"

She met his gaze. *Nothing.*

He seemed to read her answer. "He can't do that. I knew he had his way of doing things," he said, his voice hard, "but now it makes sense why he hounds you the way he does. Ain't right."

She remembered her conversation with Rose about someone running against Volz in the next election when Mr. Weldon came out of the back office. "Miss Holte," he said over a stack of papers, "the lunch hour is at twelve. Please save your pleasantries for then."

"Yes, sir," she replied, tossing Ralph an apologetic look. "Thank you."

He smiled. "I hope Eleanor gets well."

Julia thanked him again. She wanted to run around the desk and hug him. Ralph was a good man. She would be better, she told herself as he left. Now that the truth was out, she'd treat him better, not push him away. She thought back to how she'd pushed Eleanor away before. A dreadful thought struck her then: what if I never get the chance to change things? As she found the clock, watching the hand slowly tick on, Julia had the terrible fear that she might have missed her chance.

CHAPTER THIRTY

Eleanor's feet slipped on the ice. She stumbled, arms out, and tried to steady herself. Wind howled, pulling on her clothes, cutting into her chest. Breathing was a battle against the dark as she searched the starless sky for a way off the frozen lake.

"Eleanor."

She spun around. Louis stood thirty yards away. She knew it was him. His voice was the same. "Louis!" Carefully, she made her way to him. "Louis, wait." The wind kicked up, snow pelting her. She shielded her eyes, and when she opened them again, he was gone. "Louis?"

Another figure appeared in the distance. Squinting against the snow, she moved carefully. The ice groaned and cracked deep beneath the surface. "Father?" She could make out his long black coat, his top hat. Even his cane was at his side. She had played with it often as an infant when he was home between trips. Before he'd packed her things and driven her to her aunt and uncle's. Before he'd left her.

"Eleanor." Turning, she found Julia standing on the ice. She wore a fur-trimmed hide coat over denim pants and boots. Her right arm was stretched toward her.

"Julia." Eleanor glanced at her father, standing stoic. His face was dark, and she couldn't make out his features. She looked between them, then started for Julia. "I'm here," she called over the sound of the wind.

She staggered over the slick ice, nearly falling as she reached for her. "Wait," she said, closer now.

Julia smiled, her eyes bright against the dark canvas behind her. Finally, Eleanor found her, taking her hand. "I've got you," Julia said. A wave of warmth washed over Eleanor then, and she knew Julia's words were true.

"I think she's waking up," a distant voice said. Eleanor didn't want to let go. She held Julia's gaze as the darkness fell away.

"Eleanor, can you hear us?"

"Julia."

"You need to take this, Eleanor." It was Sue. Eleanor shifted, her eyes opening to her bedroom. It was bright, so bright compared to her dreams. She found Sue, then Julia. Someone tugged her to sit up. Metal pressed against her lips. She wanted to ask Julia to stay. She needed to tell her things. She needed to tell her why she always kept people at arm's length. "Easy now," Sue said, nudging a spoon into her mouth. Eleanor managed to drink the tonic, coughs shaking her afterward. "Rest now, E. It's okay."

Eleanor tried to stay awake, but she was too weak, and the cold and dark overtook her once again.

Sue was heating stew for dinner when Julia slipped out. "I'll be right back," she said.

It had been a hard day for all of them. Eleanor was still asleep. Julia had heard Peter crying in his room that morning. She felt fraught, and she didn't want to share the truth: a small part of her yearned to run, to crawl under the deepest rock and give up. Her heart threatened to break each time she looked at Eleanor, at her pale complexion, her shallow breath. Rage mingled with injustice and threatened to take her down. She needed a moment, just a little time, to get her head on straight.

Walking down the drive, she had no idea where to go. Everywhere she looked, the mountains loomed, this town's rugged, barbed wire fence warning her to think twice about running.

She was surprised to find herself at the hot springs. She stood for a time, watching the water. Eleanor sometimes spoke about this place, that she had come here after Louis left. Julia admitted the waters had a soothing effect, but she was in no mood for them now. She searched the black rock, the smattering of wildflowers along the nearby slope but found no solace in them.

She sat near the smallest spring, pulling her knees to her chest. "Why is this happening?"

A swallow sang out as the water churned on, oblivious. For a long time, Julia fought her tears. She shoved the pain and uncertainty down into her chest. If she didn't let herself feel it, it wouldn't be real. Eleanor would get better, and everything would be okay.

The clouds drifted overhead. Sunlight gleamed along the mountaintop. It hit the water, dazzling. In the flash of light, Julia saw it: life without Eleanor. She saw her bed empty. She saw Peter left alone. She saw herself, bereft on her knees, furious at another wrong in her life. For what?

"No. Please no."

The pain and pressure expanded, and like most things left bottled up, they forced themselves out. Julia screamed. Her fists came down against the earth. Her shouts echoed across the field. It all came out, bounding out from her chest as unstoppable as a flood.

Julia wept, unable to hold her worst fears back. Finally, she let herself think about the reality staring her in the face. The fact that Eleanor might leave her.

Eventually, when her body stopped trembling, when her throat ached, when her breathing slowed, she wiped her tears and stood. Sunlight flashed across the springs again, marring her vision. For a moment, it looked as if the mountains shifted, their towering peaks retreating in the wake of her relinquishing everything she'd felt. Like they'd heard her and were making room for her pleas alongside the other hopes and dreams set at their feet.

Julia blinked. She raised her hand, studying the mountainside. The field was quiet, save for the springs. A lightness overcame her. Julia swallowed, eyeing the water, the peaks. She smiled, then headed back to Eleanor's.

❖

"Will the medicine work?" Julia asked the next day, sitting at Eleanor's kitchen table. Sue finished arranging the dishes on the shelf next to the sink. Julia noted that she'd put them back exactly how Eleanor had them before.

"Doctor says it's her best chance." Sue dried her hands and moved to stand behind the chair opposite. She glanced toward the stairs. They'd just sent Peter to bed.

Julia picked at the leftovers of the meat pie. Ralph had brought more by the office that morning. Rose had sent soup, too. When Sue's head fell into her open hand, Julia sat up, taken aback by the display of emotion. "Sue?"

Sue's soft cries shook her shoulders. "I'm sorry," she said, tossing her head back and blinking to halt her tears. "I'm just so frightened for her."

Julia didn't know what to say. Since she'd been coming around, Sue had acted like her role as councilwoman, doling out instructions, making sure Eleanor's laundry work was done, her hygiene was seen to, and that Peter was minded. She'd grown lax in her wariness of Julia, who was simply glad to be let in each time she stopped by to help. Sue's initial defensiveness had waned with each passing day.

"We're all scared," Julia said while Sue cried quietly, wiping her tears as fast as they came. Julia noted her frayed appearance, the shadows under her eyes. "Why don't you take a break?"

Sniffling, she asked, "A break?"

"Let me see to them," Julia said. "You have your work to get back to. Plus, I'm sure your husband would appreciate seeing you more."

Sue laughed. "We have been two ships passing of late. But he understands."

"Of course. But…" She stood. "I'd like to be here for Eleanor and Peter. I'm here anyway. It'll make things easier if I'm the one to stay overnight. You've done enough."

Sue met her gaze, tears brimming. She looked at Eleanor's closed door, then back at Julia. "You really care about her."

It wasn't a question. Sue's words reached out through the space between them, an acknowledgement Julia hadn't expected landing gently before her. An offering of peace from someone who loved Eleanor as much as she did. "I do."

Sue smiled and sniffled again. Then, she wiped her face and took a deep breath. "Well, I'll still be by to make sure things are all right. Now," she said, shifting back to her no-nonsense self, "be sure Peter gets to school. And the uniforms will have to be tended to. I don't know how she's done it all these years. Hardly any space here to keep things organized the way she does." Sue found her handbag and hat. Julia walked her to the door. "Oh, the storm that blew through yesterday left terrible debris out back." She glanced Julia over, but the look was one of kindness, not judgment. "You seem like you can handle that."

Julia smiled. "I can."

Sue nodded, seeming like she wanted to say something else before opening the door. On the front porch she turned. "Thank you, Julia."

"Of course, Sue."

Watching her go, determination settled over Julia's shoulders. She inhaled, the fall air crisp and awakening her senses. Ahead, the mountains watched. To her surprise, the mill sounded distant, hardly registering in the back of her mind. "Very well," she said to the tall pines. "Here we go."

CHAPTER THIRTY-ONE

Two days later, Julia sat in Eleanor's rocking chair. The curtains were closed, keeping the room dim. Eleanor slept, her breathing beautifully even.

"I think her fever broke," she had said when she and Peter had come to check on her after sunup. Running a hand over Eleanor's forehead, Julia had nearly leapt for joy at the cooler feeling of her skin.

Peter's wide smile echoed her sentiments. "I'll go tell Auntie Sue!" he said, running out into the kitchen.

"After breakfast," Julia called. "And not without your coat."

When he'd gone, Julia hung the clothes on the line, then settled into the rocking chair. She'd grown quite comfortable in it, having slept in the matching one in the main room the last couple of nights. A small fire crackled, and for the first time in a long time, serenity settled over her. She watched Eleanor, then let her focus wander to the sparse furniture. Remembering that Sue had brought over an extra pair of sweaters, Julia moved to the dresser to find one.

Eleanor's blouse, the one she'd been wearing the first day they'd seen each other in the office, sat folded inside the top drawer. Julia ran her fingers over the soft material. Flashes of Eleanor in other outfits emerged, like that gorgeous green dress from dinner. She bit her lip to quell the stirring in her abdomen at the image.

Julia felt something hard and cool beneath the sweater. It was a perfume vial. She lifted it to better see, curious as she had never noticed Eleanor wearing any before. The vial looked empty until a glint caught her attention. She readjusted it in her hand.

Metal flecks sat in a tiny collection at the bottom. The vial was tinted, but she thought the flecks were gold. Julia glanced at Eleanor. Where had she gotten these? Gently shaking the vial, she watched the flecks bounce against the drops of liquid. There had to be nearly an ounce in there. Excitement trilled against her spine. This could change a lot for Eleanor and Peter. Simultaneously, dozens of questions emerged. Those could wait, she decided, as she replaced the vial and quietly closed the drawer.

Eleanor stretched, opening her eyes to her darkening room. The ache that had gripped her bones and muscles was gone. She kicked the blanket off, relieved to feel hot for the first time in ages. A sulfonamide bottle sat on her bedside table, along with Peter's toy car and a glass of water. She pushed the glass back to be even with the others and smiled.

Standing, she took a moment to stabilize herself. She felt weak, and God, was she hungry. She found her reflection in the vanity and stepped back. Bags sat deep under her eyes, and she looked frightfully thinner. Her hair was greasy and matted. Her sleepshirt stuck to her chest and beneath her arms. It didn't look like the one she remembered putting on before. When had that been? She'd been sick, of course. Glancing back at the bed, she wondered how long she'd been out.

Her bedroom door was cracked open. She opened it enough to peer out into the main room. Peter and Julia sat at the table. He was hunched over a piece of paper while Julia sat next to him, saying something as he worked. Remnants of a meal sat on plates in the middle of the table. The wall lamps were on, and a candle flickered between them.

Eleanor's pulse quickened at the sight of Julia in her usual collared shirt. Her hair was pulled in a low ponytail, but the strands still seemed to fight against being contained. Julia smiled after checking what Peter had done, and he beamed proudly.

The floor creaked beneath Eleanor. They both looked up.

"Mom!"

She smiled and opened the door wider as Peter scrambled out of his chair. "Hi, sweetheart," she said, kneeling as he collided with her into a hug. "My, did you grow? How did that happen?"

He rested his head over her shoulder, squeezing her tight. She held him to her, finding Julia across the room. Her face had been one of surprise but now it settled into her signature grin, what looked like relief pouring out of her gaze. Eleanor felt something else too, something she could hardly name, yet she heard its call. It wrapped itself up with Peter's embrace, enveloping her in a daze of tenderness.

Holding Peter out in front of her, she said, "What did I miss?"

"Julia is helping me with my arithmetic."

"Is she?" Eleanor asked, glancing at Julia, who looked down.

"She also thinks I should be Davey Crockett for Halloween. Auntie Sue said she can get the hat I need on her next trip to Denver."

"Halloween?" Eleanor frowned and stood, keeping a hand on Peter's shoulder. "What day is it?

Julia looked back up, affection and hope vibrant in her gaze. "October seventeenth."

Her mouth opened, and she had to work to form a response. "I...I was sick that long?"

"You had to sleep to get better," Peter told her matter-of-factly. "You slept a lot."

Eleanor looked from him to Julia as he wandered back to the chair. She remembered the cold and dark lake. At times, it had felt like she'd spent years lost in the snow, chasing figures across the ice. Other moments had been quick as lightning, flashes of memories gone as quickly as they came. At the table, she said, "It was more than a cold, then."

Julia held her gaze, a thoughtful crease between her brows. "Pneumonia."

Eleanor pulled out the chair to sit. "Oh. Well, that explains a few things." She felt self-conscious remembering she was in her nightshirt and how dreadful she looked. Pulling at her collar, she said, "Did you..." She cleared her throat. "How long have you been here?"

Myriads of answers seemed to cross Julia's gaze before she looked at Peter. "I've come and gone a few times since the start of the month. Sue took care of you at first. Rose contributed her cooking. Ralph dropped off some things. Henry helped with Peter when he could."

"Julia took me to school," Peter said, scribbling away on his paper.

A sheepish look crossed Julia's face. "I sent Sue home three days ago to rest. Been me and this guy since." She ruffled Peter's hair. He laughed and swatted her hand away.

Eleanor let her words sink in. She'd been bedridden—she did the math quickly—over two weeks. She glanced at the back door. Seeming to read her question, Julia said, "We've taken care of the laundry. I took the liberty of picking up your pay last Friday. It's in the drawer in your bedroom."

Eleanor met her gaze. Knowing sat in Julia's eyes. Had she found the vial? Unsure what to say, she watched Peter work out a multiplication fact until Julia said, "You just missed Sue, actually. She brought those."

Eleanor followed her finger to a stack of books in Louis's rocking chair. She smiled.

"A couple of mysteries. She said those were your favorite."

"They are." Another look passed between them as Eleanor tried to reconcile the events of the past few weeks. She could hardly believe Julia had volunteered to be here while she worked to get out of the grips of her illness. Not to mention Sue, Rose, and everyone else stepping up to help.

"Done," Peter said, breaking their silence. He handed the paper to Julia, who looked it over.

"Very good. I think," she said, tossing Eleanor a wink. "Now time for your bath and off to bed."

He scooted in his chair. To Eleanor he said, "Henry promised to walk me through the mill."

Eleanor glanced at Julia, who said, "Only if you get passing marks on your arithmetic exam."

He rolled his eyes but didn't argue. "Good night, Mom," he said, kissing her cheek.

"Good night, darling."

When he was gone, Eleanor felt shy now that she was alone with Julia. She watched her gather Peter's papers and bring their dishes to the sink. When she turned, her eyes shined.

"Julia?"

She gave a shaky laugh. "Sorry. I'm just…" She cleared her throat. "I'm really glad you're okay."

Eleanor smiled. "Sorry to scare you."

Julia grinned, and Eleanor realized she could look at that smile forever. She wanted Julia here, like this, in her kitchen. She wanted to wake up to her like this, and that idea felt like a piece had fallen into place, a piece she'd given up searching for since Louis left.

She couldn't be certain, but she thought she saw those same wants in Julia's gaze that seemed to tear itself from her as she asked, "Hungry?"

Letting such wonderment settle over her, Eleanor replied, "Starving."

Chapter Thirty-two

How was the tour?" Julia asked as Henry led Peter inside the mill office.

"Really swell! We saw the machines, and one of the men even let me turn the crank." He motioned to demonstrate.

"How about that," she said smiling. Henry looked equally pleased.

"When can we go again?" Peter asked, turning to look up at him.

Mussing Peter's hair, Henry said, "Maybe after the holidays. Rose still needs to show you how to make candied apples."

The wind howled outside, and Julia glanced at the small window as snow started to fall. Thanksgiving was a week away. "Your mom should be here soon," she said. "Come sit with me while you wait."

Peter pulled up a chair while she finished sorting through the time logs. With the audit past, the tension that had gripped the office disappeared with it. The first big snowfall and upcoming holiday had everyone in high spirits. Eleanor's health, too, had been strong, much to everyone's relief.

Julia was watching Peter doodle on a scrap piece of letterhead when the door opened. To her disappointment, it was only an office man who came in, scarf wrapped around him as a burst of cold air blew through the office. He greeted someone behind her desk.

"Hey, pal, close the door, will ya?" she called.

He gave her a look but did so, then moved on to the back of the room. Peter had stopped doodling, a hand on his chest. "The air," he said, taking a slow breath.

Julia turned to face him. "I know. It's okay."

Pain filled his gaze, but he tried to smile, giving her a brave nod.

Julia placed her hand over his on his chest. "Just breathe." She took a small breath, and he matched her. They did that several times until his ability to take a breath deepened. They both exhaled as the attack passed. "Hey, that wasn't too bad."

He shook his head. "I had my tea this morning."

"Good boy," she told him, pulling him into a hug when again the door opened and was closed quickly by Eleanor. She shook out her hair, snowflakes dotting the shoulders of her coat. Julia was transfixed by the image.

"Hello, my darling," Eleanor said. Julia was certain she cut her gaze at her on the last word. They'd been in a wonderful place since her health had turned around. They'd spent Halloween together, walking Peter around town with a couple of the other schoolchildren. Sheriff Volz had been out ruining most folks' fun, destroying street bonfires as soon as they got started. Julia had felt him watching her, but he'd kept his distance.

Last weekend, Eleanor and Peter came over for dinner, and Rose had, mercifully, ordered from the local restaurant. Things felt good between them, and the tension that had sparked since their first meeting continued to burn. Julia wondered how long she could stand it before her more wanton desires needed to be met.

"You ready to go?" Eleanor asked, pulling Julia's attention away from the opening in her coat that revealed an undone button at the top of her blouse.

Julia helped Peter into his jacket and gloves. "You, uh, you should come by for Thanksgiving," she said. "That is, if you don't have any plans."

Eleanor looked thoughtful, a smile growing. Peter answered for her, "We'd love to."

Julia grinned when Eleanor said, "That does sound lovely. We typically dine with Sue, but she and I are still on uneven terms." At the door, she turned. "If you could come by this Friday, I've been meaning to ask your help. There's a peculiar sound coming from the bathroom sink."

"Oh?" She had thought she'd done a bang-up job at fixing the leak, but perhaps she'd missed something.

Peter looked up. "Mom, no, there isn't."

Eleanor looked like she was trying to push him along. "It just started today. I don't think it's anything too serious," she said quickly, a blush rising in her cheeks. "But I hear you're quite the handywoman."

Julia grinned at the flimsy excuse to see her but had no intention of arguing. "Sure. I'll come by Friday."

"If you want to join us for dinner, you're welcome to." Eleanor was nearly out the door, but the guile in her smile told Julia she was hungry for much more than just a good meal.

Julia called after them, "See you then." She caught the glee in Eleanor's eyes before the door closed. Elation filled Julia's chest as she sat back in her chair, arms behind her head. Finally, things were falling into place.

CHAPTER THIRTY-THREE

Rose stopped Julia on her way out the door on Friday. "I don't want to be late, Rose."

"Nonsense," her sister said, scurrying to her and brushing away lint from her ironed shirt. Rose looked her over, a craftswoman admiring her work. "You're sure you don't want a splash of rose water?"

"No thank you," she said, shaking back her hair. Rose looked like she wanted to reach out and comb it but resisted. Eventually, a pleased smile settled beneath shining eyes.

"You look wonderful."

Julia straightened. She caught Henry over Rose's shoulder. He nodded in agreement. "Thanks. I'll be back later."

Ushering her out the door with a jug of tea, Rose said, "Don't worry about us, Jules," and tossed her a sly grin. "We'll see you when we see you."

Anticipation leapt in her stomach, but Julia worked to corral it as she said good-bye and walked the half mile to Eleanor's. Henry had offered to drive her, but she'd insisted the walk would keep her nerves in check. It was a cold evening, the mountainside already darkening, and she pulled her coat close around her. The gray sky overhead threatened with snow.

Peter was out the door as she neared the end of the drive. "Julia's here," he cried, running out to wrap her in a hug.

"You better get inside," she told him. "It will be snowing again soon." They stomped their boots out on the front porch. She hesitated a moment at the open front door, then knocked.

Eleanor called from inside, "Come in, Julia. Peter, take her coat."

He did, and she helped him hang it. A fire blazed in the stone fireplace to her left near the rocking chair. In the middle of the room, the table was set for three.

"It smells delicious," she said, following Peter.

Eleanor glanced over her shoulder, and Julia traced her figure. To her delight, she wore the same green dress from the church social. Her throat dried at the sight. "Is that tea?"

At a loss for words as she tried to gather her thoughts, Julia held up the jug.

"Wonderful," Eleanor said. "Let's pour us all a glass. Food will be ready soon."

Julia moved to sit when she remembered Eleanor's reason for the invitation tonight. "Should I take a look at the sink before we eat?"

"Oh." Eleanor took a moment and seemed to be suddenly very focused on ensuring the stove was off. "Well, as a matter of fact, it's worked itself out. Crisis averted." She carried a pot of stew over and began scooping the meat and vegetables into their respective bowls.

Julia only admired the flush in Eleanor's cheeks, shades of pink beneath her skin.

"Take a seat, everyone," she said, cutting her gaze to Julia. "Let's eat."

❖

"But I'm not tired," Peter said, running his wooden car over the floorboards and across the rug in front of the fireplace.

"It's getting late," Eleanor said, standing to usher him upstairs. It was only nine o'clock, but the simmering tension between her and Julia felt as if it was near boiling. She had to excuse herself twice at dinner to splash water on her face after staring too long at the way Julia's shirt sat against the curve of her chest. Additionally, she'd hoped to clear the air about some things, and it was best to do that without Peter.

"But it's not a school day tomorrow."

"Peter."

Julia chuckled, and when he drove the car past her chair, she scooped it up out of his hand. "You heard your mother."

"Hey," he said with a smile. Eleanor watched as she moved the car to her lap, then prepared her hands for a round of rock, paper, scissors. They'd conducted many a round over the course of the night over trivial things: who got to check the trap next, who got the last piece of fruit tart, who had to help with the dishes. Peter had won them all, so Eleanor was surprised when Julia placed paper over his rock.

"I win," she said. "I'll hold on to this until the morning."

Peter harrumphed, then asked, "You'll be here in the morning?"

Julia opened her mouth, seeming to realize what she said. "I, um, just mean your mother will hold on to it until then."

Eleanor found her stammer utterly adorable.

Peter bid them both good night and went upstairs. "I'll bring your tea up soon," she called after him, then moved to set the kettle on. The feeling that she was a timid schoolgirl in front of her crush returned. Eleanor took a breath to ease her nerves and rejoined Julia at the table. The fire crackled, the mountainside quiet as night fell around them.

"Thank you for the meal," Julia said. Her ankle was crossed over her left knee, and she looked utterly at ease.

Eleanor found the pulse point of her neck in the dim lamplight, her own breath quickening at the image of herself pulling Julia close. Smiling through her thoughts, she replied, "We're glad you could join us."

Outside, the wind picked up. "Henry says a big snowfall is due soon. Maybe tonight."

Eleanor nodded but could hardly think about the weather when Julia was sitting across from her looking as stunning as she did in her pants and boots. Still, the talk of snow reminded her of what she'd been trying to share for weeks now.

"There's something I need to tell you."

Julia's face grew serious. "What is it? You're not feeling ill again, are you?"

"No, nothing like that."

"Good." Julia smiled, rearranging to pull her chair closer. She rested her elbows on the table, pitching her fingers beneath her chin.

Eleanor worked up her courage, then said, "When I was sick, my mind sent me somewhere." In her lap, she touched her thumb to her fingers, willing herself to get this out. "It's somewhere I've always gone. For as long I can remember."

"Like a dream?"

"It's more like a nightmare," she said sarcastically, but Julia's face was serious. "I'm always on a lake. A dark, frozen lake at night."

Julia gave a small smile. "Minnesota has a lot of lakes, so I hear."

"Yes. I suppose it's one of those. No," she corrected herself, taking a breath. "I know which one it is." It was quiet while Julia waited for her to continue. "I told you my father left me with my aunt and uncle to be raised by them. That he was too busy for his daughter. Which I suppose was true. But my mother..." Eleanor's words halted, stuck in her throat as she started to count the grains in the table wood.

"Eleanor?"

She looked up after reaching fourteen. "I'm sorry." She pulled her own chair in, resting her hands together on the table.

Julia reached out, placing one gently atop them. "You can tell me. I..." She licked her lips, drawing Eleanor's gaze to them. "I want you to tell me things."

Eleanor took another breath before continuing. "My mother died, as you know, not long after having me. But I never…I've never shared the truth of how. My aunt told me everything when I turned sixteen." She waited, letting the words find their way out across her lips. "After giving birth to me, my mother grew terribly sad. Apparently, she couldn't recover from the trauma that accompanies bringing a child into the world. She…" Her voice broke, and she found Julia's gaze to anchor herself. "One night, she left the house. It was the middle of winter. Minnesota winters are terribly cold. Blizzards that blind you and cut you to your core. You can get lost if you're not careful."

The slightest pressure of Julia's hand encouraged her to go on. "My mother went out to the lake near my father's house. It was mid-January. She…she wore only her nightgown. When they found her, it looked as if she'd lain down to sleep."

Julia sat back, one hand over her mouth. "God, Eleanor."

"After my aunt told me, I was so angry. Angry at my mother for not having more willpower, more determination to try to live. But then, well, I started to understand her. After Louis left…" She searched the room, the shotgun above the door, the snow starting to fall outside. "I wasn't sure what to do."

"But you didn't give up."

Eleanor shook her head. She hadn't. She'd fought to make ends meet, to keep a roof over her and Peter's heads. She'd leaned on Sue but drove a trench between herself and anyone else who tried to come into her and Peter's lives. She'd fought to keep him safe from anyone who might hurt him in that same way.

Until now.

"I think that's why I pushed you away. When you first met Peter, he took so quickly to you, and it terrified me. I don't want what happened to me to fall on him. The curse that's followed me all my life. He doesn't deserve it. I don't want him to feel any more abandoned than he already does. He…he shouldn't have to bear that."

She didn't realize she was crying until Julia reached out, catching a tear. "You don't deserve all that pain," Julia said softly. "I'm sorry if I ever made you feel like that."

Eleanor reached up, finding Julia's hand against her cheek. "I've just been so scared of everything for so long. One day, I looked up to find I'd shackled my own son to the chains I'd placed upon myself."

Julia tilted her head, sympathy in her gaze. "You're right to keep him away from the mill."

"I kept him away from everything."

"You were just trying to protect him." Eleanor sniffled. Julia pulled her gaze. "You were trying to protect yourself."

They looked at each other for a long time. God, Eleanor thought, she hadn't meant to lead the night to this, crying at her kitchen table. "I'm sorry," she said, pulling back and wiping her face. The kettle whistled, and she hurried to prepare Peter's tea. Cup and saucer in hand, she turned to Julia, who remained sitting at the table. "I'll just be a minute."

When she came back downstairs—her wits collected and her face dry—Julia was standing in front of the fireplace. Eleanor watched her, the cowgirl with her hands in her pockets. She let herself admire the way the denim hugged her hips. Her hair looked more golden in the firelight.

After joining her, Julia turned, smiling.

"What?" Eleanor asked.

She shrugged, reaching out to push back a strand of hair from her face. "I'm just really glad you shared all that with me." Eleanor looked down, but Julia lifted her chin. "I mean it. Thank you, Eleanor."

Letting everything she felt, and everything she'd been feeling for months, carry her forward, Eleanor kissed her. Julia leaned back before smiling and returning the kiss. Eleanor wrapped her arms around her as Julia cupped her face. Unsure whose soft breath caught between them, she pulled Julia closer, wanting to be as near to her as possible. She still felt raw, bare, after telling her everything she had. Her very heart felt as if it was beating out of her chest, offered up for Julia. If she was willing to take it.

Pulling back, she found Julia wearing a look she hadn't seen. Lust sat in her bright gaze but also something deeper. Admiration, wanting, and the one thing that Eleanor had dreamed of for so long. Love looked at her, threatening to unravel Eleanor in the best of ways.

Grinning, Julia found Eleanor's hands. She kissed her knuckles. Eleanor's body sang with desire as Julia led her to the bedroom. She couldn't help herself as she giggled in the dark, biting her lip and gently pinning Julia against the doorjamb.

"Mrs. Perry," Julia said, her eyes on Eleanor's lips. "How forward of you."

Eleanor kissed her again, longing flooding her senses. She ran her hands over Julia's backside, gripping the tight muscles. "I need to get these off you," she murmured into another kiss.

Julia groaned. "I've imagined unburdening you of this dress since summer."

After pressing kisses to Julia's neck, Eleanor found the topmost button of her shirt. She undid the first three. Her breath caught at the soft skin beneath. Heart racing, she relished the feel of Julia's firm grip on her waist. To her surprise, she felt no nerves, no anxiety at what they were about to do. Each touch, every kiss felt right, like nothing Eleanor had ever experienced. Forcing herself to focus, she took a shuddering breath and asked, "Are you sure about this?"

Julia looked as if she had to tear herself away from some distant, daring thought. Meeting her gaze, she said, "I've never been surer of anything."

Her words woke something up in Eleanor. That warm kindling in her abdomen stirred, a desire like she hadn't felt in years begging to be satisfied. She grinned, kissing Julia again before pulling her close and closing the door behind them.

❖

Kissing Eleanor was like riding a stallion at full gallop. It was driving through the open desert faster than ever before. It was a Texas sunset that left her awestruck by its beauty. It was—

"Julia," Eleanor said against her lips. "Please."

They stood in the dark of Eleanor's bedroom. The fire that had been lit earlier in the evening burned softly. Julia moved them to the bed. Eleanor found the button of her pants, tugging them down as Julia undid the rest of her shirt buttons, letting Eleanor pull it off her. She'd never taken things this slowly before, and a stark vulnerability encompassed her as Eleanor, lips swollen from their kisses, took her in.

"My God," she said, running her hands over Julia's bare breasts, her stomach, her hips. Need throbbed in Julia's center, but she willed herself to be patient as she reached out, lowering the shoulders of Eleanor's dress. It fell below her breasts. Julia leaned down, placing kisses over her supple flesh. Eleanor pulled her closer, holding her while Julia found her nipple, caressing it with her tongue. As she moved up to kiss along her collarbone, Eleanor pulled the rest of her dress down, then her tap pants. Julia followed suit, tossing aside her men's briefs.

For a time, they simply stood and took one another in. Julia lifted her chin, still feeling exposed beneath Eleanor's hungry gaze. Finally, Eleanor pulled her in for a kiss before turning her around to face the bed.

Julia pressed back against her. Eleanor wrapped one arm around her, pulling her close. Her breasts were warm against her back as Eleanor's left hand held her hip while her right moved around to Julia's center.

They both inhaled at the slick wetness. Between kisses on her neck, Eleanor said, "I want you to touch me like this." Julia could hardly breathe, her eyes finding the ceiling as Eleanor's fingers started a steady circle. Pressing herself more into Eleanor, Julia bucked as her arousal grew. She found Eleanor's hand, directing her for a time. Her breathing grew quicker, heat rising in her chest.

"Eleanor." Julia turned to kiss her as if it was everything she'd ever wanted in this life. Through the haze of desire, she realized that maybe it was.

Eleanor pulled her hand away. Julia's breath was staggered as she was left wanting. Carefully, Eleanor moved to the middle of the bed, motioning for Julia to join her.

A guttural hum accompanied each kiss down Eleanor's body. Julia lingered on her breasts, her stomach, then lower as her fingers caressed Eleanor's gloriously slick folds. Eleanor moved as if to sit up, but Julia repositioned herself, straddling Eleanor with her left hand pressed against Eleanor's sternum to keep her against the bed. She grinned and shook her head before settling between her legs.

The first stroke of Julia's tongue prompted a sharp breath. Eleanor murmured something, but she couldn't make it out. Heat ran up her own body as she took Eleanor in her mouth. Julia worked slowly, her strokes even and measured.

"Fingers," Eleanor said between breaths. Julia pressed into her, relishing the soft cry when she did. Her own arousal built, threatening to pull her down with Eleanor's whispers. For some time, she had wanted to be here like this, feeling Eleanor, loving her the way she deserved to be loved. Was this what it was like? Was this what it felt like to want to give everything to someone, to make them happy in the way only you could? When Eleanor's muscles tensed around her fingers, Julia held her as she climaxed.

After kissing the soft wet curls, Julia pulled herself up to lie prone against Eleanor. She rested her head on her open palm, watching Eleanor's breath settle. She ran her free hand through her hair. Sweat shined on her forehead.

"You look satisfied with yourself," Eleanor said, grinning.

"I hope you are," she replied, running her fingers up and down Eleanor's side. When Eleanor's leg twitched, they laughed.

They lay together a long time in the quiet dark. Julia nestled into Eleanor, wondering how she came to be here with someone so wonderful. Somebody who didn't seem to want to give up on her. Eventually, Eleanor stirred, finding Julia's lips in another kiss before rearranging herself. Julia moved so that Eleanor could straddle her. She felt dazed by her beauty, her hair a breathtaking mane framing a woman she thought might be a spirit or perhaps a goddess.

Leaning down, Eleanor kissed her again, then pulled back to hold her gaze. Julia wasn't sure what to make of the feeling that coursed through her limbs at that moment. Light and fire and ice chased each other over her skin. Words danced across her tongue, but she struggled to manage them, to find their order, and to express them the way she hoped rang true. "Eleanor…"

Kissing her again, Eleanor smiled softly, recognition in her eyes. Still, the words didn't come. So Julia pulled her down, kissing her hard, determined to say it all in a way she hoped Eleanor would understand.

Chapter Thirty-four

Eleanor woke to the exquisite sensation of Julia's lips on her neck.

"Mornin'," Julia said, her breath warm against Eleanor's skin.

She turned, and the blanket fell around her. In the light of day, she felt a moment of shame at Julia seeing her, despite everything they'd done last night. Her body wasn't like it had been when she was younger, before giving birth. Instinctually, she moved to pull the blanket up to hide her midriff.

Julia caught her hand, though, and kissed it. "You're beautiful," she said.

"I think you may be biased, Miss Holte."

Grinning, Julia said, "Maybe I am." She leaned down to kiss Eleanor's stomach, then up her body, the kisses getting faster as she went. Eleanor pulled her close when she reached her neck, and they fell into fits of laughter. Even wrapped up in a blissful tangle of limbs and blankets, Eleanor caught the sound of little steps on the staircase.

"Peter." She scrambled over Julia, her bare feet hitting the cold floor as she found her robe. She finished tying it around her when he called from the other side, and she opened the door. "Hi, darling," she said, blocking his view into the room.

"Can we have eggs for breakfast?"

"Of course, sweetheart." She ran a hand over her hair, hoping it wasn't too mussed. "Grab two extra from the shelf." At his questioning look, she bit her lip then said, "Julia stayed the night."

"She did?" he asked, his voice pitching in excitement. He tried to peer around her. "Julia?"

"She's, uh, still sleeping," she said, raising a finger to her lips.

Peter nodded, then whispered, "I'll get the eggs."

Closing the door, Eleanor hurried back to the bed. Julia laughed and sat up, one arm behind her as she leaned against the headboard. "I get to stay for breakfast?"

You could stay forever, Eleanor nearly said. She looked down, one hand on Julia's thigh. "What kind of host would I be if I sent you off without breakfast?"

That grin spread over Julia's face. "I'd say you've already been a mighty generous host, Mrs. Perry."

Eleanor crashed into her, wrapping her in another kiss.

"Mom!" Peter called. "Where's the butter?"

Eleanor sighed, tearing herself away. "Get dressed," she said to Julia, tossing her shirt toward the bed. "Breakfast awaits."

Chapter Thirty-five

M ore hot chocolate?" Eleanor asked. They sat near the uppermost hot spring, huddled beneath a heavy blanket on a gray fall day.

Julia held out her cup. "Yes, please. And tell Sue thank you. It's delicious." When Eleanor hesitated, she added, "Are you two still not talking?"

"No," she said, pouring. "Isaac gifted me this when I returned to work last week, though I knew it was from Sue." She sighed.

"She'll come around."

The overcast sky threw a somber cold over the mountains. Being outside in such weather probably wasn't ideal for Eleanor's health, but she'd pressed the matter. Julia had asked five times if she was certain she wanted to go.

"I want to get away," she had said after three days of sleeping apart. "Just us. Just for a little while," she'd said after Rose had agreed to watch Peter at the house during lunch.

They sat as close to the water as possible to get some of the heat, and Eleanor had agreed that they wouldn't stay long. She knew Julia was terrified of her getting sick again. Of course, it was the last thing she wanted, too, but she felt confident that a half hour outside would be fine.

They watched the water in companionable silence. Eleanor was remembering when she'd seen Julia here all those months ago and smiled. The pleasant memory faded, though, when Julia spoke.

"I found the vial."

Eleanor clenched her jaw and faced her. She thought it had been moved in her drawer but had put so much effort into making up for lost time since she had been sick, the vial had fallen to the back of her mind.

"Where did you get all that?"

Unease pricked her fingers. Her instinct was to share the truth, but her chest tightened, the walls she'd built to protect herself and Peter were exhumed. "I found it."

Julia searched Eleanor's gaze as if weighing what to say next. "The mill—"

"The mill doesn't need to know," she said curtly, pulling her knees close beneath the heavy blanket. Her thumb found her finger, ticking off the number of pine needles nearby.

"Eleanor."

She was at seven when Julia tugged her sleeve. "What? What do you want me to say?" Eleanor hated her defensive tone, but fear expanded in her chest.

"Does Sue know?"

"No." *Eight. Nine.* She took a drink, scooting back. Overwhelming feelings consumed her mind. She stood, needing more space. "It's not like I stole it."

Julia remained sitting, watching her. "I never said you did."

Eleanor bit her lip. The gold was for her and Peter to build a better life. Could that life include Julia? She had been beginning to think it could. She dreamt of such a life side by side with this woman she'd fallen in love with. But Eleanor's breath came quickly, and she couldn't stand the look in Julia's eyes. What if she told Henry about the gold? She could lose her job. She felt dizzy.

"Eleanor." Julia stood, setting her cup aside and grabbing her forearm. "Please, talk to me."

White blurred her vision. She could hardly think. "I should get back."

"Wait, Eleanor."

She gathered the blankets, snatching the thermos and hurrying away. The need to check the vial drove her steps. Peter's future rested against its frail glass. She needed to get home and lock the door to the world and its judgment. That was what she saw in Julia's eyes, wasn't it?

Eleanor hurried, but Julia ran after her, catching up. "Stop, Eleanor." She grabbed her, gently making her turn. Eleanor exhaled, fighting tears. "I didn't mean to upset you. I just…" Julia slowed her own breathing. "I was curious."

Hugging the blankets, Eleanor didn't know what to say. She looked down, wondering if she'd once again jumped to conclusions. She shook her head. *Why am I like this?* Quietly, she asked, "What are you going to do?"

The silence was loud until Julia asked, "Do?"

"Are you going to tell the mill?" She looked up, swallowing her nerves.

Julia blinked, incredulity in her eyes. "You think I would do that?" The hurt in her voice cut deeply.

Eleanor searched the clouds, the trees, for how to handle this. "I don't…God, Julia." She stepped closer. "I'm sorry." She reached out, finding her hand. "I'm just…so scared."

"Of me?"

Yes, I'm scared to let you in completely. What if you leave like Louis did? Peter couldn't take it. I couldn't take it. Swallowing the tremor in her voice, she said, "I'm the mill laundress, Julia. I'm supposed to wash and deliver the uniforms, that's it. I shouldn't have that gold."

Julia listened, tilting her head. She was quiet a long time until she turned Eleanor's hand over, cupping it. "Eleanor, I don't see a difference between that gold and what prospectors found when they first came here. Every man for himself, right?" She grinned.

The knot in Eleanor's stomach loosened, her fear melting with Julia's smile.

"Do you trust me?"

Sniffling, Eleanor held her gaze. She did, didn't she? After everything they'd shared, all that they'd been through? Julia had been by her side; she'd helped with Peter, made him happier than she'd seen him in years. Still, trust seemed like such a far-flung concept, an idea from another time, another place.

Eventually, she nodded.

Julia squeezed her hand, kissing her. "Then believe me when I say, your secret is safe with me."

Chapter Thirty-six

Winter opened its arms around the Rockies, encasing Idaho Springs and its residents in a picturesque wonderland.

"I like this," Julia said in late December, pulling on her boots and watching the flakes fall silently over the ground. "This stuff isn't hard like the snowfall we got in the Panhandle."

Rose brought in a quilt some of the church ladies had donated to them, an early Christmas gift to the ill-prepared souls from Texas who hadn't thought about things like extra blankets before moving to the mountains. "You don't miss that wind that could knock you down, then pick you right back up? All while it rained ice…sideways?"

Laughing, Julia said, "Nope. Can't say I do." She moved closer to the window. "This is nice. Serene." She watched the snow deepen around the base of their trees. "It sure is a lot, though. Took me and Henry over three hours to help shovel the neighborhood drives."

Rose tugged open the curtains more. "That reminds me, the Jardas left a mulberry pie as a thanks for doing that." She frowned and eyed the snow. "Not sure why I can't get mine to turn out the same."

Following Rose downstairs, Julia found her coat by the door. "Don't forget about the Jell-O. Ralph's mother needs it to pair with some kind of fruit cup."

"Yes, yes." Rose wore a flattering red dress beneath her white apron. "It's in the icebox."

Cold air blew through the front room as Henry came in the door, flourishing his hat. "It's done, the final meeting of the year," he exclaimed.

"Wonderful, dear," Rose said, greeting him with a kiss. "Now go change, or we'll be late."

Henry looked between them. "I thought the Davies' party started at four o'clock?"

"You know, Rose, early is on time, and on time is late," Julia said, buttoning her coat.

"I hear your comment, and I reject it," Rose called over her shoulder as she washed her hands at the sink. When Julia tried to snatch a cookie from the platter on the table, Rose swatted her away. The batch was mostly burned, but Julia was starved. In addition to the four long drives on their street, she'd also helped shovel the Perrys' drive this morning after another night spent there. Julia had found herself staying overnight more and more lately with the mill slowing down in winter and the workers on holiday since last Monday. Julia was at their house often, listening to Eleanor read books, building bigger traps with Peter, or—one of her favorite pastimes—lying in bed with Eleanor.

Folks around town had noticed Julia coming and going from the Perry residence, but no one had said much of anything, to her relief. She shared as much with Eleanor, who had only shrugged and said, "Doesn't make sense for people to fret about what we're doing. They've got their own lives to worry about." Julia supposed that was the case. The wives around town, including Mrs. Henley, seemed pleased to have their husbands home with the cold weather, and the mill men were generally in good spirits with the holiday season upon them. Thrasher's was less crowded, according to Ralph. Everyone seemed thrilled at the snow and the chance to be around the ones they loved.

Nearly everyone.

Last week, Julia and Eleanor had been walking along Main Street shopping for a gift for Peter when they'd had a run-in with

Sheriff Volz. He'd been leaving a music shop, his beige coat and matching hat contrasting with the bright red poinsettias and bursts of garland strung along the sidewalks. He had nearly run into them and looked up, surprise in his light gaze. That had shifted quickly to disdain when he realized it was her. She was ready for him to come after her, to give some inane explanation of how she was breaking the law by existing, but he never did. Maybe it was because it was crowded, or the air of frivolity circulating the streets had him in a good mood, or maybe it was because she was with Eleanor. Whatever the reason, he only tipped his hat and moved on.

"That was strange," Julia had said as they continued, glancing over her shoulder.

Eleanor had looped her arm through hers. "Maybe he's given up on torturing you."

Julia had shot her a look. "Not likely."

The feeling like she was holding her breath lingered over the next weeks, and she was careful to keep a watchful eye if she did walk through town on her own, always wary of Volz lurking, waiting for his next chance to harass her.

Now, though, it was two days to Christmas, and Julia—tired of being vigilant with nothing to show for it—exhaled at the idea of a holiday party. Many residents gathered annually at the Davies' bakery for what Ralph called a, "Jubilee of merriment, meat pies, and mistletoe." She'd rolled her eyes at the overly sentimental alliteration but had to admit she was excited. Besides, the invitation bridged the remaining icy gap between the two of them. She was pleasantly surprised when he'd encouraged her to bring Eleanor and Peter.

Julia said see you soon to Rose and Henry, then went to pick up the Perrys. Snow fell lightly, the air cold but not biting. It was a lovely gray winter's day.

"Hi," Eleanor said, pulling open the door. Her long dark coat was open to reveal a sapphire blue dress Julia didn't recognize.

"Wow."

Eleanor smiled. "You like it? Sue got it for me for Christmas. She sent my measurements to Denver for it and everything."

Did Julia like it? She traced the line of the long skirt up to Eleanor's waist where a black sash was tied for a belt, accentuating her figure. The neckline was lower than Julia had seen her wear, revealing the smattering of freckles above her chest. Her hair was pulled back into a low knot, but a few curly strands framed her face. Julia loved everything about this dress.

Peter waved and scampered past to get his shoes. Julia stepped forward to kiss Eleanor, saying, "You look amazing." The blush in Eleanor's cheeks still made her chest warm.

"Let's go," Peter said, bounding out between them. With Julia around so often, she knew he suspected something between them, but Eleanor explained he was too young to put any name to it. "He knows I'm happy," she had told Julia one night to quell the fears she had. "And he's happy, too."

Presently, Peter's hair was slick with oil, and his jacket looked new. Another gift from Sue, she presumed. As they walked into town, Julia listened as Eleanor told her all about Sue's presents that had appeared by car last Tuesday with a note attached.

"Her reconciliation effort," Eleanor said, "after everything."

"That's sweet." Julia felt a twinge of guilt at not having a gift prepared. She'd spotted a yo-yo for Peter, which she'd bought and had ready at her house, but no matter how many storefronts she'd browsed or shops she'd perused, nothing had seemed right for Eleanor. After their conversation about the gold last month, a gesture of some kind seemed paramount to ease Eleanor's mind. They hadn't spoken about it since, and Julia could only hope Eleanor knew she could be trusted. It was what she wanted more than anything. But finding something for Eleanor ended up being impossible.

What do you get the woman you're falling in love with? The woman who makes you feel like you are capable of anything, except, of course, picking a gift.

Not that they'd agreed upon getting one another gifts for Christmas. Eleanor had voiced her preference for Julia's company over anything else. "I just want to be with you," she'd said, her voice sleepy as she'd nuzzled into Julia last night. Julia knew she meant it but hoped some idea would come to her before Christmas day rolled around.

Downtown looked like a greeting card in the fading afternoon light. Streetlamps and storefronts were adorned with wreaths. Red ribbons dressed windows where candles shone through frosted glass. Even Julia—not one to partake in the sentimental side of holidays—had to admit it looked magical.

"Ralph says about a quarter of the residents show up for this party each year," she explained as the bakery came into view. Its blue-trimmed awning was snow-covered, warm light emitting from inside.

"That's exciting," Eleanor said, her gaze on Peter, who skipped several paces ahead of them along the damp sidewalk. "When I went years ago, it was a more intimate gathering. More like the Davies' close friends."

"Suppose a lot of people leave to visit family."

Eleanor nodded. "Others want a quiet holiday with loved ones." She squeezed Julia's hand as they reached the door. Julia's body hummed as she opened it for them. To her dismay, she caught sight of Volz across the street. He spoke with the restaurant owner outside. She ducked into the bakery before he could see her.

Peter immediately found Stuart from school, and the two boys hurried off to the back where a game of marbles was already underway. The bakery smells were heavenly: cinnamon, sugar, and mulled cider swimming in the air. People were packed into tight groups between the counter at the back and a skinny Christmas tree in the front right corner. It was trimmed with candy canes and tinsel.

"May I take your coats?" Ralph asked as he appeared through the crowd.

"Thanks," Julia said, taking Eleanor's and passing theirs over. "You clean up nice."

Ralph was rosy-cheeked as he touched the red bow tie atop the clean white shirt he wore with black trousers. "Thanks. Care for something to drink?"

"Is that wine?" Eleanor asked, pointing to a side table lined with fine glasses next to a crystal bowl.

"Mulled wine," he said. "I'll fetch two glasses."

When he left, Julia moved closer. "Mrs. Perry, I haven't known you to indulge."

Eleanor kept her gaze scanning the room as she grinned and said, "I'm glad to be able to surprise you."

Ralph returned, and they all toasted. "To friends," he said.

"To friends," Eleanor agreed, watching Julia as she took a long drink.

The evening was turning out more pleasant than Eleanor could have expected. Her mind felt lighter than it had been in a long time. The wine, she imagined, had something to do with that, but it was also the way Julia looked at her. It was the way the air vibrated when they were close and even when they weren't. Eleanor felt constantly attuned to Julia's presence. It was like a crystal sinew had strung itself between them. A thread, not unlike the shining beads of water between the edifices in winter's throes, connected them. Each day and night spent together deepened their bond. She pondered that thread with each kiss they shared and in quiet moments alone. She considered it as she counted the gold accumulated in her perfume bottle, gold that could be a way to a better life for her and Peter. Would Julia want to be a part of that, too?

Eleanor had seen the earnestness with which Julia promised to keep that secret between them. She placed that confidence in

Julia's hands, reminding herself to keep her mind and heart open to what had become the most honest relationship she'd ever had.

She kept her eye on Peter throughout the evening, but he remained glued to the other children. He ran up to her with several of them, springing for the door, exclaiming, "Snowball fight!" as he dashed by.

She reached out, an excuse at the ready for him to stay inside, but the pure elation on his face made her think better of it. She waved as he followed the others outside. After all, she reminded herself, it had been weeks since his last asthma attack. Not to mention, Dr. Wicker was in attendance.

Henry found her in the crowd as she munched on a cake. "Jell-O?" he asked, presenting a plate.

"Oh, I shouldn't even be eating this." She held up the small tea cake. "I'm full after that dinner Mrs. Davies prepared." She looked at the fruit cup, then frowned and reached out. "What happened here?"

"Rose left it too long in the icebox, bless her." He used a knuckle to knock on the green Jell-O square. "More of a decorative piece, I'm afraid." They laughed, and Henry seemed to hesitate before saying, "Your boy nearly pulled one over on me last week." Eleanor turned, taking a sip of wine. "You recall how he spent the day with me and Rose on Wednesday? He was with me in the office. I'd told him to wait for an hour, as I had to meet some of the men in the mountain to investigate a new gold vein. There we were, standing a good quarter mile into the mine, when a clatter gave us all a good fright. Young Peter had tripped on a discarded pan and scared the lot of us. He'd followed me right inside."

Eleanor's chest tightened. "Oh, Henry," she said, mortified and ashamed. "I'm so sorry."

"I'm sorry," he said, shaking his head. "Peter is strong-willed and knows what he wants." His face softened, lines crinkling around his eyes. "This was my first real taste of that stubbornness."

Eleanor's stomach turned as she searched the room for Peter, then remembered he'd gone outside. The instinct to find him, take him home, and send him to bed overran her mind. He knew better than to go into the mine. A good reprimanding was in order, she thought, shaken. She had to ask Henry to repeat himself, she was so worked up.

"That being said, I don't think he should be barred from the office."

Eleanor gripped her wineglass to rein in her focus. "Henry."

"Hear me out," he said gently. "What about fewer visits, at least for now? Obviously with winter, we won't be in for a couple weeks. But he gets only one trip to the office with me in January. Two in February if that goes well. We won't be back in the mountains until March. What do you say? I've never met anyone with such an insatiable appetite to be part of the mill. I'd hate to deny him that completely."

At first, Eleanor was taken aback by his proposition. Then, she saw the rationale of it. It was still a punishment for his reckless behavior, but it had an end in sight with standards to meet. She smiled, tension easing between her shoulders. "I like that."

"Good. And mind you, I gave him quite the talking to after that scare. He needs to understand the dangers as much as the wonders that accompany that line of work."

Exhaling, she said, "Thank you. I'll speak to him again, too. He can't seem to get the mill out of his head."

Henry raised his glass to hers and cleared his throat. When he rubbed a hand over his neck, looking unusually nervous, she said, "Is there something else?"

"Well, I've been meaning to thank you."

"Thank me? Whatever for?" she asked, catching sight of Julia near the counter having an animated conversation with Ralph.

"For letting us look after Peter some days." He looked down, his voice gruff. "Rose and me…it means a lot to us. She always wanted a family, and Peter is like a son to her. To us." When he looked up, his eyes shone.

It was only last week Eleanor had begun to stitch the pieces together regarding Julia's reason for moving to Colorado. A late-night confession from Julia had mentioned an accident involving Rose. That combined with the way the Barrows were with Peter led Eleanor to the heartbreaking conclusion of what might have happened. Not knowing what to say and surprised at the emotion he displayed, she pulled him into a hug. "You're a good man, Henry Barrow. And Rose is wonderful."

He swiped at his eyes when he stepped back. "Anyway, Merry Christmas, Eleanor. I'm glad to know you." He followed her gaze to Julia. "We all are."

Everyone milled about for the next hour. It was dusk when someone near the back called, "Pick your sides! It's snowball fight time!" The crowds dispersed as an excited murmur ran down the room. Eleanor looked around, confused since the kids were already outside doing just that.

"Snowball fight?" she asked as she was ushered forward by the crowd.

Ralph looked as giddy as a schoolboy. "Yep, it's tradition! Since last year, anyway." He pushed through several people to get outside.

Someone looped their arm through hers in the throng, and she found Rose next to her. "Looks like it's you and me against those hooligans." She grinned and nodded toward Julia and Henry, who dashed across the street. Eleanor was certain she wasn't the only one feeling like she was a kid again. A waist-high barrier was already being constructed on both sides of the road by each team. People in the restaurant across the street stood to watch the goings-on from inside.

Eleanor laughed and found a spot with Rose near Ralph, who seemed to know what he was doing as he helped his sisters amass their snowball arsenal. Their mittened hands shaped the snow like dough. "I haven't done this in years," she said, the cool air hitting her cheeks as she crouched to help.

Rose retied the cowl she wore, a mock serious expression on her face as she said, "Come on, Eleanor, let's show those two what we're made of."

The next half hour was a blur of snowballs, peals of laughter, and jovial spars tossed back and forth across the makeshift battlefield. Peter had run past, wide-eyed as Eleanor hurled a snowball that nearly took out little Stuart. The children took cover inside, taking advantage of a generous Mrs. Davies eager to feed them leftovers.

"We need more ammo," Ralph called, pulling more snow into a pile.

Rose stood, and her well-packed snowball hit Henry in the back when he wasn't looking. "Bull's-eye," she called, victorious.

"Lucky shot," Julia replied, her bright eyes and wild hair a flash as she ran by behind their barrier.

Eleanor leaned close to Rose. "She's playing safe."

Rose grinned and handed her a snowball. "I bet you can draw her out."

Eleanor agreed. Assessing the incoming barrage, she scurried down the line of her team, then stepped out onto the road. Henry threw one, but she side-stepped, and it just missed her shoulder. Moving in on Julia, Eleanor was halfway across the street when she pulled back her arm, ready. "You can't hide from me, Holte."

Julia ducked low again, though, and Eleanor lost sight of her. She tried to track her movements, dodging more snowballs as she did. She was only a few yards from the barrier when Julia sprang out, a wild smile on her face as she let a snowball go. Eleanor yelped and threw hers as she was hit in the stomach. She laughed and doubled over right after hers hit its target. The snowball exploded against Julia's shoulder as she fell into a foot of snow.

Still laughing, Eleanor straightened to brush the powder off her coat. She had hardly done so when Julia grabbed her and tugged her down onto the blanket of snow in the middle of the street. Snowballs flew overhead. "That's cheating, Miss Holte," she cried out, only half fighting against Julia. She found a fistful of snow and brought it down on Julia's arm.

Julia knelt over her. "I thought all was fair in love and snowball wars." Snow glistened in her hair and on her face. Eleanor bit her lip to keep herself from pulling Julia on top of her. Still resisting that growing urge, she found more snow, and shoved it at Julia, who cried out and dove away. Eleanor scrambled back toward her side of the street, but the snow was slick, and she slipped onto her stomach.

"Incoming!" It was Henry's voice that echoed as an onslaught of snowballs rained down. Eleanor screamed and laughed and wondered if she'd ever felt like this, so carefree and joyful, like she was living a life she'd always dreamed about with friends and community and someone she was falling utterly in love with.

More snow rained down as she rolled onto her back, still dizzy with laughter as she shielded her face. She peeked through her arms at a flurry of movement as Julia reappeared, leaning over her to take the brunt of the snowballs that fell on them.

"Whose side are you on, Jules?" Henry called out.

Julia leaned down, her hair framing her face. She reached out, her hand warm against Eleanor's cheek. She wasn't sure if it was possible but wondered if a person could combust from happiness. Eleanor certainly felt as if she might. Her chest was warm and full, and utter bliss coursed through her as Julia smiled down at her.

A figure appeared in the corner of her vision, tearing Julia away by the collar and taking Eleanor's joy with her.

"Get off her," Volz growled, dragging Julia back and throwing her into the packed snow.

Eleanor scrambled to her feet. "She didn't do anything wrong."

Volz was looking at Julia like she was some sort of grotesque demon. "Not how it looked to me, Mrs. Perry."

Julia moved to kneel, but Volz was on her in a flash, shoving her to stay down. The snowballs halted, and everyone's laughter followed suit as both sides stopped to watch. Eleanor moved to help Julia up.

"I wouldn't do that if I were you," he said, moving to stand between them. "Wouldn't want to tarnish what's left of that good name your husband gave you."

Eleanor hesitated, and she hated herself for it. Rage shook her, and she took a trembling breath to gather her thoughts. She felt like she'd missed a step on the stairs or like someone had wrenched her from a dream. Everything had been so good. Why did Volz have to take that away? Meeting his gaze, she said, "Don't touch her again, Sheriff."

He raised a brow. "That a threat, Mrs. Perry?"

She swallowed, then flinched as someone stood behind her, but it was only Henry. "I'd be careful, Sheriff Volz," he said.

Volz looked incredulous, a sneer beneath his flared nostrils. "You." He stepped closer, pointing, "You're the one who brought this vermin here in the first place." He looked Henry up and down. "You oughta be strung up with her."

Eleanor managed to move aside to help Julia stand. She wrapped an arm around her and pulled her close. Henry's gaze was hard and dark as Rose joined him, snow still on her shoulders. Her face was stoic as they stood next to Eleanor. Ralph joined next, looming a head above them all.

Finally, Volz stepped back, but the look of disgust he wore deepened. Turning to the others on the street, he spoke loudly, pointing at Julia. "You all saw that. You all saw what she is."

Eleanor inhaled but felt Julia hold tighter to her. A few people looked around, but no one said anything. Rose stepped closer as Ralph said, "Julia is a member of this community, Sheriff. But you never did care about protecting the people of this town, did you?" Volz looked wild at the accusation, his face red, but Ralph continued. "All you cared about was pocketing funds from Thrasher's and riding your high horse around like you own the place."

Volz's lip twitched, but his silence was admission enough.

"Well, you don't own Idaho Springs or its people." Ralph pulled himself up to his full height. "And I'm gonna see to it you don't get to run things anymore."

Eleanor was sure her look of surprise matched those of the onlookers. Julia looked somewhere between confused and shocked as Ralph said, "You won't be running unopposed next year."

Volz's voice betrayed his fear when he asked, "What do you mean?"

"I mean," Ralph said, stepping closer to lean over him, "you better get your debate speech ready because I'm coming for your job."

The small crowd who had gathered to listen cheered, while a few hurried into the restaurant and bakery to spread the news. Volz only glared, then spat at their feet before he turned to leave.

Through the hubbub of people encouraging Ralph, others gossiping about what this meant, and a couple questions of, "Is the snowball fight over?" Eleanor could hardly believe the news herself.

"Ralph," Julia said as he shook hands with the local fish market owner, "are you serious about this?"

He brushed back his hair, a sheen of snow giving him a shining, confident air. He smiled. "I am, Jules. Been thinkin' about it for some time. Never did like him much."

Julia laughed and hugged him as Eleanor looked on. Several people returned to the snowball shenanigans while others went inside. Rose gave her arm a squeeze before taking Julia's arm. Leaning back, Eleanor closed her eyes. Fresh snowflakes kissed her cheeks as new snow fell around them in a blanket of fresh white.

CHAPTER THIRTY-SEVEN

For her first winter away from home, Julia was surprised at how little she missed the ranch.

"Momma and Daddy sent you this," Rose said Christmas morning, handing her a small, paper-wrapped parcel. "They sent a nice note, too."

Julia held up the blue handkerchief. Her initials were embroidered in one corner, the stitching her mother's handiwork.

"That's lovely, Jules," Rose said, a handmade sweater on her lap. "Henry got one in red."

"It'll be a nice change from all the black he wears."

Rose laughed as Henry called from the stairs, "I heard that."

That evening, Rose hosted Eleanor and Peter for dinner, and Julia had walked them home afterward.

Peter had spent most of the day chasing after the new yo-yo he'd gotten that morning. "It keeps slipping off my finger," he said, scampering after it across the living room. Julia showed Peter how to wrap the yo-yo around his index finger and the proper release motion and was glad when he wandered upstairs to practice so she could sit with Eleanor.

"I'm sorry I don't have anything for you." She never had settled on the right gift for Eleanor.

She had been watching the fire, a small smile on her face. "Julia, I told you, I don't need anything." She met her gaze. "We agreed, no gifts."

Nodding, Julia watched her a moment, waiting for the flicker of disappointment in her eyes, but it never came. She wanted to give Eleanor the world, and insecurity began to rear its head. Don't get ahead of yourself, she thought. Things were going well. *Don't push it.*

❖

One cold winter's night in mid-January, they lay in bed together at Eleanor's house. The world was quiet save for the crackling of the fire.

"What do you want to do with the gold you've collected?" Julia asked carefully, splayed on her back with Eleanor's head on her shoulder.

Eleanor traced circles on her abdomen. "A storefront would be nice. 'Perry's Laundering Service.' A place in town with space and materials for me to tackle more uniforms at once."

"I can see that," Julia said, smiling and leaning to kiss Eleanor's head. Any lingering tension around the topic dissipated. It was quiet a time, and Julia imagined Eleanor was thinking the same thing when it came to such a fantasy.

"Perhaps one day, we won't need a man's approval for things like business loans."

"That'll be the day."

Eleanor leaned back to meet her gaze. "I bet it'll happen. One day."

Julia kissed her, loving her optimism. "Until then?" she asked gently.

Sighing and nuzzling into Julia's neck, Eleanor said, "I could add to the house. Would be nice to have a room dedicated to laundry. Especially when the weather turns cold."

Nodding, Julia's mind began to turn. "Now that sounds like a good plan. You know," she said, pulling Eleanor closer, "I'm pretty good with my hands when it comes to things like that."

Eleanor kissed her neck, smiling against her skin. "Is that so, Miss Holte?"

Julia found her lips, kissing her as Eleanor pushed against her. Their kiss deepened, and Julia was struck by how tender each touch was between them, how her attraction danced side by side with overwhelming love. Julia wanted all of Eleanor's dreams to come true. She wanted her to be happy. No, she realized, moving against Eleanor, she wanted to be the cause of her happiness. As the night marched on around them, their soft cries confessions against the cool air, Julia couldn't keep those sentiments to herself anymore.

While her breath calmed and Eleanor held her, Julia waited until the rapid beating of her heart slowed. Running a hand through Eleanor's hair, she met her gaze. "I love you," she said, a distant spike of fear rising in her chest after laying such a truth bare.

Eleanor's eyes, remnants of desire and affection mingling amidst the brown, shone with the response Julia had dreamed about. She grabbed her face, pulling her into a kiss. "I love you, too."

CHAPTER THIRTY-EIGHT

It was the last week of February, and the first stretch of days without consistent snowfall was upon them. "Does this mean it's done?" Julia asked, standing in the kitchen and peering out the back door. Peter played with his car on the living room rug.

"Not yet," Eleanor said, flipping an egg while strips of bacon sizzled in a separate skillet. "It could snow through the end of March."

Julia turned wearing a look of disbelief. "March? That's six months of winter."

Eleanor chuckled. "Why do you think we appreciate summer so much around here?" She counted out their plates, realizing it had been some time since she'd felt the need to do so. She hadn't even counted the eggs before starting breakfast. Eleanor smiled, knowing the reason for her calm mind was wearing one of her sweaters at the kitchen table.

"Looks like more walks to school in the snow," Julia called to Peter.

He drove the car over to the kitchen table where Eleanor brought his breakfast plate. "I don't mind," he said. "Henry carries me on his shoulders when he walks me."

Eleanor kissed the top of his head. "You're far too big to make poor Henry do that."

"He said he wants to," Peter replied, chomping on a bacon strip.

Eleanor met Julia's gaze. She shrugged. "I think they spoil you, Peter. How many cookies did you eat with Rose last week?"

He pushed his open hand forward. "Five. They were lumpy but good."

They both laughed. "I am glad you like spending nights there," Eleanor said.

Julia, joining them at the table, tossed her a wink. "Me too."

"They let me use your room," Peter said to Julia. "I like your boots."

"Thank you kindly," Julia replied. "Maybe we'll get you a pair of cowboy boots when you're older."

His eyes grew big. "Really?"

"We'll see how the school year finishes," Julia said, pointing her fork.

Peter harrumphed but dug into his food. Eleanor set her napkin across her lap, warmth kindling over her limbs as the three of them did what they'd done so often of late and enjoyed a meal together. But it was more than that. Everything about this—the three of them together, talking about school, work, and life—felt like something bigger. Something Eleanor had always been destined for. Was this what had been lurking at the edges of her mind in those shadows, a life full of love and security? Had she only been too afraid to let that in?

The first week of March, Eleanor was finishing up her personal laundry, mentally preparing for the mill to reopen soon, when there was a knock at the door. She shook out her hands, flexing her fingers that were tired from wringing out clothing for the last hour. She was surprised to find Sue on her front porch.

"Hi," she said, feeling a little awkward. It had been a long time since they'd talked. They were still friends, weren't they? Eleanor realized she wasn't sure. Sue had been generous in sending her Christmas gifts, but they hadn't seen each other since before the holidays, and Eleanor had spent those with the Barrows. Trepidation tickled her spine. She asked an obvious question to stall, "You and Isaac are back from your travels?"

Melted snow sat in slushy puddles on the drive behind Sue. She wore a lovely fur coat and a winter hat with earmuffs and matching mittens. Eleanor smiled to see the boots she'd given her. "Just got in yesterday," Sue said, stomping snow off them. "First time visiting Isaac's brother in Oregon. Beautiful place, Oregon." Sue cut herself off, though it seemed like she wanted to share more. Her recounting of their trips typically took an entire afternoon.

Eleanor bit her lip. It felt like a dark cloud still hung over them despite Sue's efforts at natural conversation. Plus, she was still upset, wasn't she? Time had cooled her head since their spat about Julia. Besides, that seemed so far away now. It also seemed a little silly after everything that had happened when she had been sick. Sue had been there for her through it all. Obviously, Sue still cared about her.

Plus, she was here now and had extended an olive branch of sorts with all those Christmas gifts. But still…

Ugh, how terribly awkward. "I'm about to hang some clothes," she said. "It's just me here right now." Sue seemed surprised to hear that, so she explained, "Julia and Peter are with the Barrows. They're in town to do some shopping. Would you like to come in?"

"I could go for a cup of tea if you have it." Inside, Sue unbuttoned her coat and stood near the table while Eleanor put on a kettle. She headed toward the back door, and Sue followed. "How were your holidays?"

Outside, Eleanor shook out one of Julia's shirts and pinned it to the line. The air was crisp, but the sun was out. Even a few birds chirped near the river. Spring was around the corner. "Lovely, actually." She replayed the last few months. Julia had been here often. She'd become a part of her life. Like a family.

"Good, good," Sue said. "We got a telegram from Mrs. Davies when our train stopped in Utah. You recall her late husband and Isaac were old friends. Well, you can imagine my surprise when she shared that her boy Ralph will be running for town sheriff."

Eleanor's jaw tightened, recalling Sheriff Volz's conduct at the holiday party. "It's about time."

"Should be an interesting debate. I'm helping Isaac with the planning. The town hall will host it in the coming months."

Eleanor hung the rest of the clothes. Sue stepped closer. There was still an air of uncertainty between them. How to break through this awful unease?

After fiddling with the same shirt sleeve for over a minute, Sue finally said, "There was this radio program I listened to over the holidays, on Station Nineteen. Its subject matter was darker than *A Guiding Light*, you remember that one? But not as gritty as *The Shadow*." Eleanor only eyed her over the clothesline. "Anyway, it featured these two friends, see. Detectives. They'd been chums for years at the start. But they have a terrible row. Raised voices, slammed doors, the whole shebang. It was terribly dramatic," she explained, her voice rising with her enthusiasm. "Well, it was dreadful to hear it all play out." Her gaze fell, her voice dipping with it. "Heart-wrenching, truly, for such good friends to come to blows like that."

The breeze picked up as Eleanor hung one of Peter's sweaters. "I imagine they had their reasons."

Sue wrung her hands, avoiding Eleanor's gaze. "They did." When Eleanor reached for a pin, Sue handed her one. Then, she held Peter's sleeve up on the line. "What I'm getting at, E, is that two good friends might have it out now and then, but it doesn't mean they turn their backs on each other forever."

Eleanor eyed her, the resolve she'd had when Sue first arrived withering. Sue, who'd stood watch over her when she'd needed her most. Her first true friend in this town, whose shoulder she'd leaned on when Louis left. Her best friend who'd taken care of her with Julia when she had been deathly sick. Taking a long breath, she decided Sue was right. How could they abandon years of friendship? After all, Sue was here, trying, wasn't she? "I wonder if it's a good thing for friends to have it out from time to time," she eventually said, adding the last article to the line.

Sue's gaze was bright but cut away, guilt creeping across her face. "Sometimes, good friends can be very wrong about certain things. I misjudged Miss Holte."

Eleanor gave her a look. "And the Barrows?"

"And the Barrows." She rested a hand on Eleanor's. "I'm sorry, E. I should have said it a long time ago."

The breeze blew past, taking the tension between them with it. "I'm sorry, too, about what I said to you before."

A relieved smile lit up Sue's face. She swatted the air as if to move these apologies along. "Oh, Eleanor. You were right to say it. I got carried away, and I must admit that I was afraid." She looked down. "I think I was a little jealous, too. You spent all that time with Miss Holte. Julia," she corrected.

"I understand," Eleanor said. "I didn't expect everything to happen the way it did. I didn't expect...her."

Sue's gaze was sincere when she asked, "She makes you happy?"

Eleanor smiled, warmth filling her. "She does."

Nodding, Sue couldn't seem to find her words, so she decided to pat Eleanor's hand, giving it a loving squeeze.

Eleanor laughed, relieved at the return of their easy conversation. "All is forgiven, Sue."

Sue stepped under the clothes, pulling Eleanor into a firm hug. "I love you, you know that?" Holding Eleanor at arm's length, eyes teary, she said, "Let's never spend the holidays apart again."

Eleanor laughed, swiping at her own tears. "Agreed." The kettle whistled inside. "Come on," she said, leading Sue. "I want to hear all about Oregon."

CHAPTER THIRTY-NINE

Peter tugged her sleeve. "Julia, can we go outside? It's hot in here."

"Hot? The window's open." She looked up from her desk. Peter looked terribly bored. It was Friday, and Eleanor had agreed to him skipping school since she had a lot of laundry to get through, and the office kept him out of the house longer. But Julia was behind on work herself and searched for something to keep him busy. "I know, why don't you help Mr. Weldon with a few things? You can restock the coffee."

He looked unimpressed. "That's boring." He tossed his car in the air and caught it. "Where's Henry?"

"A meeting, I think." She said, turning her attention back to her papers. "He should be done soon."

Peter sighed, then scurried across the office. Julia watched him for a moment and finished checking the time logs. Most of the men were used to Peter being around. Any grumblings had been shut down by Henry. For the most part, Peter kept out of the way and was quite helpful a lot of the time. He would stack papers, count pencils, go hunting for things a clerk needed. He seemed to like feeling useful with the men in the office, especially when it came to Henry.

On cue, Henry appeared through the back door, and Peter ran up to him. "Easy there," Henry said, meeting him in a hug. "Are you minding yourself with Julia?"

Peter nodded. "Can we go see what they're doing?" He pointed toward the office door left open to let the warm breeze in. A group of boys—most of Peter's age—were hopping into the back of a wagon before it started away.

Henry laughed, but Julia could hear the nerves in it. "Not today, Peter. They have a very special job that requires training."

"Not even to watch?" Henry gave him a look. "Fine," Peter said, throwing his head back and trudging over to Julia's desk.

As Peter drove his car around the floor next to her chair, Julia went over to the stove to pour another mug. Passing one to Henry, she asked how his meeting went.

"Oh, fine. Same old stuff. A few men have come down with an illness, so we're working to get their stations covered. Nothing out of the ordinary."

Julia sipped her coffee, readjusting the handkerchief around her neck. "Illness like a cold?"

"No," he said, looking at his mug. "Headaches, trembling hands, that sort of thing."

Julia had heard those symptoms before. Eleanor had told her about Louis and what had happened to him. "I wouldn't ignore that, Henry," she said. "That sort of thing keeps happening, doesn't it?"

He sighed. "Yes, often."

"I think it's worth looking into more. I know Eleanor has spoken to Mr. Weldon about it. Those men work hard and don't deserve to succumb to whatever that is." Henry replied, but she didn't hear it. Worry drowned out his words when she looked back at her desk. "Peter?" She glanced around but couldn't find him.

Henry frowned. "He was just here." They exchanged looks, then moved through the office. "Did anyone see where Peter went?" All the men looked up from their respective tasks, shaking their heads.

Julia searched under her desk, in the corners of the office. Panic prickled at the back of her neck as she remembered he'd wanted to go outside. She tore out the front door, turning, searching for him. "Peter?" she called, keeping her voice light. "Come on, Peter. Where are you?"

A pit dug into her stomach at the sight of his toy car near where the wagon cart had been, the one carrying the group of children up the mountain. "Henry," she said as he jogged after her outside, "what was that group doing, the one who was here?"

His face paled, and she wasn't sure if there was anything more alarming than the look in his eyes. "They're today's powder monkeys."

Julia's heart sank. She felt sick but swallowed the bile in her throat. "Where are they headed?"

He looked ready to faint. "Copper Bend, two miles east." Seeming to gather himself, he checked his pocket watch. "Detonation scheduled for one o'clock." She grabbed it from him to check the time.

"That's in fifteen minutes."

Henry's look said it all, but Julia refused to accept the impending doom writhing in her stomach. He ran inside, hollering orders for a telegraph to be sent up to the station at Copper's Bend to halt detonation. Julia knew that even if they did get a message up there, it would likely be ignored. Progress into the mine was more important than anything. Children's lives were expendable. For a moment, she felt like she had all those months ago when Peter had stood before her in the Barrows' backyard, eyes wide in fear as his breathing constricted. She hadn't known what to do then. What could she do now? What power did she possibly possess to help him?

Another horse-drawn wagon pulled around the drive. Piles of potato sacks labeled with various minerals sat in the wagon bed.

Julia ran over to it. "I need your horse."

The driver, an old man with gray stubble on his chin, lifted his hat to better see her. "What are you on about, girl?"

"I need your horse," she said again, already unfastening the animal from the wagon. The horse whinnied in greeting, its tail flicking as she worked quickly.

The old man stood. "I reckon you best leave my horses be, young lady."

"I'm sorry, sir, it's an emergency." She didn't stop, easing the horse forward after releasing the tug buckle. Its companion neighed in protest. "The rein, sir," she said, one hand out.

The old man looked utterly bewildered. "I will do no such thing. This transport is for official mill business."

"This is official mill business," Henry called, breathless at her side. The old man straightened at the sight of him.

"Mr. Barrow."

"I'll explain everything," he said, "but hand over the reins, please."

He did so. Julia took them and flew onto the back of the horse. She met Henry's gaze for a moment. "You'll tell Eleanor?" she asked. He nodded, fear and worry heavy on his face. "Yah," she cried, kicking the horse's flanks. It neighed and reared, but she held tight, taking control. Years of bareback riding at the ranch flew back to her. They took off, racing past the mill and the tunnel that led into the depths of the mountain. Rough roads and trails snaked like slender riverbeds through the slopes. She ran through the maps in her mind, the ones laying out the subsequent mineshafts surrounding Idaho Springs.

The horse's hooves thundered over the earth, kicking up melting snow and mud as the remnants of winter held its fading grip over the land. She evened out her breathing, surprised at how quickly she fell back into the rhythm of riding. It was just like at the ranch, like the wind itself was encouraging her on. She turned east and urged the horse up a steep incline. They stumbled on the loose rock with just under a mile to go.

"Come on," she said, trying not to imagine the terrible look on Eleanor's face if she was too late, the horror that was just around the corner if things went wrong. And they very well could. Powder monkeys were quick, but Peter had no idea what he was doing.

The mountain opened as the gravel path narrowed to the barren earth. The one-room fort-style outpost building came into view. She pulled up in front of it. A man in a flat cap and overalls stepped out of the doorway.

"Powder monkeys," she said. "Where are they?"

He pointed toward the nearest peak. "Settin' sticks on the other side." She urged her horse on again as he yelled, "I wouldn't do that if I was you! 'Bout to blow."

She ignored him, barreling on, urging the horse to go faster. She was nearly around the peak when the explosion happened.

Her horse neighed and reared. "Whoa," she said, holding tight and adjusting her weight before he tipped too far back. She fought to settle him as the earth shook. Her ears reverberated, and she searched the dirt-filled sky as rock shot up like fireworks before arcing sadly back down.

"Come on," she said, pushing the horse through the detritus. Galloping around the side of the peak, she heard voices.

"Nice one, boys," a voice called. Through the settling dust, she saw the figure of a man, also in overalls. He beckoned for the group of boys who gathered under his arms and away from the blast radius as more debris rained down. She brought her handkerchief above her nose to keep out the choking dust and called, "Peter Perry, where is he?"

The boys ran past, scrambling back down the slope. A few more emerged from the side of the mountain, but none of them were Peter.

"Perry?" he asked. "Don't recognize that name."

"He wasn't supposed to be here. Red hair."

The man's eyes flickered with recognition. "I saw him," he pointed back toward the thick cloud of dirt as the earth finally stopped its shaking. "With Stuart Weekly."

Julia rode closer to the slope. The dust was settling, and the aftermath of the blast revealed itself. The scar on the side of the mountain looked like a fresh wound; smoldering black streaks etched into the rock in a starburst pattern, creeping out from its dark center where the dynamite had been laid. Small shouts caught her ear.

"Peter?"

"Over here!"

She rode closer. Clusters of boulders lay along the sides of the path, freshly sunk into the earth.

"We're here!"

She followed Stuart's shout. He waved her over. Peter lay on the ground next to him.

"Oh God." She dismounted, keeping the end of the reins in hand as she knelt.

Both boys were covered in dust from head to toe. Stuart had dark marks on his arms and several cuts on his exposed knees. Peter's eyes were closed, his vibrant hair dull with dust and brown dirt. "His ear," Stuart said, pointing.

Blood trickled out of it. She pulled her handkerchief off, using it to wipe up the line that ran down to his neck. "Peter," she said, then again louder. "Wake up, Peter."

Nothing. She looked around the rock-littered ground, the sky slowly opening again, and Stuart's serious face. Think, Julia, she reminded herself. Keep moving forward. Grabbing Peter's shoulders, she shook him gently. "Hey, Peter, wake up." She thought she heard him groan, but that could have been wishful thinking as he remained frighteningly limp.

"Where were you when the blast happened?" she asked Stuart.

"He came with me to place the sticks over there." He pointed toward the blast point. "Told him, once it's lit, we have to run. We made it to those rocks when the dynamite went off." His voice dropped as if he was afraid Peter would hear. "He's not as fast as me."

Julia tried to piece it all together. Peter had probably been several steps behind Stuart. He might have been thrown forward by the force of the blast. She tried to imagine the possibilities, recalling times she'd seen oil rigs catch fire. She'd even heard one explode once. Men caught in its blast lost limbs, ears, and were tossed like ragdolls in a blaze. This didn't seem as intense but could still do damage, especially to a young body.

This time, Peter did groan. He turned his head, his eyes fluttering.

"Peter," she said. Stuart helped him sit up. Peter winced and grabbed his ear. "You're okay," she said.

He blinked up at her when she said it again. "What?"

"I said, you're okay. Can you walk?"

His face fell, the hand over his ear tapping anxiously. "I can't…I can't hear you."

She exhaled, smiling. "But you can talk." She scooped him up and helped him stand. His legs were shaky, but he managed to lean against her. Relief flooded her body, and she had to take a breath to keep herself from stumbling.

"I'll go tell Mr. Hanson we're okay," Stuart said matter-of-factly before hurrying off, as if everything they'd just done was as run-of-the-mill as scrubbing their faces before bed. She wished she could level a glare at the mill. So many things about this were wrong.

"Come on," she said, helping Peter onto the horse, then hopping up behind him. "I've got you. Let's go home."

CHAPTER FORTY

E leanor had just come inside from hanging more clothes on the line when someone called from the front drive. She recognized Rose's voice, but the frantic tone gave her a moment's pause when she met her at the door. "Rose, what is it?"

She took a harried breath, her eyes wide and her hair frizzing out around her face. "Peter," she said, leaning to rest a hand on her hip. She pointed toward the other side of town. "The mill."

Eleanor didn't need her to say anything else. She didn't even bother to grab her jacket and was glad she already had her boots on. "Let's go," she said, running toward the main road with Rose. They were four blocks into town on Miner Street when someone lay on their car horn. Sue's face was framed in her blue Ford's driver-side window.

"E, what's happening?"

"Peter's in trouble. At the mill," she said, not slowing down as Sue continued alongside them.

"Oh, Lord," Sue said, pulling the car closer to the sidewalk. "Get in."

Eleanor looked at Rose, who shook her head. "I'm not leaving you alone in this. Come on."

They both scrambled into the front, sliding in next to Sue, who hit the horn again. The police officer on the corner whistled, but she stuck her head out the window and said, "Emergency,

Phillip. Let us through." His face fell, and he quickly halted traffic the other way. Sue blasted through the cross street. They rounded the curved road to Monarch Mill in minutes. All the while, Eleanor's heart thundered. Rose reached for her, and she was grateful for the comforting presence.

As they neared the office, Sue broke the tense silence. "Do you know what happened?"

When Eleanor didn't answer, Rose said, "Henry said Peter snuck off with the powder monkeys." She still clutched Eleanor's hand.

Sue met their gazes as she slowed the car to a stop, and the look she wore matched the agony Eleanor felt. Rose opened the passenger door. Eleanor climbed out after her as Henry ran out from the office.

"Eleanor," he said, waving.

"Please," she said, "what happened?"

He shook his head, looking from her to the others. "He went with a group to Copper's Bend. Powder monkeys were scheduled to lay dynamite for a new site. Detonation scheduled for one o'clock."

"One o'clock," Sue said, "that's right about—"

Despite the blast's distance, the ground still shook. They all reached out to steady themselves, and Eleanor cast her gaze to the mountains. "Oh my God," she said, knees buckling. Sue and Rose caught her, keeping her upright.

"Julia went after him," Henry was saying, though Eleanor could hardly register his words amidst the blaring white fear consuming her mind.

Sue pushed Eleanor toward Rose as the ground settled. "I'll see to the office and make sure my husband sent a message out." Henry said he did, to which Sue replied, but Eleanor was still lost in the haze, leaving their words garbled. *Peter.*

"Come on, Eleanor," Rose said, lifting her up. "We'll take you."

Somehow, she was back in Sue's car, but Sue wasn't driving. Henry was, and she sat between him and Rose. Rose, who kept whispering things like, "It'll be all right. It has to be all right. God, Henry, what about Julia?" Eleanor's mind spun as they trudged around the mountain, and she willed the wheels to turn faster.

Finally, a mile and a half up, the path narrowed. "We'll have to do the rest on foot," Henry said. "The outpost isn't far."

They got out, and Eleanor took off running. Up here, the sky still held remnants of dust and dirt. Slush and mud kicked up around her. Wind pulled at her skirt, her sleeves. The mountains passed in blurs of brown and gray until the small outpost appeared.

She stumbled at the sight of Julia on a horse. Relief flooded her, but a heavy dread followed when she saw Peter's limp body slumped in front of her.

Julia dismounted, careful to cradle him in her arms. Eleanor ran. "What happened?" she asked, kneeling opposite Julia as she laid Peter on the ground.

"He snuck off with Stuart. He…he was caught in the outskirts of the blast."

Eleanor looked from her to Peter, running her hands over him gingerly, checking for injuries and surprised at the lack of blood.

"I don't think he broke anything, somehow. But…" Julia gestured to his ear and gently tilted his head. Dark blood was drying in a thin line down the side of his face.

Peter groaned. "Mom." His voice was scratchy, and he coughed.

Eleanor leaned over him. "I'm here, my love. You're okay."

"He needs a doctor," Julia said.

Eleanor met her gaze, the look in it startlingly familiar. It was the look of a mother, someone who loved Peter as much as she did. Such a look shook Eleanor, and she could only nod.

Julia scooped him back up into her arms.

The next half hour was a blur. They made it down the mountain, meeting Sue, who seemed to have donned her councilwoman hat, barking orders at anyone in their way. She took her car back from Henry and Rose and drove Eleanor, Julia, and Peter to the physician's house in record time.

"Isaac called ahead and told them we're coming." She turned sharply onto the road and stayed with the car when they stopped.

Julia trotted inside the modest home, still carrying Peter. Eleanor was at her heels. Peter protested, small whines and cries coming now that the shock of the blast seemed to have worn off. Julia laid him down on Dr. Wicker's sofa.

"The doctor needs to make sure you're okay," Julia said, swiping the hair from his forehead the way Eleanor had done thousands of times. Eleanor would have wept at the tenderness of the gesture, but every part of her felt frayed. She couldn't unravel, though, not yet. Gathering herself, she knelt to hold Peter's hand when Dr. Wicker approached, wiping his beard like he'd just come from lunch.

"My, what do we have here?" He gave Eleanor a look that said he could take it from there.

She moved to stand near Julia in the parlor entryway. They didn't say anything as the doctor examined Peter. Eleanor felt like she was stuck in a sieve, every part of her being pushed through this terrible moment. Surely, all that would be left were pieces impossible to put back together. Her thumb found her forefinger as she started to count the roses on the wallpaper. *One, two, three.* She tried to ignore that dread and reminded herself to be strong. *Four, five, six.* She had to be brave for Peter. He needed her. He needed—

She jumped when Julia took her hand. Eleanor swiped at tears she hadn't realized were there. The reassurance in Julia's gaze loosened the fear that bound her. Her mind quieted. She wasn't alone. Not this time.

The examination done, Dr. Wicker cleared his throat and crossed the room to join them. Eleanor looked at Julia, then released her hand as he spoke. "Looks like a badly burst eardrum, most likely from the blast. I see it a lot."

Eleanor looked past him to Peter. "Is that...will he..."

"He'll heal in a month or two. Maybe longer. I recommend he keep that ear away from water in the meantime to avoid infection."

"So," she asked, wringing her hands, "his hearing…"

"Should come back, but he may experience things like headaches and dizzy spells in the meantime. He'll need ample rest for the next week." He looked between them. "No broken bones, just a few lumps from where he fell. He's one of the lucky ones."

Eleanor leapt forward to hug him. "Thank you," she said over his shoulder, "thank you."

After cleaning and dressing Peter's ear, they piled back into Sue's car. She dropped them off at home. "I'll come by tomorrow to see how you're doing," Sue said. "I've got to talk to my husband about this. No oversight at all, that's how these things happen. I've had enough."

Rose and Henry dropped off food at sundown, but Eleanor didn't have an appetite. She got Peter to bed. He seemed reluctant to look any of them in the eye. There would be time for a lecture, they both knew. Now was the time to rest.

As Eleanor descended the stairs, the fearsome grip the day had held on her relaxed. Exhaustion followed, sinking into her bones. She stumbled on the last step.

Julia, sitting at the kitchen table, ran to her. "Easy there." She caught Eleanor's waist, bracing her until she could steady herself.

Finding Julia's shoulders, Eleanor swallowed. Everything seemed to be happening at once. Her limbs shook with fatigue, her mind sang with gratitude that Peter was alive, and weariness pulled across her mind. "Julia…"

"It's okay." She led Eleanor to the table. She poured a cup of hot water, preparing Eleanor's tea exactly how she liked it. She even placed the sugar spoon parallel to her cup before pulling her chair around to sit closer. Eleanor sank over the table, her head in her hands. Julia rubbed circles on her back. "You can let it out now, Eleanor. It's okay."

She had no idea she'd been waiting for permission. Tears flowed freely, her shoulders shook as she cried and expended all the emotions she'd tamped down over the last few hours. The fear, the unknown, and all the dread that had been sitting in her chest dissipated. While she let it out, Julia sat with her, never letting Eleanor forget she wasn't alone.

She wasn't sure when she moved to lean into Julia, nor when Julia helped her to stand and led her into the washroom. Eleanor was still crying as Julia helped her out of her boots and prepared a hot bath.

After Eleanor fumbled with the shoulders of her dress, Julia gently said, "Let me." She eased the material down. Eleanor, catching her breath and wiping her face, stepped out of the dress while Julia brought in another pot of water and poured it into the steaming tub. "Take as long as you need," she said, cupping her face.

The tunnel vision that had overwhelmed her widened, and Julia's face came into focus. Eleanor found her hand. It still felt strong but tender and warm against her skin. "Stay with me?"

Surprise graced Julia's eyes before she nodded. They didn't say anything as they finished disrobing. Julia helped Eleanor into the tub, then slid in behind her. Eleanor let herself fall against Julia, let herself be wrapped carefully in her arms. She leaned back, resting her temple against Julia's cheek. Breathing in the steam, she let the water and Julia wash away the scathing marks the day had left upon her heart.

CHAPTER FORTY-ONE

"Jules."

Startled, Julia turned, the hammer poised mid-strike. "Henry?"

He stood near where she knelt next to the garden, his hands in his pockets and a peculiar look on his face. "How long have you been standing there?"

"A minute or two. Everything okay?"

She huffed and gave the stake one more swing, then tried to move the wooden frame. It didn't budge. "Fine. This timber had been kicked loose. Fixing it for Rose."

"She should be back from the Perrys' soon." He moved into her line of sight, examining a nearby tomato plant. "Surprised you didn't accompany her."

Julia didn't respond.

"How long are you going to avoid them?"

"Avoid who?"

She could feel his stare. He sighed and faced her. "Peter was lucky. Not to mention, he's strong. I think he gets that from his mom."

Julia shook her head, standing. It had been over a week since the incident, but she could still see the blood running down Peter's face when she closed her eyes. She could still feel the dread heavy on her limbs. "He's a child, Henry. A child I was responsible for, and who I let get into a terrible accident."

"Julia—"

She pointed the hammer at her chest. "It's my fault. He was with me. I was supposed to be watching him."

Henry reached out a cautious hand. "Peter made up his own mind when he ran off. You know how single-minded he can be."

Julia looked down, kicking at the dirt. What happened at the mill had been her worst fear coming to fruition, and now a terrible anxiety sat in her stomach. She muttered, "I turned my back for one minute."

"Julia." He stepped closer, taking the hammer. "Don't go there."

Too late, she thought, pinching the bridge of her nose to stop the tears. The image of Rose on the ground at the ranch flooded her mind, the sounds of her pained moans all she could hear.

"Look at me."

Reluctantly, she did. "This is not like what happened with your sister."

"Isn't it? That was my fault, and so is this. Eleanor left him with me. She trusted me." She choked back a sob. "She trusted me, and I let her down."

Henry held her gaze, his own as steady as his voice. "Julia, listen to me. Peter chose to leave. He hopped into the back of that wagon all by himself."

"I should have stopped him."

"You can't think like that."

She sniffled as Rose called from inside. Henry waited, perhaps to see if she was going to try to bolt, before he turned to go. She clenched her fist, wishing she still had the hammer to hit something. Disappointment battled with guilt and old shame. Why did it feel like a never-ending endeavor to escape her mistakes? Why did those damned feelings always find their way back?

She ruined things. And now, she'd ruined things with the woman she loved.

Julia tilted her head back, blinking at the bright sky. Eleanor hadn't said anything that day, or that night after the incident when they'd lain in bed together. But Julia didn't miss the way Eleanor hovered over Peter now, how she didn't let him out of her sight. She'd placed another burden on Eleanor's shoulders. Julia couldn't face her, not when it was just a matter of time before Eleanor realized she wasn't good enough. Sooner or later, Eleanor would see that Julia couldn't be trusted with the people she cared about most.

Pain seared through her chest and stomach. Rage succumbed to exhaustion, and she knelt again, weeping. She wept for Peter. She wept for Eleanor. More than anything, she wept for herself and for the possibility of a life she had come so close to calling her own.

A knock on her bedroom door was followed by Rose's voice. "You're up early."

Julia sat on the edge of her bed, rag in hand as she polished her boots. Morning light streamed between the curtains. "Couldn't sleep."

"Again?" Julia eyed her but didn't reply. Rose entered, casting her gaze around, moving toward the open window. "You cleaned again."

She worked to rub out a scuff near the heel of her boot. "Thought you'd be glad."

"Oh, I'm not complaining," Rose said, putting up her hands before they landed back in the pockets of her apron. A smattering of flour lay across it. Julia had thought she'd smelled bread baking. "It's just a little unusual, that's all."

"Maybe I've had a change of heart."

She caught Rose's concerned look. "Tidy room, a thriving garden, and the entire house is spotless."

"I have a new fondness for dusting."

Rose snorted. She seemed to wait for Julia to elaborate, but when she didn't, she asked, "Julia, what's really going on?"

She stiffened at her sister's concerned tone. "Nothing."

Rose moved to sit next to her. "Again, I'm not complaining about all the help. The house looks pristine. Our Wednesday church group couldn't stop singing my praises when they were here. But…" She gave a small laugh. "You polished all the china. You've pulled every single weed in the front lawn. Seems you've done just about everything you can to keep yourself tied to this house."

Pushing the rag against the leather, Julia relaxed when Rose reached out. "Henry said you went to the train station yesterday."

Swallowing, Julia set the boot and rag down, managing only a shrug.

"You're not really considering leaving, are you?"

Feeling small, she hugged herself. "Why not?"

Rose's brows rose in surprise. "Julia—"

"What? Why would I stay here, Rose? All I've done is hurt the people I love."

"Peter is fine, Julia."

"No thanks to me. What if…what if it happens again?" She turned to face her. "We got so lucky, but next time…What if it's worse?"

Rose searched her gaze. Julia saw disbelief in it, followed by sympathy and the look she knew well: weariness. "Julia, you can't go on like this."

She stood, unable to stand the look on her sister's face. At the window, she turned. "You're right. I can't go on like this. Not here. Not when Eleanor hasn't spoken to me in a week. Not when I'm a danger to her, to Peter, to everyone."

Rose seemed unmoved, crossing her arms. "And why hasn't Eleanor spoken to you, Julia? Maybe because you've locked yourself in this house? You could have come with me the other day to see them."

"She doesn't want to see me."

"Bull," Rose said.

Julia blinked, taken aback by her language. "Rose, I—"

"No. I'm sorry Jules, but you're being immature. Peter is going to be fine. Eleanor…" She took a breath, "Yes, all right, I'll admit, she does seem preoccupied. She follows Peter like a shadow. Reminds me of someone else, once upon a time."

Julia met her gaze. She'd wrestled with guilt for so long. Part of her was proud she hadn't run to Thrasher's or sought another night of outlandish bets. She knew she was stronger than all that, but guilt was so hard to shake. She just wanted to be rid of it.

"She needs you, Jules. You love her, don't you?"

"Yes." They let that declaration hang between them. Julia tried to follow the words, tried to find courage in her desires. "Rose," she finally said. "What do I do? I don't want to let her down."

Rose moved to join her near the window. "Julia, relationships aren't about being perfect all the time. Ain't no such thing as perfect."

"But you and Henry…"

Rose laughed. "Me and Henry? You think we're perfect? Jules, you've heard us fight."

"Yeah, but—"

"No. That's what marriage is. That's what," she said, hesitating, "any relationship is. It's about communicating, even when it's hard. Even when you're terrified of being judged. Love is about trust. That's what you're worried Eleanor's lost in you, right?"

She nodded.

"Trust that she loves you, Julia. Trust that she'll listen, and that she wants to hear what you have to say."

A breeze moved the curtain. A beam of sunlight shone across the floor. "If I run, I'll never even get the chance to try." Julia swiped at her nose, tears blurring her vision.

"Exactly. Oh, Jules, come here." Rose pulled her into a hug.

Over her shoulder, Julia said, "I'm scared."

"I'd be worried if you weren't." Leaning back, she held Julia at arm's length, meeting her gaze. "Promise me you won't do anything rash."

Taking a deep breath, Julia wanted to promise that. She wanted to be the person Rose always challenged her to be. She wanted to be good enough for her, for Eleanor. But the words never found her tongue. Instead, she said, "Do you need help with the laundry?"

Rose studied her a moment more, then rubbed her arms. "Sure, Julia. Let's go."

CHAPTER FORTY-TWO

"Peter?"

"I'm here, Mom." He popped up behind the tall grass twenty feet away. "Laying a trap."

Eleanor inhaled to slow her heart rate. "Stay where I can see you, please."

He looked like he wanted to say something but only scratched at the bandage on his ear then disappeared back into the grass.

"Here's your tea, honey." Sue emerged from the open back door, handing her a steaming cup. "Drink that down and take a break."

"I've got another load to get through, Sue."

"And plenty of daylight to do it, E. Come on, it's a beautiful day," she added gently, leading Eleanor to the stool. "Rest a minute."

Glancing again toward where Peter was, she reluctantly sat, taking a sip of chamomile. The warm liquid soothed the anxious hitch in her throat she'd been fighting the last few days. "Thanks, Sue."

Sue unpinned a few of the dry shirts, folding them into a basket. "Don't take this the wrong way, honey, but you look like you haven't slept a wink."

Eleanor took another drink. "I'm all right."

Sue tossed her a look but continued to fold. "Saw the Barrows at church the other day. Said they were coming by to check on Peter."

"They were here on Tuesday."

"Did Julia join them?" Sue's tone was light, but Eleanor was stung by the question. No, not by her question, by the fact that Julia had *not* joined the Barrows on their visit. Julia hadn't been by since the night of Peter's accident. Maybe she was busy, but each day that passed left Eleanor unsettled with the idea that Julia was avoiding her.

Studying her tea, Eleanor sat quietly. A snapping branch sounded toward the river. She sat up, some of the tea spilling. "Peter?" She searched the yard, then called again, "Peter?"

Sue turned, stepping toward her. "E, take it easy, now."

But Eleanor hurriedly set her tea aside and jogged into the tall grass. "Peter, where are you?"

He groaned and appeared. "Mom, how am I supposed to catch anything if you're shouting?"

Eleanor stopped, one hand on her head to swipe at the perspiration. She blinked. "I'm sorry," she said, fear replaced by anger at herself. That feeling grew at Peter's frustrated face. "I'm sorry, darling," she said, turning back. She found the stool, Sue watching her the entire time.

Her lips in a thoughtful line, Sue stepped closer. "Eleanor, this isn't good for you."

She swallowed the apprehension in her throat, fighting the urge to count the number of clothes still on the line. "I'm fine, Sue."

"I don't think you are, honey."

Eleanor leaned back, closing her eyes. She worked to calm her heart again as Sue spoke. "Ain't nothing to worry about, E. Peter's right here."

"I know." She opened her eyes. "I know that Sue, but I can't..." She clenched her jaw, digging the heels of her palms into her thighs. "I can't let it go."

"Let what go, honey?"

"I can't let *him* go."

Sue frowned. "What are you talking about?"

"I almost lost him, Sue."

"But you didn't. He's all right." She hesitated a moment. "Julia made sure of that."

Eleanor shook her head, forcing the terrible visions of Peter, limp in Julia's arms, out of her mind. "I think I'm going mad, Sue." She leaned forward, head in her hands.

"Hey," Sue said, kneeling and lifting her chin to meet her gaze. "You're just frightened after what happened. Any mother would be. But you've got support, E. You're not alone."

"I know," she said. "But I can't..." *I can't sleep without Julia. I miss her.* "Julia..." The words faltered.

Sue smiled softly. "You need her."

Eleanor met her gaze. "Why isn't she here?"

Sue rocked back on her heels, lips pursed in thought. "I reckon she's scared, same as you."

"Scared?" Eleanor straightened, brushing aside tears. "Of what?"

"You haven't exactly been yourself these last two weeks." Eleanor's gaze fell, and she picked at her skirt. "Peter's gotta go back to school at some point, honey. You can't keep him from the world. From where I stand, it looks like you hardly want anyone here but you and your boy."

"That's not true." Eleanor sniffled. "Peter is happy when other people are around. When Julia is here." She smiled through more tears. "I'm happier when she's here."

Sue squeezed her knee. "I know."

Eleanor scanned the yard. Peter reappeared, skipping toward the river before disappearing down the slope. She thought better about going after him. She couldn't do that, not if she wanted to keep her son. The wedge that had come between them nearly a year ago had returned, and she was driving it deeper. She was bearing down on him, and it wasn't fair. Things had been better when she and Julia were both here, caring for Peter. Eleanor knew Julia loved him as much as she did. And Eleanor loved her, more than anything. Julia eased her mind, soothed the tension in her body that came with being a mother. Eleanor was more confident as a parent. With Julia, Eleanor could handle whatever came next.

A terrible thought struck her. Was she driving Julia away? "Sue. I need to talk to her."

Sue stood, returning to the laundry. "I agree. But we've got laundry to finish and our meeting with the bank tomorrow morning. Remember?"

Eleanor's enthusiasm dipped, but only for a moment. A newfound energy filled her as she finished her tea and started the next batch of clothes to soak. Clarity struck her like a bell: Julia was it for her. She made their lives better, and Eleanor was going to do everything she could to ensure Julia knew that. She would go to the Barrows tomorrow after her appointment and talk to her. Eleanor wasn't going to let the woman she loved go. She only hoped it wasn't too late.

CHAPTER FORTY-THREE

I think that'll do it," Julia said, tightening the lash around the pile of lumber. "Thanks for your help."

Ralph straightened, then carefully stepped across the planks piled in the back of the wagon bed before jumping down to join her. "Just glad we could borrow Mahoney's wagon." He grinned and elbowed her. "Think he's glad we haven't stolen his mules in a while."

She laughed, the memory of that last race resurfacing. It felt so long ago, almost like another lifetime, when she had done whatever she could to numb the pain of her guilt. Clapping a hand on his shoulder, she said, "You wanna ride this over to Eleanor's with me?"

He smiled but shook his head, sweat glistening from the warm April day. "I've got to help my sisters with a few pie batches." He dipped his chin. "Besides, I can't be late to pick up my date this evening."

Julia, who had moved around to pat the horses patiently waiting, turned back. "Date?"

Flush filled his cheeks. "She's new in town."

"That so?"

His eyes brightened. "Said she's lookin' for secretarial work. Maybe she could help you out at the mill?"

Situated on the wagon seat, she said, "Well, how about that? I'm happy for you, Ralph."

Handing her the reins, he waved her off. "Go on, now. Don't make this gift any later than it already is."

The bright sun was just starting to dip lower in the sky as she pulled into Eleanor's drive. She'd let herself dream about this moment since landing on this idea. In her vision, Peter ran out to greet her. Eleanor followed. Her hair shone in the afternoon light like it always did. She raised a hand to better see Julia, a warm, knowing smile on her face that erased the worry following Julia since Peter's accident.

Julia's stomach fluttered at the image. But as she slowed the wagon in front of Eleanor's, the front door remained closed. There was no sign of Peter. She frowned and waited.

"So much for that," she finally said, reality taking a strong right hook to her daydreams. Still, she hoped this would have the intended effect. She knocked and went inside. "Eleanor?"

The back door was open, letting in the breeze. Laundry hung on the lines outside. She followed the sounds of laughter into the backyard and spotted Peter's bright hair.

"Hey," she called, and he popped up the hillside. "Peter."

He waved, and Stuart hurried past behind him, tagging him and cackling with laughter as he ran around the house. "Hey, no fair," Peter cried, hurrying after him.

Julia jogged over. "Where's your mother?" she asked, trying to catch him, but he slipped out of her grasp.

"With Auntie Sue. Should be home soon."

"Oh," she said, feeling more dejected by the minute. She sure hadn't timed things right. "I'll just wait," she called as he disappeared behind the trees, his and Stuart's laughter echoing.

She decided to be useful and unpinned some of the laundry, taking it inside. Sue's car pulled into the drive behind the wagon. Julia stepped onto the porch.

Eleanor bounded out of the passenger side. Sue turned off the car and met her, both talking excitedly. Eleanor had a handbag Julia recognized as one she used for special occasions. Her dress was the lovely forest green one, too, that brought out her eyes. Where had she gone all dressed up?

Sue spotted her first. "Miss Holte." She waved, then quickly corrected herself. "Julia, how are you?"

Julia leaned against the porch post, crossing her arms. She caught Eleanor's gaze drawn to her. "Just dandy, Sue. Thank you."

Eleanor looked at the wagon, then back to her as they walked up the drive. "I didn't know you were coming by. I sent Peter over to Stuart's."

"They found their way back," Julia said, hitching her thumb over her shoulder. "Playing near the river."

"That Stuart boy comes around a lot," Sue said, adjusting her hat.

"I reckon they formed a new friendship on that mountain," said Julia.

A tense silence fell over them. Eleanor glanced at Sue, then said, "I was planning to come see you today."

Her heart fluttered, and she worked to keep an even face. "You were?"

"I'd been meaning to for a while. I just..." She looked at Sue again, who gave her a nod. "To be honest, I was shaken up by what happened. Ever since Peter..."

"I know." Relief flooded Julia. "Me too."

They shared a smile when Sue cleared her throat.

At the base of the porch, Eleanor pointed to the wagon. "What's all this?"

Julia licked her lips. She had wanted to do this with just Eleanor. *Oh well.* "I found your Christmas gift," she said, straightening and flashing a grin.

Sue's brow furrowed. "Honey, I hate to break it to you, but it's nearly May."

Julia chuckled. "It's a belated gift. I couldn't find anything last winter that seemed right." She swallowed, cutting her gaze to Eleanor. She'd planned to say, "Nothing in this world holds a candle to you, Eleanor Perry. What could I possibly get the woman I've fallen head over heels for?" but bit her tongue with Sue there.

Sue raised a brow, her face seeming to say she could read just fine between the lines of what Julia wasn't saying. "Well," she said, patting Eleanor's arm. "I'll just leave you to it. Nice to see you, Julia." To Eleanor, she whispered something in her ear. Eleanor blushed and shooed her away.

With Sue gone, Eleanor joined her on the porch. "I told you I didn't need anything for Christmas."

"I know," she said, taking one of Eleanor's hands. "I wanted to do it."

Glancing at the wagon, Eleanor asked, "Lumber?"

"For the house. I know you have dreams of a shop of your own. I figured this is the next best thing." A vee formed between Eleanor's brows. "I'm going to build you a proper laundry room."

"You're…what?"

"Well, me, Henry, and Ralph. We're gonna work all summer to add on to the back of the house. I have it all planned out. Henry and Isaac helped with the blueprint. It'll be a space just for your work. Like you've said, it'd be nice to have a place that isn't half in the kitchen. This way, you can keep everything in one spot, all your supplies. Maybe you can even take on more work from folks in town."

The spark in Eleanor's eyes had grown brighter with each sentence. Julia's chest warmed. The sun caught shades of copper in Eleanor's hair, and she reached out. "I want to give you everything you need."

Eleanor stepped closer, grabbing her waist. "Julia…"

Julia searched her gaze, and emotion threatened in her throat. Looking down, she said, "You know, I imagined being a lot smoother during this whole thing, more like Barrymore in all his movies."

Laughing, Eleanor leaned in and kissed her. "You're doing great. Better than Barrymore." After kissing her again, she said, "I love it. I love you."

Julia stepped back to find the confirmation of those words in Eleanor's eyes: tender, warm, and just like home. "I love you, too," she said, wrapping Eleanor in an embrace.

They laughed and kissed and hugged until Julia remembered the handbag. "Where'd you and Sue get to today?" Peter scampered across the front yard, Stuart waving a big stick as they faced one another and began a makeshift sword fight next to the wagon.

"I took my gold into the bank. Sue came with me to speak to the clerk."

"You'd saved up a lot. How'd it go?"

The edges of Eleanor's mouth lifted in a smile. "I had a little over an ounce." Julia's mouth fell open. "The bank had a few questions about where I got it all from."

Frowning, Julia nodded. "That makes sense. It's not every day folks walk in with that much gold. Not since the rush, anyway."

"Thank goodness for Sue." At Julia's inquisitive brow, Eleanor explained, "We may have stretched the truth ever so slightly. The gold, she claimed, came as a bonus from the mill for my service and years of dedication."

"Clever, that Sue."

Eleanor glanced around, then said, "They gave me nearly forty dollars for it."

"Forty!" Eleanor placed a hand on her arm to quiet her. "Forty," she said again, lowering her voice. "Eleanor."

"I know." She looked over at Peter. "I'm going to put some aside for him. But the rest..." She took a deep breath. "The rest can go to supplies for work, Peter's medicine," she said, finding Julia's gaze. "Maybe some new blankets for the bed."

Squeezing her hand, Julia said, "Eleanor, I'm so happy for you."

"For us."

Julia nodded, realizing how much Eleanor meant those two words. *For us.* Eleanor was imagining a future with Julia in it.

Her heart nearly burst at the fact. Overcome, Julia hugged her again.

So what if this afternoon hadn't gone exactly the way she'd planned? Sometimes, the best plans were made better by upending them and shaping them into something only fathomable in a dream. And that, Julia realized, was what was happening now, right here on this front porch. Her future wasn't some distant, hazy dream she could never see because she was too focused on the past, too focused on things she couldn't control. Julia saw her future clear as glass. She could feel it in Eleanor's arms. Her future was as real as the woman in front of her. The woman who loved her and wanted her in her life, in Peter's life. This was right where she was supposed to be.

Julia gave a small laugh over Eleanor's shoulder.

"What?" asked Eleanor, pulling back but keeping her hands in Julia's.

Julia looked at her, let herself admire the woman she'd been searching for all her life. "I never expected to meet anyone in this town," she said finally. "I didn't expect much."

Eleanor smiled. "Life is funny that way. Shows you what you need. Like that advertisement I answered all those years ago for a new life." She shook her head. "It wasn't the life I expected to have. But it brought me here. Brought me to you." Looking down, she said, "I want you, Julia. I want you here. So does Peter. We…I was scared. These past weeks…"

Julia found her gaze. "Scared?"

"I had the terrible thought that you didn't want anything to do with us anymore. That this life wasn't for you."

Swallowing the trepidation in her throat, Julia said, "I'd be lying if I said the thought of leaving didn't cross my mind." Eleanor's gaze widened. She reached out, finding Julia's hand. "Not because I don't want this. God, Eleanor, I want this more than anything. But I was scared, too, scared I'd messed this up. I never want to make things harder for you. I want to be the person you can trust."

Eleanor's teary gaze searched hers, the start of a smile on her lips. "I do, Julia. I trust you more than anyone. I love you. We both do," she said, nodding toward where Peter had run off. "I can't imagine our lives without you."

Julia let the emotions carry her forward into another kiss. She pulled Eleanor close, hoping she could feel every ounce of joy and light she felt radiating from her chest. Solace at Eleanor's words filled her. Pulling back, she traced a finger down Eleanor's cheek. "Merry Christmas, Eleanor."

Eleanor laughed. "Merry Christmas, my love."

CHAPTER FORTY-FOUR

Everyone packed into the town hall the first Monday in May for Idaho Springs' first public office debate in twenty-six years.

"Like the pennants?" Sue asked, her gloved hand pointing to the small dais encircled with miniature American flags.

"How patriotic." Eleanor scooted into her seat in the row behind Sue and Isaac, who nodded his hello. He seemed already focused on the main event, like most of the townsfolk packed into thirty rows of chairs that evening. The stuffy room buzzed with anticipation for the first debate between an incumbent public servant and the man running against him that most of them had ever witnessed.

Glancing over her shoulder, she spotted the Barrows make their way inside. She waved. Rose saw her and ushered Henry through the crowd. Before Eleanor could ask where Julia was, Rose said, "She's helping Ralph with his tie outside." Lowering her voice, she added, "Never seen a man sweat so much in my life."

"He's nervous?"

"Shaking like a leaf," Henry added, smiling to Mr. Jarda across the room. Most of the seats were taken, so people took to lining the walls and standing in the back.

Rose sat and smoothed her skirt. "I hope he does all right."

"People love the Davies," Henry said, and Eleanor agreed. "Volz has lost a lot of support in the last few months. He harps on anyone who even looks at him sideways. People are ready for something different."

Eleanor took a breath. "I sure hope so."

The murmur of the crowd grew, and everyone turned when Sheriff Volz walked in. He arrived alone. His pressed brown pants fell over his shined boots and were paired with a crimson red button-down beneath an off-white vest. Every stitch looked so freshly ironed and starched, Eleanor wondered how he could move, which probably explained the rigid way he maneuvered down the walkway dividing the room.

The mayor, Mr. Bancroft, stood from his seat in the first row and shook Volz's hand. Another murmur from the crowd, and Ralph walked in, Julia at his heels. A few folks whistled and clapped.

"Oh, Lord," Rose said, fanning herself with a pamphlet Sue had handed her. "He looks like a bull without a horn, bless his heart."

Eleanor hated to agree, but Ralph needed to pull himself together. His hair was slicked back behind his ears with oil. A pattern of sweat sat in the middle of his blue shirt, and his face was already red. He only stopped wringing his hands to wave in their direction, which led him to stumble. He just managed to collect himself before falling onto Mr. Bancroft.

With all the seats taken, Eleanor waved to Julia to stand near them. She swapped seats with Henry to be at the end of the row. "How's he doing?" she asked.

Julia was still watching Ralph as she knelt. "We practiced his speech more times than I can count. Of course, he waited until this morning to tell me he's never spoken publicly before."

"Oh gosh." They both turned as Mr. Bancroft raised his hands to quiet the crowd.

"Thank you, everyone, for joining us today. The post of Idaho Springs sheriff has been a proud, respected position in this community for decades. It pleases me to see the long-standing tradition," he said, gesturing to Volz, "meet the vim and vigor of the future. Either way, we can't go wrong."

Julia snorted, and Eleanor shushed her, squeezing her arm before Julia moved to stand against the wall.

"Each man will have ten minutes to state their case on why they should represent us and oversee the safety of our town as its sheriff. After, we'll put it to a vote. May the best man win."

Eleanor wasn't surprised when Sheriff Volz took to the dais first, using the entire allotted time to make his case. Most of his speech was what she expected: droll, fire-and-brimstone adages designed to instill fear. "Think about what this town has always valued," he said, his voice raising like a preacher's, "tradition, hard work, and the Christian values that make not just Idaho Springs but this entire state, a safe and decent place to live."

She could see Julia bristle and was glad only a few people in the crowd seemed fired up by Volz's words. Mrs. Henley, sitting a few rows ahead, nodded approvingly.

He continued, "I promise to uphold those values, no matter what. Without a strong hand to guide, only God knows where we may end up. My father believed the same thing and would be proud to see me continue his legacy."

Between a whisper of claps, someone near the back said, "You ain't nothin' like your daddy, Lee."

Volz looked up as if searching for whoever said that. He smiled tightly. "Nobody's perfect. But my vision is clear when it comes to what we need. And I'm willing to do the work others can't...or won't."

"What about Thrasher's?" This voice was familiar, and Eleanor recognized one of the clerks from the office. "I hear you pocket half the funds."

Eleanor was sure concern flashed in Volz's gaze as more chatter started over the audience. She glanced at Julia, who had her arms crossed and looked utterly amused.

"I'll be happy to take any actual questions if you've got 'em," Volz said through a smile, half the crowd now tossing unpleasant remarks his way.

Mr. Bancroft stood again, waving his arms to tame the crowd. "That's enough now. Thank you, Sheriff." Ralph, who'd been standing behind the dais staring into the middle distance since Volz started speaking, snapped to attention. "Davies, you're up."

A bout of cheers filled the room. Ralph smiled meekly, still wringing his hands. He looked around. He found Julia, who made a gesture reminding him to breathe. He did, then shoved his hands into his front pockets.

"Hi, everyone," he finally said.

"Hiya, Ralph!"

Laughter echoed from the back of the room. Eleanor turned just in time to see Mrs. Davies pop someone on the head with a pamphlet.

"Well, as you probably know, I'm here running opposite Lee Volz for town sheriff." The room held a quiet anticipation. Ralph didn't say anything for a time, and Eleanor wondered if he'd forgotten his speech. Eventually, he turned to Volz. "Sheriff Volz had some real good points. Used some nice words like tradition, hard work, and values." Turning back to the spectators, he said, "My definition of those words might be a little different."

"Not unlike Volz, my family has deep roots in this town. My grandparents settled here in 1877 and opened our bakery. My mother was born into that family business, and then me and my sisters came along to help. I think most of you know our place over on 4th Street."

Soft laughter came in reply. "I'm proud to be a part of this community. The bakery has given me a chance to get to know a lot of people." He smiled. "I know most of your orders by heart." He seemed to relax, pointing to someone in the crowd. "Hank, that vanilla cake you always get for your wife each September on your anniversary. And Mrs. Shifton, you always order the snickerdoodles for your daughter's birthday." He found Henry next. "Mr. Barrow, those meat pies are always ready for your Friday lunch."

Henry gave a slight shake of his head as Rose turned, a confused line between her brows.

"Those are the traditions I think of when I hear that word. Your traditions: all the things each of you do every day are just as important as anything else. The little things that make your day worth getting up for. Because our days aren't easy. Most of us aren't kicking back behind a desk, waiting for something to go wrong. We're out there working around the clock at the mill or the market or seeing to it our town gets the electric streetlamps it's been promised."

Sue sat up straighter, beaming.

"Without you all, this town falls apart. Every single person in here is important." He found Eleanor's gaze. She smiled and looked at Julia, who seemed to glow with pride. Blinking, Ralph shrugged. "The sheriff's job isn't to seek out the destitute, the wrong, or whatever it is they deem unfit. A sheriff's job is to protect its citizens, to make them feel safe on their own streets. A sheriff's job is *not* to make its own residents afraid of setting one foot out of line. That ain't no way to be." He took a deep breath, a smile spreading. "If I'm elected, that's my promise to you: to ensure everyone has the right to home and happiness. That's what every person here deserves. Thank you."

Cheers erupted, and Eleanor clapped along with them. A faint boo was heard near the back, but it was drowned out by the joy and congratulations for Ralph. Volz, meanwhile, glowered behind him.

"All right, all right." Mr. Bancroft stood to quiet everyone down. "Now you'll have some time to consider your candidates. Please feel free to step outside. My dear wife and her women's society has prepared lemonade and sustenance for everyone to enjoy. We'll prepare the ballot boxes and call everyone back soon. Mrs. Weldon?" Sue stood and led her row outside, others following suit.

Eleanor took Peter outside with the Barrows. Like most folks, they found shelter from the sun beneath a large elm tree. "I think it went well," she said, watching Peter run off with some boys from school.

"I agree," Henry said, "though I wonder if folks will actually vote the way they seemed to be leaning in there."

Rose, who'd been squinting at Henry and didn't seem to hear him, asked, "What did he mean about the Friday lunches?"

"Oh, well, um…" Henry stumbled on his words, shooting a pleading look to Eleanor. Fortunately, Julia joined them.

"Glad that part's done," she said, running a hand through her hair as she sidled up to Eleanor. Julia took a sip of her lemonade. "Thanks," she said.

"No matter what happens, I'm just glad someone is standing up to Volz," Eleanor said. "He thinks no one can touch him."

"Would be somethin' for a new sheriff to be elected. Isaac said they haven't had a sheriff named anything but Volz in over thirty years," Henry said, and Eleanor could sense the unease flit between them. It was a long shot for such a long-standing position to change, even if everyone seemed to be supporting Ralph. Eleanor watched Julia speak to Rose, who was interrogating her about the meat pies. She could only hope that something new was possible. Surely, it was. If her life could change the way it had over the last year, anything could happen. Couldn't it?

Mr. Bancroft appeared in the doorway, waving folks inside. "Moment of truth," Henry said, leading Rose back into the town hall. Eleanor started forward, but Julia grabbed her elbow, keeping her back under the shade of the tree.

"What is it?"

For the first time all day, Julia looked scared. She swallowed, looking at their clasped hands. "What if he loses?"

"Ralph?" Eleanor glanced around, then stepped closer, running her hands up Julia's arms. "He made a real good case for himself in there."

"Eleanor."

She sighed, realizing she couldn't brush aside the very real possibility of a future including Volz. A future where they, especially Julia, would have to live in fear each day of his vendetta against her. She steeled herself and said, "If Ralph doesn't win, then you and I will face whatever happens together."

Julia searched her gaze. Eleanor dropped her voice, though most people were already heading toward the single file line outside the building, "I love you, Julia. Volz has another think coming if he believes we're gonna make things easy for him. Okay?" A small smile lifted Julia's face, trepidation falling away. "We're in this together. Come what may."

"Come what may," Julia echoed. "Together."

Eleanor yearned to reassure Julia with a kiss but bit her lip to resist that impulse. Instead, she squeezed Julia's hand before taking her arm. Together, they went inside.

EPILOGUE

S heriff, to what do we owe the pleasure?" Julia asked. Ralph turned, the planks on Eleanor's front porch groaning beneath him. His hair looked freshly cut, the shining sheriff's badge gleaming on his vest. He tossed her a relaxed smile as the September sun faded behind the mountains at his back. "Heya, Jules. Just doing my rounds, seeing if there's anything y'all need."

"Slow night?" she asked, glancing over her shoulder as Eleanor hurried into the room. She waved before helping Peter to the table where she showed him how to tie a bow on a small parcel.

Ralph shrugged. "A little. But I can't complain. Gave Billy the night off. Also wanted to give y'all this." From behind his back, he pulled out a small gift box. "My mom made it for Rose."

Julia took it. "That's awful nice. She can't make it tonight?"

"Afraid not. She and my sisters are working on a bulk order of pies. Apparently, some mine owners from Utah are coming by next week to tour Monarch. Isaac made the national papers with how well it's done lately."

"Henry mentioned something about that." She handed the parcel to Eleanor, who joined them outside. Peter scampered by, bounding onto the drive.

Closing the door, Eleanor said, "It's good to see you, Ralph. We'll tell the Barrows hello from you."

"Thank you," he said.

"How's Katherine doing?" Eleanor asked. Julia gave her a grateful look, as she'd been trying to remember the name of Ralph's paramour since he'd arrived.

He smiled and looked down. "Swell, thanks for asking." He looked up. "She's grateful for all the training you gave her, Jules."

They all started down the drive. "Hey, I'm glad for the help. Her being in the office lets me get home a little early some days," she said, bumping Eleanor with her hip. Eleanor gave her a smile, then caught up to Peter.

When they reached town, Ralph said, "Well, better get over to the old Volz property."

"What is it this time?"

"Oh, just some kids trespassing. Been like clockwork since he left." Julia could hardly believe that less than one week after the election results were released, Volz had hightailed it out of town. She'd expected him to put up a fight, gather his few followers, and contest the outcome until he was blue in the face. But the Monday after, someone said they'd heard his car leave in the middle of the night. Sure enough, the house he and his father had lived in was vacant. And he hadn't come back.

"Don't be too quick to get there," she said with a wink.

Ralph gave her a dubious look. "Have fun, Jules. See ya around."

Henry answered the door when they arrived. "Come in," he said, stepping back to let them pass. Eleanor handed him the gifts. "Thank you." He tussled Peter's hair. "My, you've grown another inch."

Peter looked up proudly. "I can outrun Stuart now, too."

Eleanor pulled him into a side hug. "His lungs have been good," she said to Henry, but Julia noted the disbelief in her voice. "Sue brought another bottle of medicine from Denver last month, but it's gone untouched."

"Is it possible…could he grow out of something like that?" Julia asked.

Eleanor shook her head. "God knows."

"Well, I'm glad to hear it, either way," Henry said. To Peter he said, "There's a new machine we just got in. Care to take a look next week?"

Peter fiddled with his sleeve, glancing sideways. He shrugged. "Maybe. I have a reading for school to prepare, right, Mom?" He looked up at Eleanor, and Julia didn't miss the surprise on her face.

"That's true, darling."

Rose called from the kitchen. "Can someone help me with these cookies?"

"Cookies?" Peter dashed away.

They laughed, and Henry said, "I see his hearing is back in order."

Julia said, "Good as new, it seems."

There was a knock at the door. Eleanor stiffened. Julia squeezed her hand. "Are you nervous?"

"Your parents are coming into town," she said, her gaze flitting from her to the door. "I want to make a good impression."

Julia smiled. "They'll love you." She kissed Eleanor's cheek and felt her body relax as Sue waved in the open doorway, a large parcel in her arms. "Go say hi." Then, remembering something she'd wanted to say, she added, "She had wanted to update you on Isaac's findings about the mercury they've been using, right? How it's potentially tied to what's making the men sick?"

Eleanor nodded, eyes bright. "Yes, that's right."

"Fill me in later? I'm going to see how Rose is doing."

In the kitchen, Julia opened a window. Peter walked past with a tray of delicious looking chocolate chip cookies. "The garden looks good," Julia said, peering out to see the healthy-looking tomato plants.

"Yes," Rose said, "it's come along quite nicely. I lent Mrs. Jarda some carrots last week." She passed Julia a finger sandwich. "Here, tell me what you think."

Julia lifted a corner of the white bread, eying the combination of sardine, olives, and hard-boiled egg warily. Taking a small bite, she frowned. "Rose, this is...really good."

Rose beamed but lifted her chin matter-of-factly. "Found the recipe in one of the church cookbooks. I added some lemon juice and a dash of paprika." After Julia finished the rest of the sandwich, Rose said, "You can wipe that astonished look off your face now."

Laughing, Julia took her apron and hung it up. "How are you feeling?"

Checking the food trays on the table, Rose rubbed her belly. "She's kicking like you wouldn't believe."

"She? How do you know?"

"By the way she's sitting. Here." Rose took Julia's hand, directing it to the side of her belly. They waited. Julia looked up when she felt the small pressure against her hand. Rose smiled.

Julia shook her head. "Rose…"

"I know," her sister said, clearing her throat.

Julia had cried, whooped, and hollered when she'd learned Rose was expecting. Henry had broken the news over one of their Sunday dinners not long after Ralph had been sworn in as sheriff. She had wept openly at the joy she'd felt and on her sister's face. Collecting herself now, she said, "You look radiant, by the way."

Rose laughed. "Do I? I feel like a balloon."

"Maybe Momma will have some tips for the back pain."

"Lord, I can only hope. Come on."

Julia helped her carry the trays into the parlor where everyone gathered for the dinner that, thanks to Henry's gushing around town and endless invitations, had nearly turned into an impromptu celebration in conjunction with Julia and Rose's parents coming to visit.

Conversation fluttered around the parlor as Henry stood next to Rose after passing out paper cups filled with tea. Peter, cookie in hand, returned to Eleanor's side with Julia.

"I do hope she finds the crib mobile to her liking," Sue was saying. "It's handmade by a Denver artisan."

"I'm sure she'll love it, Sue," Eleanor was saying, passing Julia a cup. Rose looked flushed but utterly beautiful as she stood next to Henry. Julia pressed her hand against the small of Eleanor's back, rubbing circles with her thumb, relishing the happiness and love filling her sister's house.

Henry asked for their attention. "Please, if I may."

"Speech," Julia called, prompting laughter among the attendees.

Henry waved her off. "I just wanted to thank everyone for being here. It means the world to us to have our closest friends here with us to celebrate." He and Rose shared a look, and Julia smiled at the affection emanating between them. Eleanor leaned against her. "Each of you has made our lives in Idaho Springs brighter and better than we could have imagined. We know our little one will be just as loved from the moment he—" Rose shot him a look. "I mean, she, arrives."

More soft laughter. Henry kissed Rose's cheek. She raised her cup, finding Julia's gaze. "To family."

Everyone echoed the cheer. Julia bit her cheek, surprised at the emotion welling in her chest. She looked at Peter brushing crumbs off his clean shirt, then met Eleanor's gaze. Who would have guessed, she thought, taking in everything. She pictured the ranch and how things used to be. Julia had been determined to hate it here, to hate everything about this town. The mill, the people, the mountains. *Now look at us.*

Life really did have a funny way of dealing them exactly the hand they needed. And always the one they least expected.

She raised her cup to join the others, smiling. "To family."

About the Author

Sam Ledel grew up in the sprawling DFW Metroplex of Texas. After graduating with her BA in creative writing, she found a calling in education and has worked in the field for more than a decade, including during her time in Peru serving in the Peace Corps.

Her debut novel, *Rocks and Stars*, was a Golden Crown Literary Society finalist for Young Adult fiction. *Wildflower Words*, a historical romance, was a 2023 LGBTQ+ finalist in the Next Generation Indie Book Awards.

Ledel enjoys being able to write in her free time, usually with a cup of coffee in hand, and her Jack Russell terrier snuggled close by. She currently resides in Denver and is working on her next novel.

Books Available from Bold Strokes Books

Discovering Gold by Sam Ledel. In 1920s Colorado, a single mother and a rowdy cowgirl must set aside their fears and initial reservations about one another if they want to find love in the mining town each of them calls home. (978-1-63679-786-1)

Dream a Little Dream by Melissa Brayden. Savanna can't believe it when Dr. Kyle Remington, the woman who left her feeling like a fool, shows up in Dreamer's Bay. Life is too complicated for second chances. Or is it? (978-1-63679-839-4)

Emma by the Sea by Sarah G. Levine. A delightful modern-day romance inspired by Emma, one of Jane Austen's most beloved novels. (978-1-63679-879-0)

Goodbye, Hello by Heather K O'Malley. With so much time apart and the challenges of a long-distance relationship, Kelly and Teresa's second chance at love may end just as awkwardly as the first. (978-1-63679-790-8)

One Measure of Love by Annie McDonald. Vancouver's hit competitive cooking show Recipe for Success has begun filming its second season and two talented young chefs are desperate for more than a winning dish. (978-1-63679-827-1)

The Smallest Day by J.M. Redmann. The first bullet missed— can Micky Knight stop the second bullet from finding its target? (978-1-63679-854-7)

To Please Her by Elena Abbott. A spilled coffee leads Sabrina into a world of erotic BDSM that may just land her the love of her life. (978-1-63679-849-3)

Two Weddings and a Funeral by Claudia Parr. Stella and Theo have spent the last thirteen years pretending they can be just friends, but surely "just friends" don't make out every chance they get. (978-1-63679-820-2)

Coming Up Clutch by Anna Gram. College softball star Kelly "Razor" Mitchell hung up her cleats early, but when former crush, now coach Ashton Sharpe shows up on her doorstep seven years later, beautiful as ever, Razor hopes the longing in her gaze has nothing to do with softball. (978-1-63679-817-2)

Firecamp by Jaycie Morrison. Going their separate ways seemed inevitable for two people as different as Fallon and Nora, while meeting up again is strictly coincidental. (978-1-63679-753-3)

Fixed Up by Aurora Rey. When electrician Jack Barrow and artist Ellie Lancaster get stuck on a job site during a blizzard, close quarters send all sorts of sparks flying. (978-1-63679-788-5)

Stranded by Ronica Black. Can Abigail and Whitley overcome their personal hang-ups and stubbornness to survive not only Alaska, but a dangerous stalker as well? (978-1-63679-761-8)

Whisk Me Away by Georgia Beers. Regan's a gorgeous flake. Ava, a beautiful untouchable ice queen. When they meet again at a retreat for up-and-coming pastry chefs, the competition, and the ovens, heat up. (978-1-63679-796-0)

Across the Enchanted Border by Crin Claxton. Magic, telepathy, swordsmanship, tyranny, and tenderness abound in a tale of two lands separated by the enchanted border. (978-1-63679-804-2)

Deep Cover by Kara A. McLeod. Running from your problems by pretending to be someone else only works if the person you're pretending to be doesn't have even bigger problems. (978-1-63679-808-0)

Good Game by Suzanne Lenoir. Even though Lauren has sworn off dating gamers, it's becoming hard to resist the multifaceted Sam. An opposites attract lesbian romance. (978-1-63679-764-9)

Innocence of the Maiden by Ileandra Young. Three powerful women. Two covens at war. One horrifying murder. When mighty and powerful witches begin to butt heads, who out there is strong enough to mediate? (978-1-63679-765-6)

Protection in Paradise by Julia Underwood. When arson forces them together, the flames between chief of police Eve Maguire and librarian Shaye Hayden aren't that easy to extinguish. (978-1-63679-847-9)

Too Forward by Krystina Rivers. Just as professional basketball player Jane May's career finally starts heating up, a new relationship with her team's brand consultant could derail the success and happiness she's struggled so long to find. (978-1-63679-717-5)

Worth Waiting For by Kristin Keppler. For Peyton and Hanna, reliving the past is painful, but looking back might be the only way to move forward. (978-1-63679-773-1)

Flowers and Gemstones by Alaina Erdell. Caught between past loves and present secrets, Hannah and Vanessa must each decide if the other is worth making difficult changes for a shot at happiness. (978-1-63679-745-8)

Foul Play by Erin Kaste. Music librarian Kirsten Lindquist knows someone is stalking the symphony musicians, but can she prove that a string of murders and suspicious accidents are connected, all without becoming a victim herself? (978-1-63679-689-5)

Hollywood Hearts by Toni Logan. What happens when an A-list actress falls for a paparazzo, having no idea her love interest is the one responsible for the photos in a troublesome tabloid scandal targeting her? (978-1-63679-695-6)

Ride It Out by Jenna Jarvis. When the COVID-19 lockdown traps Mick and Katy in situations they'd convinced themselves were temporary, they're forced to face what they really want from their lives, and who they want to share them with. (978-1-63679-709-0)

Scarlet Love by Gun Brooke. Felicienne de Montagne is content with her hybrid flowers and greenhouses—until she finds adventurer Puck Aston on her doorstep and realizes nothing will ever be the same. (978-1-63679-721-2)

The Hard Stuff by Ana Hartnett. When Hannah, the sales manager for a big liquor brand, moves to Alexandra's hometown and rivals her local distillery, sparks of friction and attraction fly. It turns out the liquor is the least of the hard stuff. (978-1-63679-599-7)

The Hunter and Her Witch by Rachel Sullivan. When an ex-witch-hunter falls for a witch, buried pasts are unearthed, and love is placed on trial. (978-1-63679-830-1)

Trustfall by Patricia Evans. Devri and Shiv never expect their feelings for each other to linger, but sometimes what you've always wanted has a way of leading you to who you've always needed. (978-1-63679-705-2)

BOLDSTROKESBOOKS.COM

Looking for your next great read?

Visit BOLDSTROKESBOOKS.COM
to browse our entire catalog of paperbacks, ebooks,
and audiobooks.

Want the first word on what's new?
Visit our website for event info,
author interviews, and blogs.

Subscribe to our free newsletter for sneak peeks,
new releases, plus first notice of promos
and daily bargains.

SIGN UP AT
BOLDSTROKESBOOKS.COM/signup

Quality and Diversity in LGBTQ Literature

*Bold Strokes Books is an award-winning publisher
committed to quality and diversity in LGBTQ fiction.*

www.ingramcontent.com/pod-product-compliance
Lightning Source LLC
Chambersburg PA
CBHW021951010726
47494CB00003B/692